Readers everywhere are in love with the new series by Lisa Renee Jones

THE CARELESS WHISPERS SERIES

"*Denial* is a stunning mix of mystery and eroticism that had me immediately wanting the second book to come out!"

—*Ramblings from a Chaotic Mind*

"*Denial* has everything you are looking for in a romance suspenseful read, with mystery, danger, action, romance, and of course twists along the way!" —*Jacqueline's Reads*

"Lisa Renee Jones is fantastic at drawing the reader in from the first page." —*OwlAlwaysBeReading*

THE SECRET LIFE OF AMY BENSEN SERIES

"Intoxicating, intense, and deeply seductive."

—*RT Book Reviews* (Top Pick) on *Escaping Reality*

"Suspenseful and packed with questions."

—*Fiction Vixen*

"The slaps to the face, the sucker punches, and the too-good-to-be-true moments will have you audibly gasping and wondering if you're going to get your HEA and still be in one piece." —*The Book Vamps*

"Suspense, suspense, suspense . . . all over the place and within every page." —*Cristina Loves Writing*

"It has everything anyone could want. Mystery, intrigue, suspense, enough heat to melt an iceberg, and characters with depth. Do yourself a favor and start this one now!"

—*The Book Hookers*

"A great story that's wrought with tension and fear of kidnapping and murder." —*Diary of an Eager Reader*

"An amazing story line with twists and turns; a roller coaster of highs and lows; and at no point could you sit back and relax. Lisa Renee Jones has stepped forward and claimed her place in the new adult category, and *Infinite Possibilities* will leave you breathless and wondering where it will all end." —*The Reading Café*

"Lisa Renee Jones will have you gripping the edge of your seat and biting your nails, and will leave you with a book hangover."

—*Lisa's Book Reviews*

Praise for the "passionate, all-consuming" (*PopSugar*)

INSIDE OUT SERIES

"If you haven't started this series yet, run to grab the first book and dive in! This easy-reading series is compelling—sucking the reader into a dark and seductively dangerous world of art, BDSM, and murder." —*Fresh Fiction*

"Lots of dark, suspenseful twists."

—*USA Today* (A Must-Read Romance)

"Great characters, angsty and real, that draw me in to their worlds, and storylines that hook me every single time."

—*Smut Book Junkie Book Reviews*

"Darkly intense and deeply erotic. . . ." —*RT Book Reviews*

"Intimately erotic . . . Jones did not hold back on the steam factor." —*Under the Covers Book Blog*

"A series that will completely captivate you—heart, mind, and soul." —*Romancing the Book*

"Powerfully written. . . . A tumultuous journey."

—*Guilty Pleasures Book Reviews*

"A crazy, emotional roller-coaster ride. . . ."

—*Fiction Vixen*

"Brilliantly beautiful in its complexity. . . . This book had my heart racing." —*Scandalicious Book Reviews*

"Breathtaking in its suspense and intrigue."

—*Heroes and Heartbreakers*

"Leaves you begging for more!"

—*Tough Critic Book Reviews*

"Dark and edgy erotica that hit all my buttons just right."

—*Romantic Book Affairs*

"If you haven't read Lisa Renee Jones's Inside Out series then you are seriously missing out on something fierce! It's a great blend of sexy, suspense, and kink." —*Talk Supe*

"These stories just keep getting better and better. . . . Every single one of them leaves you wanting more!"

—*Ramblings From This Chick*

Also by Lisa Renee Jones

The Inside Out Series

If I Were You

Being Me

Revealing Us

His Secrets *

Rebecca's Lost Journals

The Master Undone *

My Hunger *

No In Between

My Control *

I Belong to You

All of Me *

The Secret Life of Amy Bensen

Escaping Reality

Infinite Possibilities

Forsaken

Unbroken *

The Careless Whispers Series

Denial

---

*Ebook only

demand

LISA RENEE JONES

G

GALLERY BOOKS

New York London Toronto Sydney New Delhi

G

Gallery Books
An Imprint of Simon & Schuster, Inc.
1230 Avenue of the Americas
New York, NY 10020

This book is a work of fiction. Any references to historical events, real people, or real places are used fictitiously. Other names, characters, places, and events are products of the author's imagination, and any resemblance to actual events or places or persons, living or dead, is entirely coincidental.

First Gallery Books trade paperback edition May 2016

GALLERY BOOKS and colophon are registered trademarks of Simon & Schuster, Inc.

For information about special discounts for bulk purchases, please contact Simon & Schuster Special Sales at 1-866-506-1949 or business@simonandschuster.com.

The Simon & Schuster Speakers Bureau can bring authors to your live event. For more information or to book an event, contact the Simon & Schuster Speakers Bureau at 1-866-248-3049 or visit our website at www.simonspeakers.com.

Manufactured in the United States of America

10 9 8 7 6 5 4 3 2 1

Library of Congress Cataloging-in-Publication Data

Names: Jones, Lisa Renee, author.
Title: Demand / Lisa Renee Jones.
Description: First Gallery Books trade paperback edition. | New York : Gallery Books, 2016. | Series: Careless whispers ; 2
Identifiers: LCCN 2015047542 (print) | LCCN 2016000186 (ebook)
Subjects: | BISAC: FICTION / Romance / Suspense. | FICTION / Romance / Contemporary. | FICTION / Contemporary Women. | GSAFD: Romantic suspense fiction. | Erotic fiction.
Classification: LCC PS3610.O627 D45 2016 (print) | LCC PS3610.O627 (ebook) DDC 813/.6—dc23
LC record available at http://lccn.loc.gov/2015047542

ISBN 978-1-5011-2287-3
ISBN 978-1-5011-2293-4 (ebook)

Dear Readers:

I'm so excited to share part two of Ella's story with you! *Demand* starts the moment after *Denial* ends, so you will want to be sure you've read *Denial* in advance. If you haven't read it, *DON'T READ ON*, because I'm about to deliver major spoilers as I recap for readers who have read *Denial*. . . .

In *Denial*, Ella wakes up in a hospital with amnesia to find a gorgeous man by her side. He claims to have rescued her from an alleyway where he found her passed out. Kayden Wilkens is that man, and he goes on to tell her she's being hunted by a dangerous mobster, and he vows to protect her. And considering Kayden turns out to be the powerful leader of a major branch of The Underground, a group of sophisticated Treasure Hunters, he has the resources to make good on that promise. Together, Kayden and Ella seek answers as to her identity and begin a passionate, intense affair that leads to an emotional bond and, ultimately, to trust.

In the last chapters of *Denial*, Ella still has amnesia, but her memories are returning. One of her recovered memories is of a butterfly necklace with a note inside. She tells Kayden about this necklace, and he claims to have no knowledge of it at all. However, in the final chapter, Ella finds a photograph of that necklace in his office. Right after making this discovery, Enzo, one of Kayden's Hunters, ends up at the castle, bleeding to death, having been shot while trying to recover a piece of art from the leader of a drug cartel. Ella helps stabilize him while waiting for Nathan, the doctor for Kayden's branch of The Underground, to arrive to tend to Enzo's injury.

We end the book with Ella and Kayden in the shower, both fully dressed and washing off Enzo's blood. It is in this moment that all the danger and unknowns finally take a toll on Ella, leaving her shaken and afraid that Kayden isn't what he seems. The idea of his betrayal is too much to bear, and she pulls a gun on him, demanding the truth about who she is and how he came to rescue her. So *Demand* begins as we return to that shower. . . .

characters

Ella Ferguson (25)—Heroine in the series. Woke alone in Italy, saved by our hero, Kayden Wilkens. Best friend to Sara McMillan from the Inside Out series.

Kayden Wilkens (32)—Our hero in the series. Leader of the Italian branch of The Underground (a treasure-hunting operation). Saves Ella and brings her to live in his castle while she recovers.

Niccolo—Very dangerous Italian mobster. Ella has some sense of unease and knowledge of this man that she can't quite grasp.

Matteo—Works for Kayden and The Underground as a hacker. He helps create Ella's new identity as Rae Eleana Ward, and continues to try to find out who Ella is.

Adriel Santaro—Both lives and works for Kayden running a high-end collectibles store from the castle. Kayden fired him from The Underground after Adriel's father was killed on a hunt.

Giada Santaro—Adriel's sister. Also works in the collectibles store. Has a very hard time coping with her mother and father's deaths. Blames Kayden and The Underground for her father's untimely murder.

Marabella—Kayden's housekeeper, lives on the premises. Very close to Kayden, Adriel, and Giada. Is considered a mother figure to them all.

Detective Gallo—Kayden's greatest adversary. Very intent on making trouble for Kayden, and on finding out who Ella really is.

Chief Donati—The chief of police; Detective Gallo's boss. Friendly with Kayden, yet hiding secrets of his own.

Sasha—A Hunter. Her family is made up of Hunters and Hawks that used to run the French branch of The Underground, before Kayden took over for them. She befriends Ella and has quite the personality.

Blake Walker—A transplant from both the Tall, Dark and Deadly series (you can read his and Kara's story in *Beneath the Secrets*) and the Inside Out series. Chris Merit (Inside Out) hired Blake to help him and Sara find Ella after she ran off to elope with David and disappeared. At the end of the Inside Out series, Blake was still searching for her.

Enzo—One of The Underground's newest and youngest members. Sent on a dangerous mission and goes missing, only to be brought back with life-threatening injuries.

Elizabeth—Kayden's deceased fiancée. She was murdered in the castle five years ago.

Nathan—Physician for The Underground who helps Ella as she recovers from her severe concussion. While very charismatic, he is also incredibly tough and implacable.

David—Ella's ex-fiancé (mentioned in the Inside Out series). He swept Ella off to Paris to elope. Very vivid and shocking memories return to Ella of her time with David. A lot of arguing and anguish. At the end of *Denial* Ella still cannot remember all that transpired between her and David, but she does know she didn't love him.

Kevin—Kayden's adoptive father. He was the original owner of the castle and previous leader of the Italian branch of The Underground. After he was murdered along with Elizabeth five years ago, Kayden took over his post in The Underground and ownership of the castle. Best friend to Kayden's father.

Tyler—A resource of Kayden's. Helps sketch both the necklace and David from Ella's memory. Former FBI, whom The Underground has always had a connection to.

one

I sit inside the shower, the water's spray washing blood from my jeans and T-shirt and splattering Kayden, who kneels in front of me. And while my hand trembles with the weight of the Glock I point at him, the lies I'm certain he's told me shred my heart. "I want the truth," I demand.

"Give me the gun, Ella," he orders softly, his voice a tight band of control I want to break, his piercing blue eyes unreadable, the absence of a real answer painfully telling.

"Make me trust you and I will."

"You already trust me, and with good reason. I would die for you."

"Because I'm important to you," I say, and I don't even try to keep the accusation from my voice. "The question is *why*."

"Ella," he breathes out. "Don't do this."

"Do you know who I am? Not this 'Rae Eleana Ward' person you turned me into. Do you know who I was before I was attacked in that alleyway?"

"No, I do not."

"Yet I just told you about that butterfly necklace, and you already have a photo of it in your office."

"Put the gun down, Ella."

"That's not an answer. That's a dodge and weave, and you never dodge and weave with me. And I *hate* what that means."

"You're jumping to conclusions."

"Were you after the necklace when you found me in that alleyway? Were you *always* after it?"

"Damn it, Ella. *Give me the gun.*"

"No. I *will not* give you the gun. Answer the damn questions."

His hands flatten on his jean-clad knees. "Listen to me, sweetheart. This is not about a dodge and weave. It's about this being the wrong time to do this."

"Is there ever a good time to have a gun held on you?"

He stares at me, his eyes unreadable, but then I'm not sure they ever were readable. "I haven't lied to you, Ella," he says. "Not one lie."

"You just omitted facts."

His answer is to move before I can, leaning under the spray of water and closing his hand over mine and the gun. I have a split second to decide whether to pull the trigger or let him take my weapon . . . but I can't hurt him—even if he might hurt me. I relax my grip and stand up, shoving open the door and exiting the shower.

"I let you have the gun," I hiss, whirling on him, the puddle at my feet instant, the chill in my bones getting colder with every word I want him to say. "I could have shot you before you took it."

"But you didn't," he says, setting the gun on the counter, drops of water clinging to his naked chest while it literally pours off of me. "Because you care about me, just like I do you. Before I go attend to business, we need to cut through your anger."

"*Anger* isn't what this is."

"Then tell me. What is it?"

"Apparently business."

"You are not business," he says, taking a step toward me.

"Stop," I warn, backing into the counter, my hands grabbing it behind me, but he doesn't listen. He closes in on me, his big, overwhelmingly hard body caging mine, the heat of that connection a drug threatening to consume me. "Maybe I should have shot you," I hiss in frustration, my hands moving to grip his unmovable shoulders, stupid tingling sensations shooting up my arms.

"You don't mean that," he says. "And I know *you* know that there are times I have to put business front and center."

"Am I one of those times?"

"I'm not using you, Ella. Nothing could be further from the truth. You are in my bed. You are in my life. And you are in parts of me I didn't think anyone could find again."

It's so much of what I want to hear, and yet not enough. "Then tell me that you didn't know about the necklace before I told you about it."

"I swear to you, I didn't know *you* knew about the necklace."

"So you knew about it."

"Yes," he confirms. "I knew."

"And yet you didn't tell me that when I brought it up."

"Like you said. You'd *just* told me. I hadn't had time to try and put together the puzzle."

"The puzzle is *me*. *Me*, Kayden. And I'm not supposed to

be in the dark about me." I shove against him, growling with how ineffective I am. "Damn it, stop trapping me and bullying me! Let me go—then *you* go."

"I already told you," he says, holding me easily, his hands tightening at my waist, "I'm not letting you go. You matter too much to me. *We* matter to me."

More words that I want to hear, which scares me. Am I blind with this man? Am I falling in love, and into stupidity? "I have so many reasons to kick and scream and push you away right now."

"You do," he agrees. "You probably should, but please don't." In contrast to that plea, he releases me, his hands coming down on the counter on either side of me, boxing me in. "And not tonight. Not with Enzo fighting for his life."

It is a plea; raw and real, that no one can fake, and the anger I've denied but feel evaporates and my hands go to his arms. "I don't want to leave. I just want to know the truth you haven't told me, whatever it is. We'll figure out where to go from there."

"There are many truths I want to tell you, and others I do not—starting with the truth about tonight."

Dread fills me. "What about tonight?"

"I killed Raul's brother after he shot Enzo. And that will not come without consequence."

"Isn't Raul the kingpin of the cartel?"

"Yes."

"Oh God." My hands go to his chest, his heart thundering under my palms. "Do they know it was you or The Underground?"

"If they don't, they're too damn resourceful not to find out."

"What does that mean? What are we going to do now?"

"We? *Is* there a 'we,' Ella?"

"Kayden!" Adriel shouts from down the hall. "Where the hell are you?"

"Fuck," Kayden murmurs, straightening and cupping my face. "I have to go. He would have waited downstairs if this wasn't important." He kisses me fast, hard, and it's over far too soon. He releases me and turns away, and in a blink he's gone.

In about two seconds, I've decided I can't stay in this tower and wonder if we're about to be attacked. I grab the gun from the counter and shove it into my dripping-wet purse, then snatch up a towel before dashing out of the bathroom and through the spare bedroom. Exiting into the chilly long hallway, I see no sign of Kayden or Adriel. I run to the center stairs and lean over the railing. "Kayden! Is everything okay?"

Silence replies, confirming I've taken too long to catch him. I start down the stairs, only to see splattered blood and water all over the place. Freezing for a moment, in my mind's eye, I am back in the foyer of the castle, and Enzo is lying in the center of the floor, blood pouring from his body. Suddenly, I need out of these clothes, and I hurry back up the stairs, cutting left toward the room I share with Kayden, and . . . oh wow.

I am dizzy, and I grab the wall, holding on. Abruptly, I am transported back to my old family home, kneeling next to my father as he bleeds to death, begging him to wake up, *demand-*

ing that he wake up, and . . . God. Wake up! Get up! *The scent of the fresh-baked cookies we'd been eating before the attack brushes my nostrils, turning my stomach.* Wake up! *I shake him—and then everything goes black.*

Dizziness overtakes me again, and I try to focus, finally blinking in light, and then my surroundings, and . . . oh God. I'm not in the hallway anymore. I am standing in the closet of our bedroom, and I am not sure how I got here. My hand goes to my head and I breathe in and out, trying to remember the walk here, scared when I can't. "What just happened? What the hell *just happened*?"

Trying the blinking thing again, since it worked once, I lower and lift my lashes, but I still have no clue how I got here. My only comfort is that I *am* still here—not somewhere else. I tell myself this is a residual effect from my healing concussion, but my attack in the alleyway was more than a week ago now. And a blackout when I'm this far into healing can't be a good sign. But neither is Kayden's rapid departure, on the tail end of telling me he's killed the kingpin's brother.

I towel off my hair, strip off my wet, bloody clothes, and quickly dress in black jeans and a black T-shirt, hating that I make those choices because of possible exposure to more blood. But that is the reality, and exactly why I shove my feet into black Keds and pull on a black hoodie. Walking into the bathroom, I grab the hair dryer and put it to use on my hair, my purse, and even my phone. As I do so, I wonder what it would be like if my dyed-brown hair were red again. What would it be like if I knew the truth of how I got here? What would it mean if Kayden and I had answers, not questions, between us?

Shaking off the thought, I test my phone, which somehow still works, and I stick it and my gun in my now semidry purse. Shoving the strap over my head and across my chest, I step into the cozy bedroom of brown and cream with high ceilings and bring the massive bed, which I hope to continue to share with Kayden, into view. Memories and emotions created in this room stir inside me, only to be muted by the sound of the alarm going off inside the security closet, by the fireplace.

Startled, I go to the closet and punch the button by the mantel to enter, then sit down at the desk built into the wall to quickly scan the exterior castle's camera footage, but I find nothing obvious. Certain the alarm wasn't an error, I waste no time making my way out of the bedroom, down the hall and winding tower steps, to the arched wooden door separating our tower from the rest of the castle. Punching the button on the wall next to the door, I watch it lift, and before it's even at the halfway point I'm under it, exiting to the castle's center foyer. I expect to find commotion filling the room, and my heart falls when I discover I am alone—and all remnants of Enzo's emergency, including the carpet he'd bled on, are missing.

Fearing the worst, I ignore the east tower where Adriel, Marabella, and Giada live, and dash toward the stone stairwell leading to the central tower, where most of The Underground business takes place. I'm two steps from the top when the sound of the east wing's door begins to hum. I whirl around and watch Giada and Adriel enter the foyer below, Adriel's big, stocky body dwarfing her petite frame. Both seem to be scowling.

"Adriel, stop walking," Giada demands, her dark wavy hair bouncing around her face. "Stop and talk to me." He keeps walking, but she stays with him. "You said you were done with The Underground." She switches to Italian, as if that might make him listen.

Seeming to be at his wits' end, Adriel turns to face off with her, and I have a bad feeling that his choice of all black isn't about hiding blood. It's about fighting. It's about the cartel and war.

"Ella."

At the sound of Kayden's voice, I turn to find him standing just at the top of the stairs, and he's also wearing black jeans and a black T-shirt, with a double shoulder holster, the attire seeming to confirm my concern. This *is* war.

"What's happening?" I ask, hurrying to the landing to join him, one main worry overtaking all else. "Please tell me Enzo's not dead."

"He's alive, thanks to you." Kayden motions down the hallway to his right. "We moved him to a bedroom and Nathan's working to stabilize him."

"If he's not stable, why was he moved?"

"Gallo triggered the alarms, snooping around outside the gates. He can't get onto the grounds, but the timing is of enough concern that we can't ignore it."

"Did he see something when you were rescuing Enzo?"

"Nothing that we're aware of. But where Gallo is concerned anything is possible."

"Damn you, Adriel!" Giada yells on a sob, and I twist around to watch her march toward the east tower while Adriel walks toward us.

"It's time that girl is relocated," Kayden murmurs irritably. "No matter how Adriel feels about it."

I turn back to him. "She's afraid he's going to fight and die, like Kevin, her father, and maybe Enzo. Has the cartel found us?"

"If things go as planned, we won't be fighting."

"Considering you're heavily armed, I'm not comforted. What does that mean?"

"You're safe here now. I contacted the cartel and headed off an attack."

"You did *what*?"

"I don't do the sitting-duck routine well, sweetheart. In fact, I don't do it at all. And as it turns out, Raul's brother was trying to challenge his role as king. Raul now wants to share an expensive bottle of tequila with me tonight, to celebrate his brother's death."

"No. No, this is a setup. This is a trick. You'll get there and he will kill you. Tell me you aren't considering this."

"We confirmed the rift between him and his brother. This is a good gamble."

"Gambling is for Vegas, not your life. Do a virtual toast with the man and forget the tequila already."

"It's not that simple, sweetheart. Nothing with these people ever is."

"Again, what does that *mean*? I'm pulling teeth here! Just tell me everything. I *need* to know everything, Kayden."

"The way Raul sees things, we've disrespected him by trying to steal from him."

"But you *didn't* try to steal from him. You told Enzo to find the painting and report the location to his client. Not take it."

"Whether Enzo followed orders or not, he is my man, my Hunter, and by default, I'm responsible for his actions. I now owe Raul a favor."

"You killed his enemy brother."

"Which many of the cartel will see as grounds for war, even if he secretly doesn't."

"What does he want from you?"

"He won't disclose the details over the phone."

"Because he can't kill you over the phone."

"That's not how this works. You need to understand that the cartels, like the mob, have rules. This is about honor to them."

"Honor among criminals? Seriously?"

"As hard to digest as that is, honor is everything to them."

"It scares me that you know that."

His eyes glint hard and he steps closer to me, anger crackling off of him. "You want more truth? Well, here it is. It should comfort you that I know about their rules and honor, because if I disrespect them, they will kill my Hunters. More truth: I am a part of that honor circle. Without hesitation, if the mobs or the cartels disrespect me, I will not hesitate to kill any one of the criminal asses reporting to them, leaving the world a better place. And if I *don't* act that decisively, and they don't fear me, I can no longer protect anyone."

"You're testing me, to see if I can handle this world, can handle this life. I told you: yes. But do not lie to me, directly or indirectly."

"You held a gun on me, Ella," he says, the anger he had not shown in the shower now front and center.

"But I didn't shoot you," I say, repeating his words.

"And that means what?"

"It means that you shook my trust, but you didn't destroy it."

He snags my hip and pulls me to him. "I did *not* lie to you."

Like lightning, my anger shifts. "Tell me later," I say, my throat thickening. "After you cancel this meeting."

"You just said you can handle this, as long as you have the truth. So here is the absolute truth. There will be times I walk out of the door that are high risk. Saving Enzo was high risk. Meeting Raul Martinez is not. He wants something from me. If I'm dead, I can't give it to him."

"When it's high risk, will you say it's high risk?"

"Will you accept that it is, without doing what you're doing right now?"

"Yes. I will. Unless it's on a night I tried to stop one of your men from bleeding to death."

"Fair enough. Then I will tell you."

"Swear to me."

"I do."

"How is a cartel even in Italy?"

"They're the mafia's source of drug distribution."

"Niccolo's source of drug distribution," I say of the mob boss, and the man we both think I know far too intimately. "He owns this city."

"But he doesn't own us. The Underground is far more powerful than you understand right now."

"You mean *you* are."

"Yes. And I didn't get that way by being stupid or nice."

"Is Adriel going with you?"

"Yes."

"You know that once he's back in The Underground, he's not getting out."

"His father and Enzo's were best friends. I can't keep him out of this."

"I'm not suggesting that you do. I'm just making sure that beyond the moment, this is what you want."

He says something that's swallowed by a sudden series of fast, loud beeps. "What was that?"

"A warning that someone breached the fence," Kayden says, stepping around me and starting down the stairs.

I follow him, discovering that Adriel is now at the bottom of the stairs and a thirty-something man with long dark hair tied at his nape has joined him. "Were you followed inside the gates?" Kayden asks, stopping in front of the stranger.

"This is me you're talking to," the man says as I step to Kayden's side. "In five years, when have I ever been careless?"

"It's Gallo," Matteo calls out from the top of the stairs, diving frustrated fingers through his wavy brown hair on his way to us. "And he's making a beeline for the porch."

"There's no way he followed me in," the stranger reiterates.

"He's right," Matteo confirms, joining us and placing Kayden and Adriel in profile. "I was watching the security feed when Carlo and his team entered," he said, clearly naming the stranger. "No one slipped in with them," he adds.

"Then how the hell did he get in?" Kayden asks.

"We're secure," Matteo insists.

"Are we in the same fucking universe here?" the man I

now know as Carlo asks. "Because in mine, Gallo is in the gate, and we are not fucking secure."

"Do you ever get tired of being a little bitch?" Matteo surprises me by snapping. "He'd need a passcode for the gate, and since Gallo doesn't even play video games, he'd have to have hired someone to hack the system."

"I'm confused," I dare to interject. "Isn't there a way for visitors to enter the property? Otherwise, how did Gallo get to the door the night Giada was drunk and on the front porch?"

Kayden glances down at me. "She claims he must have snuck in behind her." He eyes Adriel. "And to Ella's point, if I find out she let Gallo in—"

A sudden incessant ringing of the doorbell begins and Gallo shouts, "Kayden, open up!"

"Fuck me," Kayden curses, scrubbing his jaw.

"*He's* the little bitch," Carlo says. Proving that his five years of service has come with intimate knowledge of Kayden's relationships, he asks, "Can you call his boss?"

"Kayden!" Gallo shouts again, abandoning the doorbell to pound on the door.

"I'm not owing the police chief another favor over Gallo," Kayden says.

More shouting and knocking ensues.

"Gallo's going to follow us when we leave," Adriel warns.

I have no idea why, but suddenly Carlo's piercing green eyes are locked on mine, and there is something dark and dangerous in his stare, something that sends a shiver down my spine.

"You're Ella," he states, and before I can confirm, he adds,

"You saved Enzo." His tone is flat, void of emotion, as if it's an observation rather than a celebration.

But whatever it is to him, it's gut-wrenching to me. "I bought him time," I say, and I swear I can almost feel the blood that must be on my skin beneath my clothes. "I pray Nathan can save him."

"Carlo," Kayden says, dragging the man's attention from me to him. "I'm going to ride with you and your men." Shifting his gaze to Adriel, Kayden directs him, "You'll drive the F-TYPE that I favor and lure Gallo in the wrong direction. Then circle back here and hold down the castle so Matteo and Nathan can focus on their jobs."

Adriel's expression hardens. "You know I want in on this. And you need a man on your left and right—not just Carlo."

"Get your fucking sister out of here," Kayden states, making it clear that he heard what I said to him and actually listened. "Then, and only then, can you exit retirement. Until then, you tend your store."

Adriel's eyes flash with fury, but he wordlessly drops back from the group, disappearing in the direction of the garage.

"Kayden!" Gallo shouts. "Open the fuck up."

Kayden gives Carlo a two-finger wave. "Go get your men ready."

Carlo turns away, but not before I catch the gleam of satisfaction in his eyes, and the word *dangerous* comes to mind again.

"I have to go," Kayden says, facing me. "Raul's a vicious, paranoid bastard, and when you make those kinds of people uneasy, someone ends up dead."

"You know this kingpin well enough to know that about

him?" I ask, still trying to get a grip on the politics of this, and really not sure how I feel about it all.

"I know the police chief's favorite beer, too, sweetheart," he says, and before I know his intent I'm in his arms, his mouth slanting over mine, his tongue doing a deep, passionate stroke before he releases me, and without a word he turns away and starts walking.

"Fuck," Matteo curses, and I whirl around to face him.

"What's wrong?"

"Note the silence," he says, holding out his arms. "Gallo heard the garage door open, and he's standing in the middle of the driveway, clearly intending to stop Kayden from leaving."

While a paranoid cartel leader with an impatient trigger finger waits for him. I can't do nothing, and there is no way that doing *something* won't have consequences.

In what's sure to be a defining moment in my life, I walk toward the front door and unlock it.

two

"No, Ella," Matteo shouts, lunging in my direction, but I gamble that he won't risk a confrontation with Gallo by following me outside.

I step onto the porch and shut the door behind me. The lawn is alight thanks to the motion detectors Gallo has obviously triggered, but I don't seem to be able to locate him. Hurrying across the porch and directly into a gust of air that reminds me a hoodie is not a coat, I scan for Gallo and suck in a breath as the wind punishes me for wearing just a hoodie in February. It's not until I'm down the steps and on the circular drive that I spy Gallo to the left, just in front of the garage, and thankfully the door is now shut. "Detective!" I shout urgently, running toward him. "Detective!"

He faces me, another gust of wind lifting his trench coat, and even his suit beneath is flapping around. I hug myself and run toward him, trying to convince him he needs to do the same, and it works. He jogs forward to meet me, away from the garage, and the instant I am in front of him, his hands come down on my shoulders. "Are you all right, Eleana?"

"Yes. Of course." I resist the urge to back away from his touch for fear it will shift his attention back to the garage and delay Kayden's departure. "It's just—"

"Is Giada okay?"

"Giada?" I blink in confusion. "What are you talking about?"

The garage door opens behind him, and he releases me, turning toward it at the same moment that Kayden's ice-blue F-TYPE Jag exits the castle, immediately followed by a black sedan and several motorcycles. Gallo murmurs something fierce in Italian, scrubbing his perpetual two-day stubble before fixing me in a fierce glower. "Did you distract me on purpose?"

"Distract you from what?" I ask, because what else am I supposed to say?

"Don't play coy with me, little one," he warns, closing the space between us to tower over me, taller and broader than I remember but just as cranky as ever. "We both know he was in one of those cars you helped to escape."

"Since when did driving out of your own garage become escaping?" This time I do take a step backward.

"My badge and I were at his door and he knew it."

"The problem with you stalking him is that you're always at his door, in one way, shape, or form."

"Stalking him?" he repeats. "He really is in your head now, isn't he? I came to your rescue."

Now he's making me angry. "You're here because it's Kayden's home." I fold my arms in front of me. "He's had to leave. He asked me to talk to you."

"Kayden asked you to talk to me," he repeats dryly. "Forgive me if I'm not buying the swampland you're selling. And since when did you become an expert on his business?"

"I'm pretty sure neither one of us are experts on his business."

"Indeed, and since he wants to keep it that way, this conversation is perfect timing, isn't it?" He doesn't give those words time to sting, moving on with, "You might not be frank with me, but others have been. Giada told me there's trouble in the castle tonight. I need to see her."

More dread fills me, followed by a hot spike of anger at Giada, who I'm now certain gave him the code to the gate. I force myself to contain my fury. "Giada," I say, thinking, plotting as I speak, "is trying to make you fight her schoolgirl battles for her. Bottom line, she slept with one of Kayden's Hunters and her brother found out. The Hunter left and Kayden followed him to ensure this isn't going to become a problem."

"What Hunter?"

"I'm not going to tell you that."

His lips thin. "Of course you aren't. I'll need to talk to Giada to confirm your story. I'm certain you understand my duty to ensure she's safe."

"Did she ever tell you she wasn't okay?"

"I need to talk to her. Bring her outside." A cold breeze rips over us and I hug myself, prompting him to add, "Or invite me inside, where it's warm."

"This is a family drama that doesn't require your intervention."

"Half of what we do is family drama." He reaches into his pocket. "I'll call her and tell her to come outside."

This announcement jolts me, shifting my anger from Giada to him. "You want revenge against Kayden. Using a young, confused girl for that goal makes you a monster. *A monster*, Detective. Is that what the woman you lost would want you to be?"

"She's a grown adult who seems to see Kayden far more clearly than you do."

"That's not the denial I'd hoped you'd give me."

"She called for police intervention."

"No, she didn't," I spout back. "She called you because she wanted to lash out at Kayden and Adriel. I won't let you hurt her. I'll call your boss. I'll do whatever it takes to protect her."

"Whatever it takes? You'd think Kayden just spoke, not you."

"Said the man risking his career to hurt another. He didn't kill the woman you loved. A car accident killed her."

"Right. He just fucked her *and* me. Am I calling Giada, or are we going inside?"

"I'm not disrespecting Kayden by inviting you inside his home."

"Kayden isn't here."

"It's *his* home."

"It seems it's become yours. A lot seems to have become yours—a topic we're going to discuss once I've seen that Giada is safe and well. What are you hiding . . ." He pauses and adds, "*Eleana*?"

A shiver of foreboding slides down my spine at the way he says the name, but I decide to walk right through the flames. "I'm still remembering my favorite foods. What am I supposed to hide?"

"Maybe you remember and aren't telling me."

"I *wish* that accusation were right," I say, thinking of the necklace, the uncertainty about my life, the gun, and that man I keep remembering who I do not want to be Niccolo.

"You don't want me in that house," he accuses.

"You're right," I declare. "I'm protecting Kayden's privacy from a man who's determined to destroy him."

"I'm protecting Giada, a young woman who called me sounding frantic and worried. And I'm protecting you, even if you don't see it yet." He punches a number on the phone, obviously calling her, and at this point, I have to expect the worst from Giada. But if I stop him from calling, it will only make him more suspicious. Considering I don't know the laws of Rome, I can't be certain what will constitute his freedom to enter the castle, which means I can't be certain what he will do next, either.

But remarkably, Giada doesn't seem to be answering the call, and with each passing second, I can breathe easier, while Gallo's jaw sets a bit firmer, until finally he removes the cell from his ear. "She didn't answer, and my concern for her safety constitutes my right to enter the castle. We're going inside." He doesn't wait for my agreement, walking toward the castle, and I tell myself Matteo is watching; he'll stop Gallo before he gets too far. But what if he doesn't?

I start to pursue while my cell phone rings. Praying it's Giada and I can get her to call off Gallo, I glance at the caller

ID and find Kayden's number. I stop walking and punch the "answer" button to hear Kayden say, "Why the hell are you with Gallo?"

"He was standing in the driveway, intending to stop you from leaving, and you said people die when Raul gets uneasy. Kayden, listen to me. Gallo claims Giada called him, frantic over trouble in the castle." Gallo starts up the front steps. "And right now, he's headed to the front door with the intent of going inside."

"Matteo won't let that happen."

"He has yet to show himself." No sooner than I say the words, Matteo steps onto the porch. "Okay, I was wrong. Matteo just headed him off at the door."

"And the police chief is about to call Gallo."

"Thank God," I say, air gushing from my lungs. "He's trying too hard to get into the house for comfort." I shove fingers through my hair. "I can't believe Giada did this."

"She's a problem I can't ignore any longer."

"Aren't you supposed to be in your meeting?"

"I'm about to walk in now." He changes the subject. "You protected me and The Underground."

"You doubted that I would?"

"You pulled a gun on me," he reminds me yet again.

"Because of the blood, and the necklace, and the moment."

"I *can* explain the photo."

"Good. I want you to." I glance toward the porch again, and report, "Gallo just gave Matteo his back and took a phone call."

"Then it's about to be over," he says. "I have to go now,

but if you need me, *really need me*, call me. I'll find a way to answer. But be sure it's an emergency—and take Giada's damn phone from her."

"Happily," I say, and the idea of hanging up and maybe never seeing him again has me grinding out, "Don't get killed. I'm the only one who can kill you. Understand?"

"Today is not the day I die, or the day Gallo wins."

"Promise—" The line goes dead and my stomach knots. He's about to negotiate with a kingpin, and considering Gallo is charging toward me, I can't even fully digest that reality. I stuff my phone back in my pocket and step forward once again, meeting him halfway.

"We need to talk," he announces.

"Talk about what?"

"You," he replies, "and believe me when I say that you're going to want to hear what I have to say." His cell phone starts to ring in his hand. He glances at the number. "I have to take this call." He steps around me.

Turning, I am stunned to discover he's heading toward the gate, obviously intending to leave. "Jerk," I whisper, certain he's just playing a game with me, taunting me, and no doubt hoping I worry and squirm.

"Ella!"

At the sound of Matteo's voice, I turn again to find him waving me forward. Jogging toward him, I am certain of three things. One, Gallo's not going to stop coming at Kayden until he destroys him. Two, if he keeps digging around, he's going to get me attention from Niccolo that could get us all killed. And three, Giada, in her immature, self-centered way, helped Gallo get dangerously close to all of us.

Suddenly furious over her careless actions, my pace quickens and I climb the porch steps two at a time, Matteo backing into the foyer to allow my reentry into the castle. "What the hell were you thinking, running out there like that?" he demands, shutting us inside and locking the door.

"Someone had to distract him, and we both know that couldn't be you without creating more trouble. And it's a good thing I did go out there, because now we know that Giada is the one who let Gallo onto the property."

"That little bitch."

I wish I could disagree with him, but right now, I can't. "Kayden wants us to take her phone."

"And lock her in her room," he growls, already stalking toward her tower, while I quickly follow, shocked when he keys in the entry code by the arched wooden door.

"You have the entry code?"

"Not to Kayden's tower."

Which is mine, and I'm not sure why I'm relieved. "You could hack it."

"I can," he says. "But no one else can. I set it and I'm that good." The door begins to lift.

I duck under the barely open door, and into the foyer of the section of the castle I've never visited.

Straightening, I find this tower to be identical to the one Kayden and I share, with a library directly in front of me and a huge, winding stairwell to my right that I know will lead to a top level. Matteo joins me and we start up the steps, the anger

I'd felt at Giada a few minutes ago a stone in my chest that's quickly becoming a boulder.

"What did Giada say to Gallo? And since Kayden told you to take her phone, I assume he knows?"

"I told him," I say, glancing in his direction. "And all I know is that Gallo claims that she called him in a frenzy of some sort, and reported trouble in the castle."

We step to the landing and find Giada and Marabella waiting for us at the top, Marabella's blue dress covered by an apron, while Giada is in jeans, a sweater, and a jacket, with her purse cross-body style.

"Going somewhere?" Matteo asks her.

She glowers at him. "When a man is bleeding to death in your home, and the cartel is after him, it's smart to be ready to run if necessary."

"Necessary?" Marabella demands, her tone proving her kindly nature toward Giada is as tested as mine. "What's necessary is that you respect this house and Kayden, which you did not, and do not, do." She holds up a phone and looks to me and Matteo. "She won't be making any more phone calls, but I can't get her to go to her room."

"I was trying to protect my brother," Giada states, arguing her case, and looking to me as she adds, "You *know* I have to protect him."

That's it. She's officially turned the pebble into a boulder, and I close the space between us, stepping toe-to-toe with her. "That man who was bleeding in your home is named Enzo, and I can still smell his blood and feel it on my skin."

"Ella—"

"He's barely started his life, and he, too, is mourning the

loss of a father who just happened to be close to *your* father. And he now has less chance of surviving, because we had to move him too soon. And do you know why we had to move him? Because *you* let Gallo onto the property. Enzo could die because of you."

Her chin lifts defiantly. "He could die because of The Underground."

"If Enzo weren't working for Kayden, he'd be working for someone else, who wouldn't tell him to stay away from trouble."

"He's dying," she hisses. "He didn't stay away from trouble."

"He disobeyed orders, and why is this your judgment? Why?"

"The Underground is why my father is dead."

My mind flashes to me leaning over someone I can't picture. Someone bloody and dead, and I'm crying and scared and certain I'm next. "You're going to be the reason some of *us* are dead. If you keep bringing attention to me, you'll be the reason *I'm* dead! I don't need attention, Giada. Stop getting me attention. Just stop!"

"Ella. *Ella*, easy now."

I blink at the sound of Matteo's voice, becoming aware of him to my left and Marabella at my right.

"Ella," Marabella repeats. "You're okay."

I blink again and realize I'm gripping Giada's shoulders, and I'm not sure if I'm shaking or she is. "Ella," she pleads, tears streaming down her cheeks. "Ella, I—"

"Need to go to your room, like Marabella said."

I let her go, turning and starting down the stairs, my legs trembling with each step. Who was the man who was dead?

Who was I afraid of? I try to replay the memory in my mind, to will the images to materialize, but they don't. I am a blank space, and it's infuriating. I want my memories back, and, ironically, I barely remember the walk to the foyer, or the moment I punch the button to raise the door again. But it's lifting and I impatiently duck underneath again, making a beeline for the stairwell leading to the central tower, and hoping for good news about Enzo. I really need some good news right now.

three

I'm halfway to the landing when I'm suddenly in *his* bedroom, whoever *he* is, and I'm on my knees in front of a drawer, staring down at a gun. I blink and I'm on the landing, staring at the closed door to Adriel's collectibles store, and it just plain freaks me out that I seem to be blacking out. What is *wrong* with me? Aside from a man nearly bleeding to death while I held his wound shut?

I turn left, the direction Kayden had indicated I'd find Enzo, and travel down the stone hallway, the many closed doors reminding me that this entire tower was shut for years for a very good reason. This is where Kayden's fiancée and mentor were slaughtered. The very idea has me shoving my hands in the pockets of my hoodie, with the impossible hope of warming any part of me. I just pray that maybe, just maybe, this place can now be the tower where Enzo gets a second chance at life.

Finally I reach an open room, pausing a moment before entering to steel myself for whatever awaits me inside. Inhaling, I round the corner, finding a room one might expect to be a getaway at an inn, with crackling flames in the fireplace framed by a pair of narrow, rectangular windows, and a sleigh bed directly in front of me, sitting on a blue-and-gray rug. But any coziness it might hold is turned bitter and chilled by the sight of Enzo lying in the bed, an IV feeding a bag of blood into his arm and a beeping heart monitor sitting next to the headboard. He is pale and lifeless, and I have a bad feeling about how this is going to turn out.

"Ella."

At the sound of my name, I look to the far left corner to find Nathan sitting in a large leather chair, his white button-down shirt stained with blood. His hands are scrubbed clean, telling me he's done what he can for Enzo. I walk toward him and tentatively claim the ottoman in front of him. "How bad is it?"

"The next few hours are going to be touch and go."

"Should he be in a hospital?"

"What he needed was blood. We got that for him. The question is whether it was soon enough."

"An hour ago, I didn't want to know where that blood came from," I say. "Now I do."

"Kayden donates generously to a hospital nearby," he supplies.

"That was a fast answer."

"And an honest one," he says.

"If it is—"

"It is," he says firmly.

"Then it's a better answer than I'd expected."

He studies me a long moment, his intelligent brown eyes weary. "You're very calm about all of this."

"Considering I drew a gun on Kayden, I doubt he'd

agree," I surprise myself by saying, not sure what I hope to get in reply.

"There's a new twist on foreplay," he says, and any other time it would be funny. But not now. Not in this room.

"You aren't going to ask why I did it?"

"Having someone's life in your hands is a lot of pressure," he says, getting right to the crux of my emotions.

"Says the doctor covered in the blood of the man I tried to save."

"He wouldn't be alive right now, if not for you. What you did took a level head and training."

"Tell me that if Enzo lives." I glance at his blood-soaked clothes. "Do you want me to get you something of Kayden's to change into?"

"My clothes are the least of my worries right now," he says, a hint of his native Canadian accent in his voice I've never noticed before. It must be stress induced. "But thank you." He studies me intently. "Where did you get medical training?"

"My father was some sort of Special Forces and trained as a medic. He taught me."

He arches a surprised brow. "Did you get your memory back and forget to tell your doctor?"

"Small pieces of things are slowly coming back to me, as you said they would. But I'm a little concerned. Tonight I blacked out in the middle of my flashbacks."

"Define 'blacked out.'"

"I was angry at Giada for calling Gallo and—"

"*She's* why he was here?"

"Yes, she is. I was furious at her, and it triggered a memory. One minute I was giving her a piece of my mind, and the next I was shaking her shoulders without any memory of doing so."

"She's the reason we had to move Enzo. She's lucky it wasn't me. What else?"

"When I was walking up the stairs to find you, I got lost in a memory, and then I was at the top level and I don't remember the steps. It also happened about an hour ago, when I was changing clothes."

"Has it happened before tonight?"

"No. Not like this."

"Then I'd say it's stress and trauma. If it continues for more than twenty-four hours we'll run tests, but I don't think it will."

I give a nod, comforted by his lack of concern, and by the easy friendship I feel with him. "I know Kayden hasn't told me everything."

He doesn't so much as blink at my sudden change of topic. "In our world, everyone is an enemy until they're not. And sometimes even then, they are."

It's not the answer I want, but perhaps, as Kayden said earlier, it's the one I need. "Does it ever get to you?"

"It gets to all of us."

"Then why do it?" I press.

"I believe in Kayden."

"Why?"

"Do you know how many men in The Underground would be criminals, if not for Kayden? He shows them another way. He wants more for them and the organization, and he keeps order in his two countries in ways you can't even begin to comprehend yet. So my answer is, I'm here because he's here."

Footsteps sound and I push to my feet, standing next to Nathan. A moment later Adriel appears in the doorway, his hands on the frame, still dressed in black, still wearing guns, his gaze flicking to Enzo, then us. "How is he?" he asks.

Nathan gives a grim shake of his head and Adriel inhales sharply, his expression hardening, and I have a sense of him trying to rein in the emotions he never shows. I wonder if those emotions are why he's not dealing with Giada right now.

"Do you know what happened with Giada and Gallo?"

"I know," he confirms, "and I'll deal with her. But it's not in my sister's best interest for me to do that now."

It's at that moment that the machine next to Enzo starts screeching and the green lines go flat. Nathan is on his feet in an instant, running across the room and pulling some sort of cart with an electronic box on top of it to the edge of the bed. "Get the sheets off of him," he orders, yanking open a drawer in the cart and removing paddles that begin to hum in his hands.

I pull down the sheets and Adriel appears at the end of the bed, helping me get them all the way down Enzo's body.

Nathan shocks Enzo with the paddles, and Enzo's body lifts and trembles. Seconds tick by and we watch the monitor, but the green line remains flat. Nathan shocks him again, and again without success. The next few minutes become a blur of shocks and failures, until the dreaded moment arrives.

Nathan shoves the paddles into the drawer and announces, "It's done. He's gone."

He pulls the sheet over Enzo's face, and watching it is like being punched in the chest. I sink against the wall, squeezing my eyes shut, fighting images that I can't escape. Suddenly I am transported into the past, leaning over that bleeding man again. I try to hone in on his face when I hear Adriel say, "I'll call Kayden."

My eyes snap open and I shove off of the wall. "You can't call Kayden when he's with Raul. He'll be furious with Raul. He'll get killed."

"Like I said," Adriel replies, "I'm calling Kayden."

"You're going to get him killed," I accuse.

"Because you fuck Kayden," Adriel bites out, "does not make you an expert on how he wants things done." He rounds the bed, heading for the door.

"Adriel!" I shout. "Wait!" And when he doesn't stop, I turn to Nathan. "Stop him, before you're covering another man with a sheet!"

He shakes his head. "Kayden's orders were specific. He wanted to know any news on Enzo immediately."

"You have to see why that's a problem!"

"He *wants* to know. Let it go, Ella."

"I won't let it go," I say, dashing for the door and the hallway to find Adriel nowhere in sight until I reach the stairs. I see him in the foyer below, his back to me. I run down the stairs, and watch as he slips his phone into his pocket and turns to face me. "You told him, didn't you?" I demand, walking up to him.

"I left him a specific message. Yes."

"If he dies—"

"He won't, because he's not dictated by his emotions. And

if you can't remove yours, to stand by his side, *you* will get him killed. You will be no different from Giada, who doesn't belong here."

"I'm not—"

"This is *not* your world," he says from between gritted teeth. "And people who don't belong in this world, but stay here, end up like Enzo. *Dead.*" He steps around me and starts walking, his boots sounding on the stone floor, no longer covered in a rug, and each booted step echoes, not like a warning, but a threat.

I decide right then that my uneasiness with Adriel isn't going away, no matter how much Kayden trusts him. But now, when we're all riding an emotional roller coaster, is not the time to go to war with him. Especially since I'm fairly sure that the only thing I'm objective about right now is the fact that I'm not objective.

Inhaling, I walk to the front door, open it, and exit, a motion detector triggering lights that cast the porch in a dim glow. Ignoring the cold night air, I shut myself outside, sit on the top step, and dig my phone from my purse, noting the ten o'clock hour. I tab to Kayden's phone number, my finger lingering above it, but I remember my vow to only call in an emergency so I don't hit it. And I quickly rule out a text as distracting and potentially dangerous.

The door opens behind me, and I twist around to find Matteo joining me. "What are you doing out here?"

"I need a few minutes of air."

"It's cold."

"Is it?"

He studies me for several beats and shrugs out of his

black leather jacket I don't remember him wearing, offering it to me. "Kayden will kill me if I let you freeze."

Kill me. I hate those two words right now, though of course I know they aren't literal. It's just . . . oh God. He doesn't know. I accept the heavy weight of the jacket and manage a soft "Thank you," hesitating to add, "Matteo . . . I . . . Enzo . . ."

His eyes shut, his chin falling to his chest, a guttural curse sliding from his lips, his reaction chilling me way beyond the cold breeze.

"I'm sorry," I say. "We tried. . . . Nathan—"

"I know," he says, looking at me again. "I know." He scrubs his jaw. "Don't stay out here long." He doesn't wait for a reply, turning away.

"Wait!"

He turns to look at me.

"They told Kayden."

Understanding fills his eyes. "He's The Hawk, Ella," he says, as if that should explain everything. And I never get the chance to ask for more. He enters the castle and shuts the door firmly behind him.

I face forward to stare across the dark expanse of the yard, settling the jacket around my shoulders, and while Matteo might have given it to me, in doing so, he made it clear that Kayden is looking out for me even when he's not here. He is The Hawk. The protector of his people. *I would die for you*, he had said to me, but the word *die* shifts me back to the moment Nathan said, "He's gone," and tears prickle in my eyes. He's gone. He's gone. Damn it. *He's gone.*

My cell phone rings and I glance at the caller ID, hoping

it's Kayden. But it's the number from Gallo's business card—and like Kayden, I question his timing. My gaze lifts, scanning the darkness, looking for a way he might be able to see me. But there's really no way to know, thus no certainty he won't know I am ignoring him. I decide it's best to avoid any more of his wrath.

I hit the "answer" button. "Hello."

"We need to meet," he says. "Tomorrow morning for coffee. There's a place in the neighborhood called Caffè del Cinque. Be there at eight. *Alone*."

"I can't do that."

"Do you want me to take a photo of my badge and text it to you? Or perhaps your temporary visa?" He doesn't wait for a reply. "You can meet me, and you will."

"What is this about?"

"You."

"What does—?"

The line goes dead.

Though I'm certain Kayden has more power than he does, I am afraid that Gallo will deport me, but I don't think he has anything substantial on me, or he'd be dragging me out of the castle right now. It's a game. He's always playing games. I shove my phone back inside my purse and zip it up, glancing around the expansive yard, darkness consuming the walls blocking us from the public. Eerie silence surrounds me, the inky black almost a living creature, and suddenly I feel very exposed out here. I stand up, the leather draping my shoulders heavier than moments before, and hurry to the door.

Once I'm inside I lock the door, rush to Kayden's private tower, and punch in the security code. The instant the heavy wooden door starts to slide up, I impatiently want to duck under, but Matteo's jacket is too big and awkward. Forced to wait, I replay Gallo's words, wondering why he didn't insist on meeting tonight, since he knows Kayden is gone. Maybe he was baiting me, or us. Maybe he thought I'd panic and go somewhere he could follow? Perhaps to Kayden? Whatever the case, he's playing head games and it's working.

The door opens fully, a pool of light pouring in from the hall, and I hurry into the private foyer of the tower, pausing to push the button on the wall to shut the door again. And though normally I'd head right up the stairs, and let it close on its own, I'm antsy enough to watch it slide shut and know that I'm alone, considering Kayden guards our entry code like gold. Hurrying up the winding stone staircase, I reach the landing and pause, glancing down the hallway toward the bedroom, but the idea of being secluded in that room without Kayden hits all the wrong spots. Instead, I find myself walking straight ahead into the dimly lit living area, where I claim a seat on the couch, two chairs framing me, a big-screen television on the wall in front of me. The gas fireplace glows in the far left corner, warming the room, but it can't thaw the chill deep in my bones and my soul from the death of Enzo.

Pulling my purse over my head, I set it on the floor by the couch, then lie down and cover myself with the jacket, staring at the high ceiling without seeing it, tormented by the death I've lived through tonight and taunted by Gallo's phone call. I replay the important part of the conversation, honing in on my query about tomorrow's meeting: "What is this about?" I'd asked.

And his reply: "You."

It's then that images flash in my mind, as if in answer to some question I haven't asked, and I close my eyes, knowing even before I fully visualize the scene that this is the memory I was having right after Enzo died.

I am in the hotel room where David and I are staying. The room where I ripped the butterfly necklace off my neck and found the note inside. The phone rings and I rush over to it, hoping it's David, who has been gone for an hour.

"Hello?"

A female voice says, "He's at Seventy-fifth Avenue. . . ."

I open my eyes, frustrated that I can't remember the address. Seventy-fifth Avenue what? And who was it who called me? The voice was strongly accented, but was it Italian? My brows furrow. I don't think it was. I shut my eyes again, and will more to come to me.

It is dark outside when I reach the address the caller gave me—a restaurant. I enter and walk to the hostess stand, and spot David with a beautiful blonde, who I believe is American. I quickly move out of his line of sight, and dash back outside to the busy sidewalk. I don't think they're lovers, but I don't know. I wait outside, the hood of my jacket covering much of my face, and he finally exits, and the woman is not with him, but he turns away from our hotel, and I follow, sheltering myself in the crowded sidewalk, where shops line our path. For blocks we walk like this, him in front of me, me praying I find the truth about the man I foolishly planned to marry. Love wasn't in the equation. Normalcy was. I wanted to be normal. To be secure. To forget the dangerous past I don't want to exist.

Abruptly David turns down a side street and two women block my path. I cut around them just in time to see David disappear. I run after him, but pause at the corner. Peeking down the sidewalk,

I find it dark, lined with brownstones, and no pedestrians, not even David to mark my path. Inhaling, I dare to turn down the path he'd taken, hurrying forward until I reach an open gate leading to a private garden. It's then that I see a man on the ground. . . . David on the ground.

I rush to him, and there is blood oozing from his chest. "I'll get help! Hold on. I'll get help."

I start to get up and he grips my arm. "Wait," he hisses. "Don't . . . give . . . him the necklace."

"Him who?"

But the memory goes blank and my eyes pop open, my heart racing a million miles an hour. "Don't give him the necklace," I whisper, repeating his words and then my own. "Him who?"

And I can come to only one conclusion. He didn't use a name because he believed I knew who he was talking about.

four

"Ella."

At the sound of my name, my lashes lift and I blink the gorgeous man leaning over me into view, my mind flickering back to the hospital room where I'd done the same. "Kayden?" I ask, rising up on my elbows to find him kneeling beside me.

"Why are you on the couch?" he asks, his voice a soft but evident demand.

"I must have fallen asleep. What time is it?"

"Two in the morning."

"Two," I repeat. "The last time I looked it was ten, and—" Everything comes crashing back to me. Raul. Enzo. Adriel. Gallo and Giada. The flashback of David dying on that cobblestone walkway. My fear that Kayden would also die. "Oh God." I throw aside the heavy weight of Matteo's jacket, sit up, and fling my arms around Kayden's neck. "You're alive. You're okay. I'm so glad you're here."

But he doesn't hug me; his hands settle at my waist. "But you didn't want to be in my bedroom, in *our* room, Ella."

I lean back to look at him, shadows stroking his face that

have nothing to do with the ones I see in his eyes. "I just . . . I needed to be right here while you were gone."

"Because you don't trust me right now."

"But I do," I confess, no matter how right or wrong that decision may be. "Beyond reason, I do, which is why the idea of you betraying me guts me."

"The truth is not as simple as a betrayal. And what guts me is the idea of losing you."

"I don't know what the future holds, Kayden. I barely know how I got here. I can't promise how I'll react to what you tell me. But I know that we're here, and Enzo is gone, and I can't lose you tonight."

His hand slides under my hair, folding around my neck. "I can't lose you *ever*." His mouth slants over mine, his tongue stroking deep, and suddenly we are crazy, wildly kissing, touching each other like we will never touch again, two people who value control and have lost it, as if every emotion we've bottled up tonight has exploded right here and now, and become this moment that is all about need, passion, and hunger. My hand slides under his T-shirt, and only then do I realize his guns are gone. The hell is done and over, at least for now, and I press my palms to his warm, taut skin, reveling in this escape that I know will not last.

"Kayden," I find myself whispering, his name a plea for some unknown something that only he can give me.

His answer is to kiss me again, and I feel the deep, seductive stroke of his tongue in every part of me. I moan and arch into him, and a frenzied rush of our hands on each other's bodies ends in our shirts disappearing and my bra falling to the floor. It's then that we slow down and his gaze rakes over my breasts, a hot inspection that tightens my nipples and my sex.

"You are beautiful," he declares, flattening his hand between my shoulder blades, molding my naked chest to his, skin against skin. "If I can hold you like this every day for the rest of my life, I'll die a happy man."

"*If*," I repeat. "I hate that word. I hate all of the uncertainty between us."

He stands and takes me with him, stroking the hair from my face and tilting my mouth to his. "*If* is a reminder to never take anything for granted. That every day, and every moment—"

"Could be our last," I supply, the words reminding me of Enzo, of his loss, and our fight to save his life, which ended in his death.

"Which is exactly why we need to fuck like it is." He kisses me then, a short, hot claiming that is all about demand, two parts fierce, one part a question I don't understand, before he tears his mouth from mine and walks me backward. "You have too many clothes on," he declares, going down on one knee again and wasting no time removing my Keds.

My hands settle on his shoulders, his mouth finding my belly, his tongue flicking here and there, and my nipples ache to feel the same. And when he moves lower, exploring the bare expanse of skin just above my waistband, my fingers slide into his hair, tangling in the soft stands. But they do not stay.

Almost instantly, Kayden catches my wrist and presses my arms and hands behind me. "Lace your fingers together."

"What?"

"I'm going to make sure you can think of nothing but us. That's what you want, isn't it?"

"Yes," I say, my certainty that I want whatever he offers absolute. "That's what I want."

"Then do as I say. Lace your fingers together and don't release them until I tell you to."

The idea of submitting to him, of willingly giving him control, is sexy in ways that defy what I know of my past. I am even wetter and hotter than moments before. But Kayden has declared my submission to be my choice, while the man of my past took it. I twine my fingers beneath his grip, and there's no mistaking the satisfaction that lights his eyes, a satisfaction that I know isn't about sex. It's about trust—something that I don't believe either of us have known much of in our lives.

His finger trails my waistband, his mouth following, his tongue flickering above the denim, a touch and a lick I feel in places he hasn't yet explored, but I have no question he will. My lashes lower, my breasts feel heavy, my sex is tight, slick, ready for the moment Kayden is inside me.

"Ella," he says, softly, the rough timbre of his voice compelling me to look at him. "Tell me that the birth control you started has kicked in, and I can be inside you with nothing between us."

"It has," I say, and for several beats we stare at each other, a new level of intimacy between us that has nothing to do with our naked bodies, but everything to do with our newly formed, fragile commitment to each other.

He suddenly averts his gaze, resting his cheek on my belly, his energy shifting, darkening, several heavy beats passing. I want to touch him, to drive away the torment coming from him. "Kayden," I whisper softly, and when he looks at me, those shadows of minutes before are thicker, more intense.

"I'm going to make you forget everything but us. I'm going to make *me* forget. I'm going to fuck you every possible way I can before this night is over." He cups my sex. "I'm going to lick you here, over and over, until you cry out because you want to come so badly it hurts. I'm going to make you say please. Do you have a problem with that?"

"Maybe I should just say please now."

"No. When it hurts so good that it's almost pain, you say please."

He unsnaps my jeans and then unzips them, his hands slipping under the denim, and my panties, to my hips, sliding them down. They pool at my feet and I have a second at most to be self-conscious before he's standing. He wraps his arms around me, covering my hands with his behind me, and then he arches backward, lifting me as he kicks away my pants. But he doesn't put me down. He holds me there, cradling my body with his, and I can't move, but I don't want to. I just want *him*. This. Nothing else. The air around us crackles, stealing my breath. Stealing time and washing away everything else before this moment.

Slowly he lowers me, walking me backward, and then easing us down again so I'm sitting on the couch, and he is in front of me between my open legs. Leaning into me, he presses my hands into the cushion behind me, and then drags my hips forward, forcing me to support my weight on them. I've barely steadied myself when he twines rough, erotic fingers in my hair and kisses me, before ordering,

"Shut your eyes." I do it, no hesitation, wanting whatever unknown he intends, and when I do, he adds, "Don't move."

And then he is gone, and I can hear the sounds of him undressing, an erotic thrill that promises soon he will be naked, inside me, touching me. Me touching him. But unbidden, an image of that necklace is in my mind and then me holding a gun on Kayden. I jolt upward. "Kayden," I say, at the very moment he shoves his jeans and underwear down his legs, giving me a delicious view of his amazing backside and the circle of skulls tattooed on his back.

He faces me, tossing his jeans aside as he does, and I inhale at the sight of him, every delicious, long, muscular inch of him now exposed, his thick shaft jutting forward. And somehow we are frozen in place. He doesn't move. I don't move. Seconds tick by, and every moment we've ever shared, including the one in the shower with me holding the gun on him, is between us, but there is only one question that I have to have answered right now. Before I can ask, though, he's walking toward me, and in another few beats, he is sitting on the couch, pulling me over his lap to straddle him, his erection pressed to my belly between us.

"You want to know about the necklace now," he says, his voice low, terse, his expression stark.

"No," I whisper. "I want to know what really matters."

"Which is what?"

"I want to know that we're real. Tell me we're—"

He kisses me, cupping the back of my head and dragging my mouth to his, the taste of him wickedly erotic, and almost angry, bleeding into my senses a moment before he demands, "Does that taste real?" And he gives me no time to reply as his mouth closes down on mine again, and this time it's a claiming, a possession that ends with another demand of, "Do we *taste* real?"

"Yes," I whisper.

"You aren't saying it like you mean it." He lifts me, pressing his shaft inside me, and pulling me down the hard length of his erection. "Let's try this again." He shifts himself, burying his cock in the deepest part of me. "Does that *feel* real?"

My lashes lower, my breath lodged in my throat. "Yes."

He cups my head again and rests his cheek against mine. "Do you know what I feel? Too much."

"And yet I want more," I whisper.

"Now," he says. "You want more now."

There is an odd ring of finality to that statement, as if there won't be more later, but he holds me to him, driving into me, and we are rocking and swaying, and everything else fades away. Wildness takes us again; we can't kiss each other enough or touch each other enough. Harder and faster, we move, we grind, he drives, and the edge of no return is threatening to steal the here and now. I'm not ready to let go of it, but it's too late. It's here, and I cry out, "Kayden!" a moment before my sex clenches onto his cock, and I bury my face in his neck to ride out the sensations.

His arm wraps my waist and he pulls me against him, a low guttural groan coming from his throat, and our bodies shake. Pleasure trembles through me, the world fading, time standing still until I finally return to the present, resting against Kayden, his arm holding on to me.

For a long time we sit like that, huddled together, refusing to accept whatever comes next, until dampness spreads on our legs and reality scrapes away at our escape. Kayden turns me and lays me on my back, leaning over me, staring down at me. "Ella," he whispers, and I know he feels what I do. We can't just fuck away the night. Neither of us can take the unknowns between us.

"When you said that right *now* I want more—"

"Right now we both want more." His lips and his voice tighten. "Until we don't."

"Until we don't," I repeat. The reference to both of our withdrawals implies a much bigger problem than I know of.

"Yes," he confirms, drawing a deep breath to pull out of me and sit up, giving me his profile. "Until we don't."

I grab my shirt lying next to me, pressing it between my legs. "As in *when* we don't." Suddenly needing the shelter of being covered, I reach for the soft brown blanket on the back of the couch, and wrap it around myself. "I guess it's time you tell me everything."

"I'd have to know everything to tell you, and I still don't." He stands and grabs his black jeans, shoving his legs inside them.

"But you knew about the necklace."

Forgoing his zipper, he sits on the stone coffee table in front of me, resting his hands on his legs. "I knew about the necklace."

His cell phone rings, and he grimaces. "Holy fuck, I can't even get an hour." He stands and retrieves his phone from his pocket, answering the call in Italian. He listens a few beats and then replies, before giving me his back and ending the call, tension radiating off of him.

He finally faces me. "Matteo is making Enzo disappear,

disconnecting him from The Underground. That means his mother can't know he's dead—and I'm not sure if I'm doing her a favor or a disservice." He scrubs his jaw. "I need a shower to wash some of the death off of me." He doesn't wait for a reply or invite me to follow, he simply turns and walks toward the hallway.

I sit there a moment, not sure if I should go after him, repeating his words in my mind: *wash some of the death off of me.* And I think it's more about guilt that he wants to wash away. He blames himself for every death that touches his life, including Enzo's. My mind flashes back to my father lying in a pool of his blood and again, I wonder what I have wondered over and over in my life: could I have done something different and saved his life? Maybe if I hadn't hidden in the pantry with my mother when intruders came into our home. Maybe if I had stood and fought by my father's side. Maybe if I had come out of that closet just three minutes earlier. Guilt sucks. Questioning yourself sucks.

No one needs to deal with that alone. And Kayden's been alone a long time. I think . . . I think that I have, too.

I stand up, allowing my shirt to drop to the ground, and I hold the blanket around me as I hurry toward the hallway, cutting left toward Kayden's bedroom, *our* bedroom, cold stone beneath my bare feet. And I know what I had not admitted until now. Kayden had been right. I didn't want to go back to the intimate place we share until after we had talked. Now I can't wait to get there, where he is and probably thinks I will not follow. I reach the giant wooden door, finding it cracked open, and since Kayden does nothing by accident, I'm aware of the invitation it represents.

I enter the room, the fireplace warming the space, crackling with warming flames just beyond the bed I pray I'll still share with Kayden when this night is over. The bathroom door is open, and I hear the sound of water running. I drop the blanket and stand in the doorway of the white glistening room, an oval tub before me, and directly beside it, the deep, stone-encased shower making it impossible for me to see Kayden inside.

Walking to it, I enter, shocked to find a dripping-wet Kayden now out of the spray and sitting on the floor in the corner, his head resting against the wall, eyes shut. I sense that he knows I'm here, but he doesn't move, so I close the distance between us and sit down beside him, facing him, my hand on his knee. He lifts his head to look at me, immediately letting me inside the cage holding him captive. "If you could have remembered your father without knowing the brutal way he died, would you have chosen that path?"

"You're worried about Enzo's mother."

"Yes. I'm worried about his mother."

I consider his question, shutting my eyes as I remember the moment I grabbed my father's gun and shot and killed one of his attackers. And then the next. I look at Kayden. "I want to know who sent the men who killed my father. I want to know justice was served on his behalf. I need to know justice was served. I won't let it go."

"What are you telling me?"

"That if you love someone, you look for them, you fight for them, you have to have answers. But the more you know, the more you want to know."

"Meaning I need to give her closure."

"Yes. You do. Does she know about The Underground?"

"No. She can't. In other words, she can't have the truth."

"Can you at least give her a goodbye, not a disappearance? Make it seem like a car accident or some other accident? If not now, then later, to give her closure?"

"Gallo will dig around."

"Matteo is good at painting a perfect picture."

His cell phone starts ringing again, and he looks upward. "Jesus, I just need a fucking hour." He starts to get up.

I grab his arm. "Let it ring."

"I can't do that tonight." He stands and helps me up. "No one else can know I'm struggling with this. They can't know I need five minutes, let alone an hour."

"Of course not. But it's got to be at least four in the morning. Seriously, can't you let it go?" His phone stops ringing and almost immediately starts again.

"They're moving the body while the police chief has Gallo on a leash. I have to take it."

I suck in air at the announcement, and he exits the shower. The reality of what he's just spoken a little too brutal, and suddenly I need to wash the death off of me, too. I turn and grab the sweet-smelling shampoo Marabella bought me, wet my hair with the quickly chilling water, and suds up my hair and body. Images start flickering without definition in my head and while I try to invite and embrace memories, I'm not sure now is the time. I try to shove them away, pouring conditioner into my palm and running it through my hair. More images flicker.

"No," I whisper. "Not now."

I rinse my hair and find myself standing there as I lose the battle and images begin flowing freely. I relive the moment I grabbed my father's gun, the kitchen door flew open, and I shot and killed the man in black who entered. I am tormented. I am heartbroken. I am angry. The next moment, I'm in the foyer of the castle, wrapping a torn shirt around Enzo's wound, blood gushing everywhere, while I scream orders at Kayden's men to help me. I'm terrified for him. I am terrified of failing to save him. Finally, I'm leaning over David, blood gushing from his chest as he whispers, "Don't give him the necklace." And I feel angry. So very angry, and I don't understand why I'm not trying to save him.

"They're connected," I whisper. These three events are connected. One dot, two dots, three dots. *That's* why I'm remembering them together. *They're connected—but how? It makes no sense.*

"Ella. Sweetheart."

I blink again and see Kayden, and I'm sitting in the corner of the shower, with no memory of how I got there, and he's kneeling in front of me.

"Are you okay?" he asks. "Let's get you out of here."

"David's dead," I say. "Did you know that?" I don't give him a chance to answer. "But before he died, he lay there in his own blood and told me not to give '*him*' the necklace." My eyes meet Kayden's. "Was he talking about you?"

five

Kayden's hands come down on my arms and he stands, taking me with him. "Let's get you out of the shower." He reaches over and turns off the water.

"That's not a *no*, Kayden. Was David talking about you?"

"I had no idea David was dead," he says, wrapping his arm around me and urging me out of the shower.

"That's still not an answer," I say, grabbing a towel and knotting it at my chest. "*Was* he talking about you?"

"That's a complicated question, which I will answer. But here's how this is going to happen. We're going to get some clothes on and I'm going to make a pot of coffee. Then we'll sit at the kitchen table and have a past-due talk."

"Just tell me now and get it over with."

"Like I said, you asked a complicated question that has a complicated answer. And while we're both naked, and emotions are high—"

"I'm calm and rational."

"You are *always* remarkably calm and rational. Two of the many things I love about you, Ella. But you're wet, cold, and exhausted, not to mention affected by losing Enzo. Although this is the wrong time for this conversation, we need to have it—but my way. And that means that I'm going to get dressed and get that coffee going. You take time to dry your hair, and I'll be waiting when you're ready." He steps around me and heads for the closet.

He's right. We need to have this conversation in the kitchen. I grab another towel and partially dry my hair. It's then that Kayden reenters the bathroom, wearing gray sweats, running shoes, and a white T-shirt stretched over his broad, muscled chest. His light brown hair lies in damp tendrils framing his handsome face.

He doesn't immediately touch me, and despite every reason I have to doubt him right now, I *want* him to. "I need you to be the man I think you are."

"I have been completely honest with you about who and what I am. I'll be in the kitchen when you're ready. Don't feel rushed."

"No problem there," I say, a knot forming in my belly. "I suddenly seem to have gone from demanding answers to not being sure I'm ready for them."

"I understand," he says, caressing my cheek with two fingers, my skin tingling beneath his touch. "If I didn't," he adds, letting his touch fall away, "we would have had this conversation the first time you told me about the necklace." He starts to step around me, but stops, and his hands go to the sides of my breasts as he kisses me firmly on the mouth. And then he is gone, leaving me aching for his touch and praying for answers I can live with.

I do not turn to watch his departure, but instead find myself replaying something he said. *"I didn't know David was dead." Does that mean he knew David?* That's a bad thought I dismiss. He'd been upset over David, almost jealous.

Whatever the case, I'm suddenly over the dread that made me linger in the bathroom. I go to the closet and pull on black sweats and a black tank top, then shove my feet into slippers. Still cold, I pull on a matching black jacket and then return to the sink to use the hair dryer. As the wet strands become a sleek and shiny dark brown, I wonder if Kayden knows the me that had red hair. If he does and didn't tell me, that will be a hard pill to swallow—especially since *I* still can't remember my past.

That's enough to launch me toward the bedroom, and I suddenly stop, staring at the massive king-sized bed I share with Kayden. My mind is searching for the secrets of my past and I have a flickering image of me naked and tied to a bed, and another image of David and me fighting in our hotel room, and I'm not sure why I'm thinking of these two things right now. How do they connect to this room, and this moment? They feel nothing like any experience I have ever had with Kayden. But then, maybe that's the point: he is different. My instincts about him say he's different. But if my instincts are good, how the heck did I have those prior experiences?

Shaking off the questions, I leave the bedroom, entering the hallway with an odd sense of being watched. Ridiculous, since Kayden doesn't allow cameras in our tower, but I leave the bedroom door open and peer at the high ceiling as I start to walk, deciding I'm just spooked due to Enzo's death. How can I not be? Still, I rub the prickling sensation on the back of my neck, and it feels like forever before I turn into the living room. Crossing behind the couch toward the kitchen, I find myself remembering those naked, intimate moments with Kayden only a short time ago. The passion. The trust I'd felt for him. And then his words: "We both want more. Until we don't." The words send a surge of adrenaline and nerves through my body.

The scent of freshly brewed coffee teases my nostrils as I reach the kitchen, where I immediately find Kayden standing behind the island. But it's not him that makes my heart lurch, as usual. It's my gun that's lying on the counter between us. And when I should perhaps step backward I find myself charging forward to claim the other side of the counter. "What is that for?"

"You thought you needed it earlier," he says. "I want you to have it now."

My fingers curl on the tiled counter. "Do I need it?"

"That's for you to decide."

"That isn't the answer I want."

His jaw sets hard. "If you're expecting an answer you'll want, you'd better pick up that gun."

We stare at each other, a push and pull between us that has nothing to do with fear or intimidation, and everything to do with a bond we both know is being tested. "I know what you're doing."

"What am I doing?"

"The same thing you did outside that church, when you helped me hold the gun to your chest."

"Which is what?"

"Offering me the façade of control."

"You holding a loaded gun on me in no way equals a façade."

"I know you now," I counter. "You don't give up control, even when you say you are."

He rests his hands on the counter, one turned just enough for me to catch a glimpse of the hawk inked on his wrist, its wings spread, the mark of a man whose rules of many must dictate his actions. "There are two sides to this coin," he says, his words drawing my attention, his pale blue eyes piercing mine. "The me with you, and the me with everyone else."

"We barely knew each other at the church."

"I'd already decided you were mine. You just didn't know it yet."

I glower at him, frustratingly aroused and angry. "I know you haven't lived in America in a long time, but that's a very caveman-like, antifeminist statement to make."

"I wasn't aware you were a feminist."

"Yes, well, I wasn't either specifically, but my skill with a gun and my attitude say I am."

"Then let me say this to this new feminist side of you. You own me in ways I do not want to be owned, and should not be owned as The Hawk of The Underground. That is power. That is control, whether you want it or understand it. That is what you do to me."

Now he's the one who sounds angry, as if he doesn't quite comprehend how this has happened, either—how I have control he doesn't want to cede. And once again, without even trying, he has taken control, and given it, in a way that balances out the overwhelming alpha part of him. "Kayden—"

"Pick up the gun. Hear me out. And then decide what to do with it."

"I don't want the gun," I say, pushing off the island and

going around it to the coffeepot on the counter behind him. I'm aware of him right behind me, and I inhale, his spicy scent mingling with the richness of coffee, wreaking havoc on my senses, and it's all I can do to open the cabinet and grab a mug.

Kayden steps to my side, and I turn and offer him a cup. He closes his hand around mine instead, and heat rushes up my arm and into my chest. "Ella," he says softly, and my name on his lips slides under my skin and nestles deep in my soul. And Lord help me, I don't know if I am even capable of being objective with this man.

He inhales, that perfect chest expanding a moment before he takes the cup and sets it on the counter. I grab another and set it down beside it, and he fills both with coffee. Part of me thinks that this domestic act should downplay my worries and calm my nerves. It doesn't even come close, but I think it should, and I stick to this strategy. *Try something normal. Do something normal.*

Kayden sets the pot on the warmer while I tear open several packages of sweetener, my stupid hand trembling with the adrenaline I'm battling, and I drop one of the packages in the cup. Frustrated at my lack of control, I hold up my hands. "What are we doing? I don't want coffee. You don't want coffee. We're just going through the motions."

"Come on," he says, lacing our fingers together in that intimate, familiar way and leading me to the table. Rather than putting it between us, he pulls two chairs out to face each other, each of us claiming one. "First," he says, resting his hands on his knees. "I want you to know that I haven't lied to you about anything. I didn't know you until I found you in the alleyway. I don't know who you are now. And I had no idea you were connected to the necklace until you remembered it."

"So you were looking for the necklace before you found me," I say, confirming what seems obvious.

"I was, but not for hire. This isn't a treasure hunt, and it has nothing to do with money. At least not for me."

"What does that mean?"

"That necklace is a century old, and property of the British government. It disappeared fifty years ago. It's worth a large enough fortune to have the Italian and French mafia looking for it, and now, it appears, Raul and the cartel, as well. In any of their hands it's dangerous, but considering Niccolo is twice as powerful as the others, in his it's downright lethal."

"And you're trying to get to it first."

"I'm *going* to get to it first and return it to the British government, where I know it won't be used to profit Niccolo or anyone else."

"Because it's stolen?

"Because it represents the kind of power we can't allow someone like Niccolo, or anyone in his class of pursuers, to have."

"When you say fortune, how much money are we talking?"

"It's valued at a hundred and fifty million euros, but there's a private collector willing to pay double that."

"Oh my *God*. I didn't even know a necklace could be worth that much money."

"There's some history to this one, including the trail of ownership."

"And it was stolen from the British government?"

"Fifty years ago. And when I say stolen, I mean, it vanished. There were occasional rumors of its reappearance, each time starting a frenzied search. Interestingly, considering your involvement, none of those rumors placed it in the United States."

"But it must have been, if I was used to transport it to Europe."

"Maybe," he says. "But I'm not convinced you weren't wearing a decoy, meant to draw attention away from the real necklace."

"Why would you think it was a decoy, if I've obviously ended up on Niccolo's radar?"

"Because from what I know of the original's construction, there would be no place to slip a note inside. And you found one."

"Could the note give the location of the real necklace?"

"More likely, it was about a payoff for transporting the decoy. But whoever's behind that transaction knows where the real necklace is located."

"In other words, I really need to remember where that necklace is."

"Not necessarily," he says. "If the necklace was a decoy, as I suspect, then the important piece of the puzzle is what was on that note."

"Which wasn't in English, so my memory won't help us. I'd have to find it, and/or the decoy, to be of any help." I tilt my head to study him. "So I'm the key to what you're trying to achieve. Why didn't you just tell me this, Kayden?"

He leans forward, his hands settling intimately just behind my knees. "I fully intended to tell you, but I wasn't ready yet."

"What exactly would have made you ready?"

"Some way to prove to you that I wasn't using you to gain the necklace. I selfishly wasn't ready for that divide. Which backfired, and delivered us to that shower, with a gun between us."

"It could have been worse," I say with a halfhearted laugh. "I could have shot you."

"Your distrust is the only bullet I care about dodging right now." He sits up again, his hands settling back on his knees. "And that's exactly why I need you to think about that alleyway."

"I have been. I don't remember it."

"I'm not talking about what happened once you were there. I'm talking about what brought us both to that place."

"Oh," I say flatly, hating where this is going. "The necklace."

"Yes. The necklace and—"

"Niccolo," I supply, his name ice and fire, and not in good ways. "I am so confused right now. If he's the man from my flashbacks, I wanted him dead. The last thing I would do is meet him to hand him a necklace that makes him more powerful."

"Unless you didn't know it was him."

"Or he's not the man from my flashbacks at all, and I'm more deeply involved with Niccolo than I think." I swallow hard and stand, putting the chair between us. "Is this the real reason you didn't tell me about this?" I demand, my fingers closing around the wooden back. "Do you think I'm part of that man's entourage? Were you trying to prove that before you revealed everything else?"

I blink, and he's beside me. "Don't create nightmares that don't exist. You were running from Niccolo's men when I found you."

"I can think of no good reason why I was there to meet him, Kayden. Not one."

"Then let me help you with three. Blackmail, survival, and revenge."

"You think he was blackmailing me?"

"Blackmail is what he does. He threatens people, those they love, or the general public, to get what he wants. And if he doesn't, he kills them." His lips thin. "I've long believed that he killed Elizabeth and Kevin."

"I thought you had no idea who killed them?"

"I have reason to believe Kevin had contact with Niccolo frequently, leading up to the murders. Does that mean he did it? No. Do I believe he did it? Yes. The point is, he will do whatever's necessary to get what he wants."

"And he wants the necklace."

"Or you." His fingers gently tangle in my hair, lifting my mouth to his. "And he can't have you." He lowers his mouth to kiss me, but I firmly press my hand on his chest.

"No. Stop. You can't kiss me. We can't do this."

"Oh, I assure you we can," he says, leaning in again.

"No. No, Kayden." I push back and his hands catch my waist before I can escape. "Don't you see?" I demand. "I am now irrefutably connected to the man who killed the people you loved most in this world. And we don't know why. We don't know my motivation, or his leverage over me. You don't know and I'm in your bed and your home."

"Our bed. *Our hom*e, now."

"I want it to be, but we have to be realistic. We don't know who I really am. We need to talk to Nathan. Could I wake up one day and be changed? A different person? I don't think I can; I feel like this is me. I do. I *feel* like this is me."

"Easy, sweetheart. I did talk to Nathan, long before I found out about your connection to the necklace."

"And—"

"And it's time to go to bed." He scoops me up and starts walking.

"Damn it, Kayden, I want to talk about this!"

"I talk better naked, and so do you."

"We don't talk better naked."

"We do a lot of things better naked."

"I'm trying to protect you."

"Protect me naked," he says.

"This isn't funny," I object.

"I don't remember laughing."

"We have to talk about this."

"We will." He enters the bedroom and kicks the door shut. "Eventually."

I open my mouth to argue, but he sets me down beside the bed and starts undressing me. And I don't know how I go from being desperate to talk this out, to being desperate to be naked with him, but it happens. Suddenly, I'm tugging on his clothes and he's tugging on mine, and I end up on my back, his thick erection between my thighs, the delicious weight of him on top of me.

"What if we're enemies?"

"If we're enemies, sweetheart, you're killing me softly, and I like it."

"Kayden—"

"We choose what we are, Ella. *We* choose. No one else." He reaches under me and cups my ass. "In the meantime, just in case we suddenly decide we hate each other, we should take precautions and use my no-fail strategy."

I instantly know what he's talking about. "Keep your friends close and your enemies closer."

"Exactly," he concurs. "That's our plan. To stay close. Real damn close." His cock is nuzzling my sex, and then pressing into me, stretching me, sinking to the deepest part of me, before he says, "How do you like my plan so far?" He doesn't give me time to reply, kissing me with one deep, possessive stroke of his tongue, followed by another, and he doesn't taste like a man with doubt. He doesn't taste like a man who's sleeping with his enemy. He tastes like a starving man who wants more of me, who takes more of me, and in a blink we're in a frenzied rush of hot, possessive passion—touching each other, kissing each other, *fucking* each other every way we can, all of which comes with his silent promise that, right or wrong, he is nowhere near done with me, nor me with him.

But a long time later, I lie in bed with Kayden wrapped around me from behind, awake when he's asleep. Staring at the glow of the fireplace with one thought. Kayden didn't tell me what Nathan said about my amnesia—and nothing Kayden does is unintentional. That tells me I won't like what Nathan said to him. It tells me we are far more fragile than the passion we share says we are.

As if on cue, Kayden pulls me a little closer, and I press

into him, gripping his arm where it drapes my upper body, and once again, we are both holding each other a little too close and too hard, and to me that reason is clear. The secrets of that dark alleyway have been haunting us since the moment I opened my eyes and called him beautiful.

six

I don't remember finally falling asleep, but I wake to the dim glow of sunshine from a nearby window, immediately aware that Kayden is no longer touching me. Rolling over I find him gone, but a piece of paper is lying on his pillow. Leaning up on my elbow, I yank the blanket up over my chilled, naked body and read the note:

> Ella,
>
> Wrapping up some loose ends from last night. I will be gone most of the day but I'll call you when I can. Adriel is in the castle if you need him, and since you're a feminist with a gun, I warned him to keep his distance.
>
> Kayden
>
> PS: Close is good.

I laugh at his joke, and yes, close is good, but my smile fades quickly with the reference to last night. And while I don't feel like I could be any other me than the me I am now, I can't seem to frame the person in my flashbacks who submitted to more than being tied to a bed and left for hours. *He* took me to a club and had me tied up and whipped, a thought that has me remembering a hard, spine-bending lash that jolts me to a sitting position, my breathing turning into panting.

The sound of my ringing phone makes me glance at the nightstand, and I find that not only has Kayden set my phone there and attached it to a charger but that my journal, gun, and purse are there as well. Needing to hear his voice, I scoot over, grab my cell, and lie back down to answer. "Hello," I say, only to hear, "You're late, Eleana."

At the sound of Gallo's voice, I momentarily twist back around to glance at the clock, noting the eight fifteen hour. "I didn't agree to this meeting," I say, flattening firmly on my pillow where I intend to stay.

"Obviously when I stated that my badge indicated that you would make this meeting, I wasn't clear enough. Consider this your notice. This is official police business related to both your present and past activities, as well as Kayden's, which is why he will not be joining us for coffee."

I jolt upward, clutching the blanket to my chest. "Activities?" I say, telling myself this is a head game. He doesn't know about Niccolo. He doesn't know about the necklace. "I have no activities."

"Furthermore," he continues, as if I haven't spoken, "it's a courtesy that I'm giving you the opportunity to discuss said activities in an unofficial capacity, outside the castle, where the walls have ears. And I strongly believe you want this conversation kept confidential."

"I have nothing to hide," I say, managing to sound convincing when the idea that he knows something that puts me at odds with The Underground, or Kayden, terrifies me.

"Awfully certain for a woman recovering from amnesia."

He's hit a nerve that Kayden and I opened last night. "We're talking now. Say what you need to say."

"On an open line, which is unacceptable. You will come and meet me, and you will do so alone."

"Detective Gallo—"

"If you'd prefer, I can send a car to pick you up and take you to the station."

"Kayden works for your boss," I remind him. "He'll never let you take me, or Giada, to the station."

"The quite disturbing text messages Giada sent me last night will ensure otherwise. How much damage do you think she can do to Kayden and his beloved Underground, by the time Kayden frees you both from the interrogation room? You will come and meet me. You will not call Kayden, who I know is not in the castle, nor will you involve Adriel, who I know *is* in the castle."

"You *do* know that using Giada like this makes you a bastard, don't you?" I demand, not sure if I'm more furious with him or her.

"So you've said, but that just tells me how brainwashed you are, and how important this meeting is. I'm waiting, Eleana."

At this point, I just need to get off of this phone call and decide what to do next. “I haven’t even gotten in the shower,” I say. “I need forty-five minutes.”

“You have thirty. And in case you get the idea to call Kayden, I’m having a car pull to the front of the castle, ready to take you and Giada downtown.”

My jaw clenches. “I don’t remember where we’re supposed to meet.”

“I’ll text it to you,” he says. “And for the record, Giada didn’t tell me who was in the castle. I know things. And you need to know what I know.” He ends the call with that bombshell, which implies that someone close to Kayden is running their mouth.

I pull up Kayden’s number, but as I start to push the “call” button, I hesitate and grab the note he left. *Wrapping up some loose ends from last night*. And last night he was with a trigger-happy drug lord. Damn it. I’m not supposed to call unless it’s an emergency, and while Giada and me ending up at the police station would be that for sure, the best way to prevent that from happening is to face Gallo and have a proverbial stare-down. If I do it right, maybe he’ll back off and give Kayden some breathing room while I find out who, if anyone, is betraying Kayden. He protects me; it’s my turn to do the same for him.

Decision made, I throw aside the blankets, rush to the bathroom, and make a beeline for the shower. Turning on the water, I let it warm up, and I’ve just stepped under the spray and tilted my head back when there’s a flickering image of a man’s hand coming down on my arm, his pressed white shirt cuff riding up and uncovering a watch. My head lowers and I stare forward. *Kayden’s watch.*

What the heck did I just see? That wasn't Kayden. It couldn't be Kayden. It's always felt familiar, but never, ever has it come to me in a flashback.

"It's not Kayden," I say firmly, reaching for the shampoo. "So who is it?" It's a question I still haven't answered when I step out of the shower and towel off, then quickly apply light makeup and dry my hair, which now shows signs of red roots. It's a reminder that there is a small possibility that Gallo might really know something of my past. And that past might, in some way, make me the enemy of The Underground, as I feared last night. Kayden might handle that well enough, but I'm not so sure about his men, especially with me in The Hawk's bed.

Suddenly eager to get to this meeting and just know what is before me, I quickly dress in dark jeans, a navy sweater, and black knee-high boots. Once I'm dressed, I grab my black Chanel trench coat and head back to the bedroom, where I toss it on the bed and slip on my cross-body purse before reaching for my gun. The minute I touch it, I flash back to standing in a firing range, firing a weapon with my father by my side. *Charlie*, I think. His name was Charlie, and my eyes lower with the wholeness of that memory. Bit by bit, my father is coming back to me.

I decide right then that my gun is now named "Charlie" and if anyone messes with me, they will know his wrath. Placing my newly named bodyguard in my purse, I'm about to zip it up when my gaze catches on my journal. Since my memories are active today, I grab it and settle it safely next to Charlie. Then I put on my coat, shove my phone in my pocket, and head for the hallway.

On my way downstairs I think about how carefully Kayden has guarded me, and I'm not sure I can leave without Adriel following. Not to mention the fact that the castle security system seems to send an alert to everyone's phone. There has to be *some* way everyone leaves without driving the other residents crazy. Stopping at the bottom of the steps, I fish out my phone and dial Giada, hoping she's gotten her phone back.

"Ella," she answers. "Hi. I wanted to call you, but I just got my phone back, and you were angry and—"

"We need to talk. Alone. Where are you?"

"My tower."

"And Adriel and Marabella?"

"Marabella's in our kitchen, baking. That's her way of coping with last night. And Adriel is holed up in his office upstairs. That's his way of sparing us all his bad mood."

"Is his office in your tower, or the store?"

"My tower, but I can come to you."

I punch the button to lift the door between our tower and the main lobby. "The walls have ears in this place," I say, ducking under the door and entering the foyer. "Can we go out to lunch?" I glance up the central tower stairs, where the huge wooden door to the store is closed. "Or will Adriel not allow you to leave after last night?"

"Why does he have to know?"

That's not the answer I want from her, but it's a good opening for the information I need. "I thought all the doors pinged his phone."

"Not the garages or the store."

Bingo. I start walking across the foyer toward the central tower steps. "We aren't going to piss everyone off more by sneaking out," I say hypocritically, since that's exactly what I'm about to do. "But we need to talk and eat." As I start up the stairs, I remember Gallo's threat and ask, "Did you send Detective Gallo any text messages?"

"*No*. Why?"

"Are you sure?"

"Positive."

"You know Matteo can hack your messages, right?"

"There's nothing to hack. What's happening?"

"We'll talk over lunch," I say. "How's one o'clock?"

"Great. Should I come to you?"

"That's not a good idea," I say, hating that her suggestion makes me suspicious.

"Because Kayden doesn't want me in your tower."

"Let's give him space to cool off," I say. "How about we meet in the store?"

"Fine. There are no text messages."

"Good. Keep it that way."

I end the call and jog my way up the stone steps to the store, where I'm forced to wait on the electronic door, wishing like heck we had one normal door I could just open and shut. Finally, though, I'm inside the store. The windows are shuttered, but the front door is not, and the lock flips easily. The process of resetting the lock isn't as easy, though, and it takes me a few tries before I figure it out. When I finally step outside, successfully locking up behind me, I'm hit by the bitter February cold. And compared to the front of the castle, the street view here is like being on another planet. Back here there's no plaza, just a wall smack in front of me, and narrow, grayish, uneven brick roads with no sidewalks.

Aware that every moment standing here is one when Adriel could intercept my departure, I turn left and start walking, then after a few feet, I turn right down another tiny street, a cold wind lifting my hair, and freezing my scarf-less neck. While this one is just as narrow, it's quieter, without retail stores and street vendors. Desperate to get away from another gust of wind, I slip into an alcove and pull out my phone. Sure enough, Gallo has indeed texted me the meeting details, and it appears that Caffè del Cinque has become Bar del Cinque. I'm not quite sure what to make of that, especially at this early hour, but whatever the case, I key the address into Google, and discover that it's straight ahead and to the right.

Pushing off the wall, I start walking again, but I've only taken a few steps when that same sense of being watched, which I felt in the castle hallway, returns. Glancing over my shoulder, I see a couple of women behind me that seem to be chatting it up, but no one else. Still, that feeling persists, and though I charge forward, I reach under my coat to unzip my purse, keeping my hand there for easy access to Charlie.

Uneventfully, I turn the corner and arrive at "Bar del Cinque." The door is standing open despite the cold, and Italian pop music drifts outside. I cross the threshold, pausing just inside the entryway to find what I'd consider a typical American hotspot with clusters of wooden tables and a few booths near the back. To my left, the half-moon-shaped bar has been transformed from a place to drink to a place to display a lineup of pastries and coffee cups, proving I have much to learn about how Rome operates. I wonder what it would feel like to know this place as home, the way Kayden does, and to do so with him. But if Kayden is one of the most powerful men in Europe, which surely he is, as is Niccolo, how can Kayden expect that I can stay long term, and never cross paths with him? Unless . . . he doesn't expect me to stay?

"Eleana!"

At the sound of my fake name, I scan the mostly full tables and finally spot Gallo standing by a booth in the back of the room. I zip my purse up, stuff my phone into my pocket, and move in his direction. He watches my approach, transfixed it seems and not in a sexual way; more clinical, assessing. If he thought it'd make me uneasy, he's failed. Instead, I have the sense that he's trying to figure me out and doesn't mind me knowing it, which is a bit unnerving yet also comforting. His gaze says he doesn't have the full picture of who I am—*yet.* But he's trying way too hard.

And too soon, I am at the side of the table facing him and I see that his normally wrinkled suit is fairly well-pressed today, while the shadow on his jawline appears as perpetual as the sharpness of his gray eyes.

"Eleana," he greets me, the name sliding off his tongue much more comfortably than it meets my ears.

"Detective."

He waves me to my seat. "Shall we?"

I take a seat and when he joins me, sitting across from me, I note the red streaking the whites of his eyes. "You look tired," I say. "Did you stay up all night, thinking about how to terrorize me today?"

"I got up early to make a meeting," he replies dryly, his eyes lighting with amusement, not irritation. "Nice of you to finally show up for it."

In this moment, with his mood slightly lighter, I'm reluctantly reminded that he's rather handsome—a detail that doesn't help me keep Giada away from him. "You said this place was a café," I say, "but the sign says *bar*. That was very confusing."

"*Bar* means 'coffee bar.' "

I want to ask about Giada's text messages, but jumping into that topic might indicate the severity of my concern, so I stick to small talk. "I've been to a bar here in Rome, and it was beer and wine."

"A bar can be many things," he says, and pauses for obvious effect. "As can a person."

"It's confusing," I comment, pretending not to notice he's talking about me, and has somehow managed to nail my fear that I am not who I think I am.

"Not to Italians," he replies, "but you, Eleana, are another story. You are one big question mark."

"I'm not even a small question mark to myself anymore. I know who I am and why I'm here—as do you, since I've shared the details with you."

"But that's not the real picture, is it?"

Alarm bells go off in my head, but I don't react beyond a curious furrowed brow. "I'm confused by that comment. What does that mean?"

"Ciao!"

I silently curse the bad timing of the bald, middle-aged waiter with a short salt-and-pepper beard who's just arrived at our table. "Would you like a coffee?"

"Yes, please," I say. "I'm American, so whatever is most popular here in Rome."

"Cappuccino is what Italy is famous for," he supplies.

"Then cappuccino it is."

The man gives me a smile and a nod before he turns to Gallo, who speaks to him in Italian. The man replies and gives me a curious look, then departs, leaving me frowning in his wake.

"Why not take your coat off and stay awhile?" Gallo challenges.

"I'm chilly."

"Nerves do that."

"I thought nerves made people warm and clammy?"

He laces his fingers together on top of the table. "Have you remembered how you ended up in that alleyway?"

"Unfortunately, no," I say, glad to have this start out with something I can answer honestly. "I remember basic things. The rest is still cloudy."

"What things are 'basic'?"

"That answer changes often," I say. "For instance, I won't remember a particular food I like or hate, until it's presented to me. But when it is, it's like a light switch being flipped. I'm a puzzle that is slowly filling in the pieces."

"And where does Kayden fit into that puzzle?"

"If you have questions about Kayden, Detective, ask Kayden."

"I asked a question about you, not him. Where does he fit into *your* puzzle?"

"At this point, I'm figuring out just about *everything* in my life."

"Including him?"

"Of course," I say, because it's what he needs to hear, not because it's what I feel. What I truly feel is connected to Kayden, right with him in ways this man cannot change.

"Are you sure?"

"Sure? How can someone with amnesia be sure of anything?" And yet, for reasons I can't explain, sitting here with Kayden's enemy, I find that nothing in me is unsure about Kayden. And with that feeling, any worry I had last night, that my memories could turn me against him, evaporates.

He studies me for several awkwardly heavy moments. "And yet you can't seem to understand that a casual stroll down memory lane in a bad neighborhood could be dangerous. Even deadly."

"I have no idea what that means, either. You're talking in code. I'm a direct person, Detective. If you have something to say to me, please just say it."

"All right, then. Kayden wasn't in that alleyway going to the damn supermarket, as he claimed. He was after something, and he ended up with you. So either he's helping you hide something—"

"Hide something?" I demand indignantly.

". . . or he's after something he thinks you can give him," he continues. "If the latter is true, what do you think will happen when he finally gets it?"

I want to lean away, to withdraw, so I flatten my hands on the table and lean forward. "I know why you hate him."

"What happens when he gets what he wants?"

"How do you know I'm not what he wants?" I challenge.

"I have no doubt he wants you, but my question is why?"

"Insulting me isn't going to win you points here."

"I don't want points," he bites out. "I want justice."

"You want revenge," I say. "And you want it to the point that it's illogical and scary. Do you even care if you hurt other people to hurt him?"

"I care if *he* hurts other people."

"And yet you're hurting Giada by using her."

"You're very hung up on Giada. She clearly worries you."

There's an implication of more than sisterly worry that I decide is going no place good, so I sidestep it. "Why am I here, Detective?"

He reaches down to his seat and sets a file on the table. "It's time you understand who, and what, he is." He opens the file and sets a picture in front of me, of a man in his mid-forties. "Do you know who this is?"

"I do not."

"He's my boss." He slides the picture down the table but still facing me, setting another one in front of me. This one is of a younger man, mid-thirties maybe, with dark, curly hair. "What about this man? Do you know him?"

"No," I answer honestly.

"His name is Raul Martinez, and he's the leader of a Mexican cartel that's in bed with the Italian mafia."

I don't react to this information, but he's too close for comfort. "Why are you telling me this?"

His answer is to flip over another photo that turns my stomach—and it's all I can do not to react. "What about him? Do you know him?"

"No. I don't know any of these people."

"Niccolo Bulgari," he supplies. "The leader of the Italian mafia. And do you know what all of these men have in common?" His reply is to start turning over photos of Kayden with each of the men. "Kayden is what they have in common."

I glance at the photos and then at Gallo. "Do you know all of these men?"

"It's my job to know them."

"So those men all have you in common as well, right?"

His jaw clenches and he turns over another photo. "This man," he says, indicating a tall, thin man in an impressive suit, "is a politician believed to have killed his wife." He shoves a photo of Kayden talking to the man in front of me. "That was taken right after she died," he continues. "For all we know, Kayden killed her."

"Kayden didn't kill her," I snap, not sure what the explanation is for this and wishing I knew.

"And you know this how?"

"Because I know."

"Because he told you."

The waiter chooses that moment to set our coffees in front of us, and it's all I can do to murmur a "thank you" and listen to Gallo do the same before we are left alone again. Gallo shoves aside his coffee and I do the same. "Because he told you," he repeats, and it's a statement, not a question.

"No," I say. "There was nothing to tell me."

"And you know this how?"

"Because I've gotten to know Kayden," I say, not even blinking before I reply.

"Then you know that Kayden is a Treasure Hunter who will do anything for money."

"You forget the part where I said I've gotten to know him—so I know that statement is false. And murder is not just anything, nor is treasure hunting *murder*."

"I'm quite clear on the meaning of the word *murder*, as is Kayden, I assure you." He narrows those shrewd eyes on me. "Just how involved in his definition of *anything* are you?"

"Enough to know your accusations are completely misplaced, and driven by bitterness that's eating you alive."

"Accusations are only misplaced if untrue, and mine are not."

"Accusations exist," I countered, "because they're without merit and fact, which you clearly don't have or you'd have arrested him already."

"You are quick-witted for a woman with amnesia, *Eleana*."

The overuse and emphasis of my fake name doesn't feel accidental, nor is the bite to my voice as I say, "Amnesia doesn't mean stupid."

"Right. Just . . . absentminded. And as eager as you are to fill in your blank spaces, I'm surprised you haven't asked about those activities that I mentioned on the phone."

"On cue to please you," I say, steeling myself for a bullet. "What activities?"

"Those that include a man who consorts with the mafia and a drug cartel. That, *Eleana*, means you are, as well. I'd have thought that would disturb you, yet you didn't even blink when I mentioned it."

"My knowledge of the mafia and cartels comes from movies like *The Godfather*. And if anything I've seen is true, they're terrifying. I've also seen enough of Kayden's world to know the difference."

"Another of those amnesia anomalies. You remember *The Godfather* but not how you got to Italy."

"I told you—"

"You have a selective memory. I get it. And since you have an apparently selective understanding of the English language, despite using it better than I do, let's go back to visuals." He grabs the picture he showed me of Kayden standing with Niccolo and points at Niccolo. "Mafia king." He points at Kayden. "The man in your bed. They're laughing. They're friends."

"Keep your friends close and your enemies closer," I say. "You, it seems, just throw daggers at yours."

"'Keep your friends close and your enemies closer.' Interesting concept there. Since you've gotten to see inside Kayden's world, maybe you can enlighten me on how that saying applies to the people around him." He sets the picture of Kayden with his boss in front of me. "Is he one of Kayden's friends or his enemy?" He replaces the photo with the one of Kayden and Niccolo again. "What about him? Because to me, it's hard to tell where his allegiances are. And you know why? Because his only real devotion is to himself. Kayden Wilkens is an opportunist."

"Says the man using a young, grieving girl to exact revenge."

He gathers the photos and stuffs them back inside the folder, then crosses his arms in front of him and levels me a hard stare. "I think you know a lot of things you aren't telling me." He leans forward again. "A good fuck does not make a good man."

Anger knifes through me. I stand, and seeming to anticipate my action, he stands as well, his folder in hand. "We're done," I say.

He studies me several moments that feel eternal. I'm not sure what he wishes to find, or if he's simply trying to intimidate me, but the result is a twist of his lips. "For now." He slaps a few euros on the table and starts to walk away.

"Wait," I say quickly, and he backs up a step and gives me another arched brow. "Leave Giada alone."

"Not until she's out of the castle. Same story with you, Eleana. Because what you can't see for the blinders you're wearing is that I care, and you need someone like me."

"Don't try to make this about me and Giada, when it's about you and Kayden. Leave us out of this."

"He hasn't, so I can't."

"So you'll hurt us to hurt him? Is that really who you are?"

"Maybe I don't show it in the way you want me to, but I'm not a man of vengeance. I'm a man of the badge. I'm protecting you."

"By treating me like a criminal?"

"I know people. I read them and I know how to get their attention. Had I pleasantly warned you that you were sleeping with the enemy, you would have dismissed me. But you aren't dismissing me. You're thinking about what I've told you now. I see it in your eyes, even if you don't see it in yourself. *I am* protecting you. Call me when you figure that out. I will be here for you." He starts walking again, and I don't stop him, a memory of my father filling my mind.

I'm standing at the window of our living room and there are two men in official Army uniforms, though my father is dressed in jeans and a T-shirt, home for a rare month. I watch as one of the men steps close to my father and they square off.

I hold my breath, afraid they'll come to blows, but abruptly they step away from each other. The two uniformed men turn and start walking away. My father watches them get into the Army jeep, and I run to the door and open it, standing on the porch and waiting. It's not until that jeep is driving away that he walks toward me, his jaw set hard, his body stiff. He climbs the porch steps, and I don't ask a question, but rather, wait for whatever lesson he will deliver, because there is always a lesson.

He stops in front of me. "Never judge a man by his uniform or his attitude, good or bad. The truth is in his eyes and his actions. Never forget that, baby girl."

"So were those men good guys or bad guys?"

"Signora? Do you need something else?"

I blink and bring our waiter into view. "The ladies' room?" I ask, struggling to bring myself back to the present. He motions to a corner sign that reads TOILET, and I murmur, "Thank you," and head in that direction, keeping my pace until I've traveled down a small hallway to the one-person bathroom.

Inside, I lock the door and sink against it, inhaling and letting it out, affected more by the memory of my father than I am by Gallo. That day was—I think—about six months before he died. Before he was murdered. Who were those men? Why were they there?

And what did Gallo say that triggered the memory? Was it his reference to murder? What the hell was that thing about Kayden and a politician and murder?

I have looked into Kayden's eyes. He wouldn't kill someone for money. And damn it, I played this all wrong. I didn't find out anything Giada has revealed to Gallo, nor did I find out who inside the Hunters is betraying Kayden. Maybe I should have pretended to doubt Kayden. No. No, that would have just empowered Gallo even more.

A piece of paper slides under the door. I frown and pick it up, opening it to read: *I know*. That's it. Just, *I know*. Nothing more. Nothing less. A chill runs down my spine and I open the door to find the hallway empty. Grinding my teeth, I whisper, "Your actions define you, Gallo. You really are an asshole."

I glance at the note again. *I know*. I have no idea what it means. Maybe it's about the butterfly? Or Niccolo? Or both? Why wouldn't he bring them up, if he knew any of this? Maybe he's just trying to spook me into a reaction I won't give him.

Officially ready to get out of here, I open my purse, wanting Charlie handy, then shove the note into my coat pocket with my phone and head back into the bar again, relieved that Gallo hasn't reappeared. Wasting no time, I cross through the seating area, and reach the front door. Exiting, the cold air makes me walk quickly down the narrow brick pavement that's now lined with pedestrians. The crowd provides coverage for me if Gallo is following, but it does the same for him.

I turn onto the quieter walkway where I'd paused to Google a map earlier, thinking about Giada and the need to rein her in. I'm halfway to the end when I pass an alcove, and to my shock, a strong hand comes down on my arm and pulls me inside.

seven

I know it's Kayden even before I see him, the familiar spice of his scent enveloping me, his big, warm body pinning me in a corner, his jean-clad legs caging mine. "What the hell were you doing there with Gallo, Ella?" he demands, his hands bracketing my waist, his tone hard. His temper is unforgiving, but I don't cower.

"Why are you here, and not attending to your business?" I retort, my fingers curling around his T-shirt, beneath his leather biker jacket. "This was not an emergency. This was not a reason for you to leave what you were doing. That you did makes me look to your men like a distraction you can't afford."

"*Why* were you with Gallo?" he demands.

"Because had I not met him for coffee, he was going to take me to the police station for questioning, and we both know that would have put me on Niccolo's radar."

"And yet," he bites out, his fingers flexing at my waist, "you didn't call me."

"You said only to call if it was an emergency, and Gallo being an asshole is not an emergency."

"*Last night*, Ella."

"Exactly. The note you left said you were wrapping up loose ends from *last night*, and I don't want you to think I don't know the definition of an emergency. That's like the boy who cried wolf, nor do I want your men to think I represent a distraction."

"Let me worry about my men."

"I'm not going to do that; not now or ever. If you want a puppet who'll burden you with everything and care about nothing you do, then I'm the wrong choice for you, Kayden. That's not who I am, or who I hope we are together. You didn't have to come here. I would have called you the moment things turned in the wrong direction."

"What part of once it's gone wrong, it's too late, don't you understand?" he demands. "Why didn't you go to Adriel?"

"Aside from the fact that he's been vocal about me being a distraction you don't need, and the reason I was worried about your men?" I don't give him time to reply, getting to the real issue. "Gallo said that any interference by Adriel, you, or anyone, would mean not only me visiting the police station, but Giada, too. And I wasn't willing to let her run her mouth in an interrogation room."

"He had no legal right to do that—which you'd have known, had you called me or gone to Adriel."

"It's more complicated than that," I say, hesitating to bring up Giada when he's this angry.

"Define *complicated*." I hesitate a moment longer and he is not willing to wait. "Ella—"

"Gallo claims Giada sent him text messages last night that were damning enough to ensure that you couldn't stop him from questioning her or me. She swears there are no messages, even though I told her Matteo would find out if she was lying. But I couldn't take the risk that there were texts."

"And yet you tried to handle this on your own."

"I *did* handle it, Kayden. I'm not arrested. I'm not at the station and on Niccolo's radar any more than I was before today. You don't owe the police chief yet another favor, and no one has told one single Underground secret. I'd be back in the castle trying to throttle Giada right now, if you hadn't just yanked me into a dark hole."

"There's a bigger picture here that you need to understand—but that isn't a conversation we can have when I have men and business waiting on me at the castle."

He reaches for my hand and I grab his jacket. "Wait. Please. If this is about my past—"

"It's not."

"I didn't betray you, Kayden. If it's about trust—"

"One of my men died last night, Ella," he says, his low voice rough, almost guttural. "The last thing I needed today was to find out that you were with Gallo, when we don't know what Giada told him. One wrong word, one careless whisper, and he will take you and my men down to destroy me."

"I promise you, when you have time to listen, I handled him well."

"Even if you did, you took a risk that didn't have to be taken. You didn't know what trigger to your past he might hit, or how you would have reacted."

I physically flinch. "And there it is. My amnesia. The monster in the closet we denied last night."

"Not a monster, and there is no denial here. Just a fact

that we both have to consider for everyone's protection." His cell phone buzzes with a text, and he reaches inside his jacket pocket to glance at it, before returning it and refocusing on me. "We need to get back to the castle." He takes my hand and leads me out of the alcove. There is no pause or opportunity to adjust to the freezing cold weather. I shove my other hand in my pocket as we head down the path, his black-laced biker boots crashing against the brick street and seeming to echo with more than his unappeased anger. There is a shift in him now, a drive that is all about power, control, and purpose, that silences anything I might say. Something is happening and he needs to focus on it, not me, which was my intent all along.

It's on that thought that Kayden turns us around the corner, directing us down the walkway that leads to the front of the castle, not to the back, where I'd exited. We've almost reached the plaza, and our point of entry, when a twenty-something man steps directly into our path, and I jolt. Kayden reacts to my reaction and the visitor, pulling me closer, bending both our arms at the elbow and aligning our hips, possessive, protective. And just like that, I feel like us again, not the divide, not the doubts I realize now that his reaction to my action has stirred in me.

The stranger speaks to Kayden in fast, clipped Italian, never looking at me. Kayden issues an equally clipped reply, and the man departs immediately while Kayden puts us back in motion.

"Who was that?" I ask.

"One of the neighborhood crowd," he says. "Niccolo might own the rest of the city, but I own this neighborhood and its ears and eyes." He halts us in front of the castle. "And Gallo's aware of that fact."

Realization delivers a painful dose of the big picture Kayden had hinted existed. "He threatened me to ensure that I didn't call you, knowing that someone else would. He wanted to cause trouble between us."

"Yes," he confirms. "But even more, your showing up to a meeting I wouldn't have allowed you to attend told him that you aren't fully aligned with me. It told him you didn't call me."

"But if I hadn't gone, it would have looked like you didn't trust me. Or like we had something to hide."

He closes the small space between us, towering over me, touching me nowhere, when I want him to touch me everywhere, anywhere. "I *do not* play Gallo's games, and if you are to be by my side, you don't, either. Period. The end. That isn't up for negotiation because it's about keeping you safe. Your safety is never a negotiation."

"You can't—"

He gently shackles my arm and pulls me to him. "I can and I will when it comes to your safety. Because I fucking care way too much for either of our good. And if you want to argue that point, we will fight and fuck this out in private."

"When exactly are we going to do this fight-and-fuck thing, because I think we'll both feel better afterward."

"We will, tonight. During and afterward." Heat rushes through me, one part anger, one part lust, just as a sleek black Porsche pulls up beside us, the windows tinted dark. Kayden motions it inside the grounds and we follow to the other side of the gate, where he hits the button to lock us inside before withdrawing his phone.

We walk the broad expanse of the front yard while he makes a phone call, saying simply, "Open the garage," before returning his cell to his pocket.

I watch the Porsche pull around the drive as the doors open. "Who's inside it?"

"Carlo," Kayden says. "Who is about to be reminded that I'm his moral compass."

"Considering he's amused at inappropriate times, that doesn't surprise me."

"Don't confuse amusement with lack of intelligence," he says. "He's cunning. He's lethal and he misses nothing."

"And the moral compass?"

"He has one, but he's about to be reminded that mine is the only one that matters." We reach the bottom of the stairs and he turns me to face him. "My men think you called me before meeting Gallo. Keep it that way and they might not ask questions. Don't talk about it. Less is more, unless it's with me."

"Because they'll see me as a weakness."

"Yes."

"Am I?" I ask. My cell phone rings from my coat pocket and Kayden's jaw sets hard. No doubt he assumes it's Gallo, as I do.

"Check it," he orders softly.

Dreading where this might be going, I fish it from my pocket and nod. "It is. It's him."

"Decline the call," he says, his mood shifting back to that dark edginess from the alcove.

I don't hesitate, not after his comment about Gallo trying to divide us in some way, which the note he stuck under the door supports as true. I hit "decline" and shove my phone back into my pocket, and the mysterious note flutters out to the ground.

Kayden bends over and snags it, reading it and looking at me. "What does 'I know' mean?"

"Gallo shoved it under the bathroom door in the coffee bar, but he said nothing to indicate he knows about my past."

"Of course he didn't," he says, balling the paper in his hand and shoving it inside his pocket, his jaw clenching at the sound of the front door opening.

"Less is more," he repeats as we start to climb up the stone steps.

I hurry to keep up, my gaze lifting to find Adriel has appeared on the top step, dressed in jeans and some sort of polo-style Italian football shirt. His features are harshly drawn, the scar lining his cheek somehow more pronounced. When he looks at me, it's brittle, and the only color in his eyes is ice. He's pissed at my bypassing him today, and my struggle to find peaceful ground with him, and I'm thinking my telling Kayden about his disapproval isn't going to help.

He speaks to Kayden in Italian and the two men talk on the porch. Eager to get out of the cold, I continue into the main castle foyer, almost running into Carlo. I back up, and I swear in morning light, dressed in jeans and a tan leather jacket and tan boots, he's far more the Italian stallion than I remember. A man I suspect could fuck you senseless and slice your throat, and I'm not sure why Kayden tolerates him.

Carlo is quick to remove the space I've just put between us, his eyes a bit too warm, too attentive. It could be flirtation, but my gut tells me that's not the case. He's testing me, trying to intimidate me, and I hold my ground. "How was coffee?"

he asks, a cynically amused quirk to his lips, arrogance wafting off of him.

I want to step backward, but refuse to give him that reaction. I fold my arms in front of me. "Uneventful and uninteresting," I say dismissively.

"Gallo is many things," he says, "but we both know *uninteresting* is not one of them. Did he fuck with your mind? He likes to fuck with people's minds."

"Spoken like a man who's been his victim."

He gives me a deadpan stare and then smirks. "Ha. Ha. Aren't you funny. And brave."

There is something brutal in in those flippantly spoken words, almost a threat, or maybe it's just that everything about the man is lethal. I stand firm, reaching for the respect I need to stand by Kayden's side. "Brave because I said that to you, or brave because I dared to suggest I fared better than you?"

The door shuts behind me and a moment later Kayden steps beside me, speaking to Carlo in clipped, thick Italian, but it is not his words that I cannot understand. It's how, without trying, he sucks all the energy from the massive castle foyer, leaving none of it for Carlo to claim as his own. Kayden has become The Hawk. He is always The Hawk, but I'm in awe of his control when he chooses to radiate that persona. Carlo's words sharpen and Kayden stares at him, seconds ticking by before without looking at me, he orders, "Wait on me in the tower, Ella."

I'd rebel against that order if he weren't The Hawk, who I've vowed to battle behind closed doors, and if I weren't certain Carlo had just challenged him over me. Which makes me want to stay and fight my own battle, and his too, but he is

The Hawk, and I can't risk working against his leadership. Knowing my show of respect is critical right now, I force myself to turn and walk to the door dividing me from our tower, jabbing the code into the keypad.

The door begins to lift, and for once, my impatience does not win as I wait for it to rise all the way up, hoping to overhear the conversation sure to take place between Kayden and Carlo. But they start talking in Italian, driving home how important it is for me to learn the language—and then Adriel's and Matteo's voices join the conversation, surprising me. Giving the door my profile, I bring the foursome into view to find Matteo standing next to Carlo, and Adriel next to Kayden. Perhaps the choice of positions is simply convenience, but I have this odd sense of a division that I do not like.

Too soon, considering I know nothing more, the door has fully lifted, and I'm forced to enter our tower, pressing the button on the other side to close the door. I rush up the stairs and go straight to our room, shutting the door behind me. Leaning against the hard surface, I stare at the bed now cast in shadows, ignoring the light switch, but I do not truly see it. Instead I think of Gallo's implication that someone is leaking information to him. And while Carlo seems an obvious choice, I'm just not sure. Someone who's a rebel and an asshole rarely finds safe haven with a police officer. And I have a flickering image of a man in a suit whose face I cannot see, saying those exact words to me.

I press my hands to my face. "My God. What is wrong with me?" I drop my hands and lean my head back against the door. "Why can't I remember? I'm not a scared person. Or do I just not remember the fear?" It's a horrible thought, and it doesn't matter anyway. I *have* to remember, or Kayden and I will always wonder about those triggers he mentioned. We will never truly have trust, and I will never really be at home here. The word *home* seems to be one of those triggers, for suddenly I'm seeing myself on a stage, dancing to an empty auditorium, and my mother *and* my father are watching. My father didn't approve of my dancing. My chest aches with the heaviness of the emotion now stirred, and I think my mind is telling me that dancing will take me places that will hurt, but I have to visit.

Ready to change clothes and go upstairs to the room Kayden has made my dance studio, I shove off of the door and make my way through the bathroom to the massive closet. *What if we're enemies?* I inhale, and reject the ridiculous notion that didn't exist at the coffee bar today. It is not possible that I could be Kayden's enemy.

Suddenly suffocating in my coat, I dig my phone out of its pocket, and then hang it up. Sitting down on the bench in the center of the closet, I have a memory of Kayden and me having sex right here, on top of it, and it's a good memory that curves my lips. *We are not enemies.* I pull my purse off and set it beside me, unzipping it to put my phone inside. Just for good measure I touch Charlie, which is one part a gift from Kayden, and another from my father, who taught me to use it. I want to say the only two men who have ever fully earned my respect and trust, but I can't know that for certain. Yet . . . I do.

The sound of the bedroom door opening and shutting has me zipping my purse and facing the door at the same moment Kayden appears, his biker jacket telling me he's not staying.

He is so damn powerfully male that he consumes the small space, and me with it.

"That was about me, right?" I ask.

"Yes, but it's handled, as is Carlo's attitude." He holds up the piece of paper Gallo left for me. "Tell me about this."

"I told you all there is to tell," I say, pressing my hands to the back of my jean-clad hips.

"Tell me again."

"Gallo took assholeness to a whole new level, and I told him we were done talking. He left, I thought, and I didn't want to be on the street with him, so I went to the bathroom. I'd barely locked the door when it was slipped underneath."

"He left?"

"He walked toward the door, but it was behind me, so he must not have."

"So you don't know that Gallo put this under the door?"

"It's logical."

"But you don't know."

"I guess not."

"What did Gallo say to you?"

I fold my arms in front of me, dreading this part of the conversation. "He all but told me one of your men was running his mouth. That's how he knew you'd be gone today."

Kayden slips the note inside his jacket pocket, his jaw hard. "I met with the police chief this morning about that favor he wants."

"And Gallo knew."

"Apparently so."

"Does that mean the police chief turned on you?"

"He isn't that foolish. Not with what he wants from me,

and what I know about him that he doesn't want anyone else to know. And the cold, hard fact, which Gallo might have told you, is that I will use it if I have to."

"You've been very honest with me about everything not being squeaky clean or easy."

Kayden stares at me for several beats. "What did he say to you?"

"He showed me pictures of you with various people he claims you consort with, while running down their list of sins."

"What people?"

"Raul. Niccolo."

"Niccolo?"

"Yes. But he didn't seem to know anything related to me and him. Except he kept overusing my fake name, after saying he wanted to talk about my activities."

"What activities?"

"It turned out to be my connection to your activities."

"What activities?" he repeats.

"The connections to Raul and Niccolo, and there was a politician whose name I regretfully missed, who Gallo says employed you to either kill his wife or cover up her murder."

He stands there, stone that cannot be broken, his eyes hard, his spine stiff, seconds ticking by before he says, "Why did you end the meeting?"

"He made a crass statement about a good fuck not making a good man."

He closes the distance between us, stopping a step from touching me, the scent of him earthy and warm. "He made you doubt me."

"No. He got me doubting *me*. He got at me and the amnesia. Part of the reason I went to that meeting was that reference to my 'activities' that I feared would sideswipe us, or get to your men before me. I know in my heart that I can't be turned, but you can't take that risk. You can't operate as The Hawk with a woman who's a mental light switch from becoming a problem."

He snags my hips, his touch spiraling through me, the way everything about this man spirals through me. "This was never about me trusting you," he declares. "This was about you trusting me. About you waiting to find out about me from me, not fucking Gallo."

Suddenly, every word he's spoken and every action he's taken since pulling me into that alcove shifts and takes on a new light. It's now about him daring to open himself up to me, about being raw and exposed, letting me see the blood of past wounds, while Gallo tries to cut them deeper.

"He can't turn me against you," I say, grabbing his jacket again. "I'm with you, Kayden. All the way, in every way."

He backs me up, pressing me against the wall. "You say that now, but being with me is not roses and chocolates, Ella. With me comes every dark, hard-to-swallow secret of The Underground."

"If Enzo's death last night, and Gallo today, doesn't prove I'm here to stay, I don't know what will. *I'm here*. I'm not leaving."

"I'm not just talking about Enzo or Gallo. I'm talking about me, and what this life does to me, and what it has made me. And I'm talking about us, and how that affects us." He cups my backside and pulls me to him, my hand flattening on the solid wall of his chest. "You have no idea how dark I can be," he declares, his voice a rough, low rumble. "You have no idea of the decisions I have to make, and how I cope with them. And if I didn't have business to attend to right now, I'd show you." His forehead touches mine. "I'd make you understand." His cheek slides to mine, his breath a warm tease on my neck and ear. "I can protect you from everyone but me."

These words hit a nerve I don't understand, and my fingers curl around his shirt. "Don't. Don't protect me from you."

"I've been cautious, Ella. I've been *gentle.* I've said I'll demand everything and more from you, but I haven't."

I shove on his chest, forcing him to lean back and look at me. "Then you deny both of us the possibilities of what we could be."

His eyes darken the pale blue to almost black. "I am—"

"*Not him,*" I say, knowing at least partially where this is coming from. "He didn't push my limits like you want to. He didn't escape with me. I was a possession he was free to punish—not please, tease, and pleasure. He took me to a sex club and tied me up and had a woman beat me. You would not do that. You are my escape. You make me forget that."

"Until you see everything I am."

"I am not afraid of who you are. I am afraid of who you *won't* be when you're with me, and what that does to us. So as of right now, be on notice. Fuck gentle. I demand everything and more. And don't you dare give me anything less."

"I am many things you haven't tasted or touched, but this conversation isn't about me denying you, or us, those things. It's about me promising you that they're coming." He releases me without warning, leaving me limp against the wall, stunned to find him walking toward the door.

"But you think it's the beginning of the end," I say, my words halting him in the archway. "So I'll just have to hang on tight enough for both of us."

He finally faces me, his face all hard lines and shadows. "Do you think I helped that man kill his wife, or at least cover it up?"

"I don't know what happened, but I believe that you make decisions that are honorable, or I wouldn't be here. And if you think you could stop me from leaving if I chose to, you're wrong. I'm resourceful."

"If you weren't, you wouldn't have made it to that alleyway alive. We're going to a formal political event tonight. I'll make sure you have what you need. Be ready for the party by eight." Then he disappears into the bathroom, his footsteps quickly fading, the bedroom door opening and closing, to seal me inside his world, not out, so much so that he's taking me to this event. At least for now.

I press my palms to the wall for much-needed stability, stunned by what just happened—but one thing is crystal clear. I have looked into his eyes and seen inside his soul, and I am deeply, passionately in love with him. But to have that matter, I can't just say the words. I have to show him. I have to fight with him and for him.

I can't speed up that process, but I can remove an obstacle. My amnesia. I hurry to the stool again and sit down, pulling my phone from my purse. Tabbing through the numbers, I pull up Nathan's number and dial the man who is not only my doctor but my hope right now.

"Ella," he says two rings later.

"Can I see you? Or can you come here?"

"Is everything okay? Is your head bothering you again?"

"I'm fine. The concussion seems to be gone. I just . . . I need to talk. About my amnesia."

"Kayden told me you might. And yes. I can come there and I will, but I'm at the hospital. It's nearly noon now; I'll be there in a couple of hours if I can. I'll meet you in the store."

"Great. Thank you, Nathan."

He hesitates. "I should warn you up front that that I might not have the answers you want."

"I want you to make me remember."

He laughs. "That's about as reasonable as you asking me to lose ten pounds in twenty-four hours. Some things take time."

"Is that what you told Kayden? That my memory will take time?"

"Let's talk when I get there."

"*Avoidance* is a four-letter word."

"You can teach me some new ones when I get there." He ends the call.

I grimace, setting the phone in my lap. *I might not have the answers you want.* That's already not the answer I want, and I now know why Kayden didn't directly respond when I asked him what Nathan had told him. Nathan didn't give him the answer he wanted, either. And suddenly I wonder if he's told Kayden that I'm unstable or unreliable. He might have even told him not to trust me.

Frustrated that I'm doing this to myself, I shove my phone back into my purse and zip it up. Standing, I slip the strap over my head and chest, keeping my phone and Charlie close at hand. My gaze travels down the closet, seeing the rows of Kayden's clothes on one side, my limited wardrobe on the other.

This place, this man, is home to me now. I'm not letting it go. I need the trigger I was after when I came in here a short while ago, and my attention lands on the pink ballet slippers sitting on a wall of shelves. An image of my mother, my first dance instructor, with a huge smile on her face. I smile, too, but abruptly the feelings and the moment in time shift. Now there is pain, loss, heartbreak. Now my mother is lying in a hospital bed, and by her side is some man I do not like. She is close to death, and I don't want to live this heartbreak again. I most definitely don't want to know the man standing by her bedside, but I have to face those things. I have to face all things.

Marching forward, I pick up the slippers, steeling myself for the pain to follow and shutting my eyes. And I wait. And wait, and I will something to come to me, but I have nothing. Frustrated, I remember my lunch with Giada, and set the slippers down. Dancing for my memories will have to wait. And I wonder, not for the first time, what can be so horrific that I refuse to remember it? I have to talk to Nathan about controlled triggers. There has to be a way to drive my progress.

Leaving the closet, I walk into the bedroom, glancing at the clock, which reads twelve fifteen. I have forty-five minutes to kill before my lunch with Giada, and I pull my journal from my purse, opening it to a random page. I find one of the many butterfly drawings there, and while I now know they represent the necklace, for some reason, it still feels like it means something else. Or maybe the butterfly is a part of a memory I can't quite reach. Desperate to fill the black holes of my mind, I decide that stimuli trigger memories, and since I won't get that alone in this room, I'll head to the store early. I shut the journal and replace it in my purse.

I quickly make my way to the main castle foyer, and as I head up the central tower steps toward the store, I hear, "Ella!"

I turn to find Giada rushing up the stairs toward me. While her all-black jeans, boots, and sweater would strike me as stylish another time, today I have a feeling she's trying to stay low-key. "Thank God you're early. I'm suffocating in that tower. Marabella and Adriel have been watching over me like a hawk."

A Hawk. *Kayden*. He is The Hawk and right now, I am an extension of him. "Because last night was bad, Giada. I need to know what you said to Gallo."

"I told him there were men here with guns. Nothing more."

"Giada—"

"I didn't tell him anything more." She tears up. "I had just seen Enzo lying in his own blood. I was supposed to go on a date with him, Ella, and he was dying. He *did* die. I didn't really know him, but I might have, and *I hate* The Underground."

Stunned by this revelation, which doesn't justify her actions but helps explain them, I pull her into a hug. "I know that hurt. I know it scared you."

She sobs and I hold her for several seconds, before she makes a low, frustrated sound and pulls away from me. "This is why I hate Kayden."

Protectiveness flares in me hard and fast, forcing me to tamp down on it just as quickly. "I know why you're connecting this to The Underground, to the many tragedies in your life—but Kayden gave Enzo specific orders that he ignored."

"Kayden tells those men when to pee."

"Kayden gave him an order that he ignored," I repeat. "And we all make choices, and we live or die with them."

"Kayden gave him the job he was on, knowing it was dangerous," she argues.

"Kayden tried to talk him out of the job. And when he finally let him take it, he told him to observe and report. Instead, Enzo charged after his prize—and he knew the risks."

She glares at me and then storms past me to the store.

I follow. "Giada," I say, but she ignores me, keying in the code to open the heavy wooden door arched in front of us, then staring forward. "Giada, damn it," I growl. "Look at me."

She faces me. "You're fucking Kayden. You're not objective."

"Kayden is much more than a *fuck* to me," I snap, irritated at her crassness, which matches Gallo's a little too closely. "Do you think I'm not terrified that when he walks out of the door, he won't come back?"

"Then get out while you can. Because mark my words: one day, he won't come back."

"Yes, he will. I have to believe that. And even if he doesn't, I'm not giving up days of my life that could be spent with him, just because there might not be one more. *This* is who they are. They *are* The Underground, Adriel included. Like my father was in the Army. He was a risk taker. Kayden and Adriel are risk takers. Loving them means accepting them." She tries to duck under the door, and I grab her arm, forcing her to look at me. "Loving them means accepting them," I repeat. "Keeping them safe means accepting them—not distracting them, which could get them killed. If you can't do that, I'm sorry, but you can't stay here. You have to leave."

"You can't say that. Adriel says that."

"This is Kayden's home. Unless you're able to do a one-eighty, you're gone. And even then, it might be too late."

"In other words, he's going to kick me out. I should have known it."

"You're right. You should have. He's The Hawk, and he carries every loss of life he's experienced as a hole in his heart. He won't let you be one of them. Or Adriel. And you're going to get Adriel killed."

"Now *I'm* the one putting him in danger?"

"Sweetie. He is part of The Underground—"

"He's not."

"He is. And every moment he denies it is misery to him."

"What about me? What about how *I* feel?"

"Not everything is about you. We all lose people. We all hurt. And we're all in danger when you act like you did last night. Grow up, Giada. And show some appreciation for Kayden, who lets you live here, and set up a fortune in a trust for you. And show some appreciation for your brother, who's miserable running a damn store, when he wants to hunt."

"You don't know him."

"Apparently, I know him better than you, because the

hunt is in that man's eyes. Let him be happy. You have a fortune in a trust fund. You can do anything. Be anything. Go anywhere."

"I'm not leaving here. I'm not leaving my brother."

"Then you have changes to make, and some real convincing to do," I say. "Think about it." I turn away and enter the store, taking broad, adrenaline-laden steps, when I stop dead in my tracks at the realization that Adriel is standing there in front of me, his legs planted in a V, his arms folded over his chest.

I hold my breath, not sure what he overheard, or how he's going to react. But as we stare at each other, there is less ice than before, and after several moments, he nods in appreciation.

I give him a nod in return. "I was going to have lunch with Giada, but I thought it best we stay in. Do Italians have pizza delivery?"

His lips quirk, his mood remarkably, palpably, lighter. "This isn't ancient Rome. Of course we have pizza delivery."

"I was hoping to hang out here. My tower is rather quiet and . . . empty."

"I know the definition of the word quite well," he surprises me by saying, lifting one hand toward an archway leading to a part of the store I've never visited. "You'll find a full living room and kitchen there."

"Thank you." I start to walk away and pause. "I mentioned to Kayden that I'd like to help out here in the store."

"And he said what?"

"He wasn't receptive at the time," I admit.

His lips quirk. "Let me guess. You plan to change his mind."

"Not change his mind. Just . . . talk."

"You talk quite effectively," he comments dryly. "Let me know when you're ready for the keys."

"So . . . you're okay with it?"

"I hate this fucking store."

"Good," I say, glancing around the store, surprised at how excited I am about where this is headed. "Because I think I could kind of love it, and I have a feeling you'll be less of an asshole if I'm running it instead of you."

"You think I'm an asshole, do you?"

"*You* think you're an asshole," I counter.

"Only when I have to be."

"You never have to be with me."

"Disproven by rethinking last night's events."

"Last night sideswiped me. It won't happen again."

He studies me a moment, and slowly, approval lights his eyes. It's the first time I've seen anything light his eyes. "I'll hold you to that."

"You won't have to," I assure him.

"You hate the store?" Giada asks, and I don't wait for Adriel's reply, which comes in Italian anyway.

I head toward the archway, glancing at the various displays in glass cases, eager to start exploring them all. Crossing under the giant arch and turning right, I discover a cozy living area with a white stone fireplace in the corner, a brown leather sofa, two oversized matching chairs, and a flat-screen television mounted on the wall. Farther right I find an open-concept kitchen with a gorgeous gray stone island, but my joy at the coziness is doused as I wonder if this was the part of the castle Kayden shared with Elizabeth before she was murdered. If that's the case, I am not bringing up the store to him again.

I return to the living room.

"Ella."

At the sound of Nathan's voice, I turn to find him standing by the couch, dressed in jeans and a long-sleeved shirt, his normally clean-shaven jaw shadowed. "My patient transferred to another hospital, so I came by on the way to meet them there." He motions to the couch. "You want to sit?"

I nod and join him on the couch, angling to face him. "You look tired."

"It was a hell of a night, and I got called into surgery this morning."

"What day of the week is it?" I ask. "I really don't know."

"Saturday. And welcome to my world, where I barely know if it's morning or night."

"We don't have to do this today."

"I'm here, and I want to be here. I assume you want to know the same things Kayden wanted to know."

I actually just wanted to pressure him for a way to trigger my memory, but I suddenly do want the answers Kayden wanted. "He told you that you could tell me?"

"Anything you want to know."

I am once again reminded of my father's advice. *The truth is in his eyes and his actions.* "What did he ask you?"

"He asked me if the return of your memory could change who you seem to be now."

"Who I seem to be," I repeat. The "seem to be" is pretty hard to swallow, but I can't fault Kayden for asking what I also want to know. "And?"

"I've studied the data on this, and there aren't enough cases like yours to be sure."

"You mean I *could* end up a completely different person?"

"Unlikely."

"Unlikely?"

"It's very individual."

"That's a nonanswer."

"It's the answer I have to give you. Not only are there a minute number of people who've gone through this, but the circumstances they find themselves in could affect the outcome. It's like a husband lost at sea for years, and when he returns his wife has remarried. Does she love him less?"

"Thank God I've remembered enough to know I'm not married," I say. "If Kayden and I had that over our heads, I'm not sure where we'd be. But there's the potential that something in my past could change us." I shake my head. "We can't live like this. He can't have unknowns."

Nathan leans closer, elbows on his knees. "Let me be as clear as possible. Do I think you will wake up and be a different person? No. Do I think you will stop caring about Kayden? No. Do I think the past could influence how either of you feel for each other? Maybe. And do I have one ounce of scientific evidence to justify those answers? Yes. But not much more."

"And that's not enough for Kayden."

"He says it is."

"And we both know it's not, Nathan," I insist, but I stick to the less-is-more idea, and leave it at that. "We both know that he deserves more than that. *Make me remember.*"

"I can't make you remember."

"What about drugs or hypnosis?"

"No to drugs, and I don't recommend hypnosis for one simple reason: risk versus reward. It's not documented as highly effective, and we'd have to step outside The Underground. Writing in your journal is the best way to bring back your memories." His phone buzzes and he pulls it from his pants pocket and glances at it. "I need to go," he says, his gaze catching on the TV remote. "This part of the castle has American news. Have you tried watching it?"

"No. I had no idea we got American news here."

"I think I remember Kayden saying it's only in this tower. Some kind of technical issue, so try it. It might be better than hypnosis." He starts to walk away.

"Wait. Nathan." He turns and arches a brow. "This room isn't where Kayden and Elizabeth lived, right?"

"No. He left that part of the tower sealed, even after he opened this part. There's a lot he keeps sealed, Ella. He's his own best enemy. Not you."

"Is that what you told him when he asked you about me?"

"Yes."

The answer is too simple. "But he wanted more, just like me."

"Of course he wanted more, and I had to tell him exactly what I'll say to you. You're suppressing something, and no matter how much you say you want to remember it, you don't. Your mind is protecting you from what it thinks you can't handle. You'll remember it when you're ready."

He leaves, having confirmed that he's all but told Kayden that I'm the potential time bomb I've feared.

eight

I stare after Nathan, watching him disappear around the corner, and I decide he's done me a favor by removing any answer to my questions but me. I have to solve this. I have to remember and stop hiding from my past, and just deal with it. That means exposing myself to triggers in every way I can.

Doing what I can right here and now, I pick up the remote and begin flipping through channels, and sure enough, I find two American news stations: CNN and Fox. Memories don't stir in my mind, but the familiarity is a welcome sensation and I keep the TV on. Obama is president. Biden is vice president. I know these things easily, but I have no clue how government works in Italy—which shores up my conclusion that I hadn't been in Italy very long when I ended up in the hospital and with Kayden.

Unzipping my purse, I remove my journal and pen, and cautiously seal Charlie back inside. Opening to a blank page, I will memories to come to me and fill the pages . . . but I am as blank as they are. I start drawing the butterfly again, tracing it over and over, outlining the curves of the wings. The sound of the newscaster talking intrudes and I decide to give up on memories, changing the channel to an Italian station, making a list of words I want to look up. Music would be even better, since songs repeat words over and over. Yes, I decide. I need music, but this Italian thing isn't going to work without a computer to look up words. I'm sure Kayden has one I can use, but for now, I start writing down words from the TV that sound familiar: *ciao*, *bello*, *prego*, *la ragazza*.

And suddenly, I'm back in that moment where I found David dying on the pavement.

I rush to him, and there is blood oozing from his chest. "I'll get help. Hold on. I'll get help." I start to get up and he grips my arm.

"Wait," he hisses. "Don't . . . give . . . him the necklace."

"Who?"

"Don't give him the necklace," he whispers. "Hide it. Hide . . . it. . . . Don't let them have . . . it. He's not what he seems."

I blink back to the present and try to collect all of my thoughts, and I write them down. *He is not what he seems* and then *THEM or HIM*, as I remember David referencing both, which could have been a misspeak considering the circumstances. Or maybe he was referencing both Niccolo and his people? Or maybe Niccolo and whoever runs the French mob Kayden had mentioned? I write down: *Who is the head of the French mafia?* And it feels important for some reason. *Who runs the French mob? Do I know?*

The TV invades my thoughts, the Italian confusing me, and I switch back to the news. "Next in headlines," a female newscaster says, her voice cutting through the memory as well, and I grab the remote to mute the volume when I hear, "Money and power—"

"Money and power," I whisper, writing those words down and staring at them, another memory taking shape. I shut my eyes and am transported to another time.

I am sitting at a restaurant with HIM, who remains faceless and nameless. I can feel his energy. I know who he is in some part of my mind, but no matter how hard I try, I cannot picture him. But still I am there, at the table. I can even see the black turtleneck sweater I'm wearing when the waitress stops beside us, speaking in a language I don't understand. HE rescues me, ordering for me, and I feel a little less out of my element.

But then the images shift and I'm back on his bed, naked and tied up. I've been there for hours. I'm cold. I'm scared and angry when finally he comes to me, but unlike the last time I lived this memory, I don't experience the moment he enters the room. He, whoever he is, is just suddenly naked and at the foot of the bed. He is standing there but I refuse to look at him. I hate him. I thought I'd loved him.

The bed shifts and his hands come down on my knees, and before I realize what is happening, he's pressing them to my chest. His fingers dig into my legs and he moves closer, leaning over me. And damn it, I am looking at him when I swore I would not. "You're angry," he says.

"Two hours," I say. "Two hours, you left me here."

"I told you not to leave the house."

"You don't own me. You can't tell me—"

"I can and I will. And I left you here to make sure you think twice the next time you consider disobeying me. A painless punishment, considering how disobeying me might have ended. I am a powerful man, angel. You know this. My enemies will lash out at anyone I care for. And that's you. So if I tell you to fucking stay in the house, I fucking mean it. Understand?"

His demand is guttural, the rasp in his tone telling me he truly feared for me. "Yes," I say, realizing now that I really was in danger today—because he isn't the only one who will do anything to win. His enemies will, too.

He stares at me for several seconds, weighing my reply before his voice softens. "Good girl." He lowers my legs and slides between them. "There is always a price for power, but losing you will not be mine. I protect what is mine." He leans into me, his cheek pressed to mine, his lips at my ear, to add, "And you are mine."

My eyes pop open at the memory that ends in the exact same place as when I'd had it before, and David's warning comes back to me. *He's not what he seems.* I write that down and underline it. *He was not what he seemed.* David was talking about the man in my flashbacks. I know it, but I'm not sure if I knew "him" before David's warning, or after.

"Ella?"

I blink and look up to find Giada rounding the couch, and only then do I realize that I'm on the floor between the couch and the table, on top of a soft brown rug.

"Can I sit?" she asks.

"Of course you can sit," I say. "It's your brother's store."

"That he hates," she says, claiming the cushion. "I am making him miserable. That's not what I wanted."

"You seem pretty miserable yourself," I say, moving to sit on the opposite end of the sofa.

Tears well in her eyes, and she glances skyward. "You think?" She swipes at her eyes, as if angry she's showing weakness, then fixes me in a surprisingly direct stare, her voice unwavering. "I just don't want The Underground to take him like it did my father."

"Like I said outside the store. There are people in life who are risk takers. We have to decide to either embrace that part of them, or to walk away. Those are the two choices."

"How do you ever leave someone you love?"

"It's not about how. It's about why. It's about not tormenting yourself and them with your fear."

"I'm not leaving," she says, straightening, her hands settling on her knees, repeating the words more fiercely. "I'm *not* leaving. Adriel is all I have. He's my family."

"You want to stay—and yet you betrayed Kayden by calling Gallo, and you did it in his own home."

"You, Adriel, and Marabella have made that mistake abundantly clear. Believe me, I get it."

"Backing down because we got upset doesn't mean you get it. It means you don't want to hear us bitch anymore."

"Enzo was bleeding to death, and Adriel wanted to go after the people who did that to him. All I was thinking about was saving Adriel. Can't you understand that? Can't any of you understand that?"

I think of my father lying in his own blood and I say, "Yes. I do. I've lost people. And so has Kayden—everyone he loves. You don't seem to understand, or even try to understand, that Kayden inherited the huge burden of being The Hawk. Losing Enzo gutted him."

She considers me a few beats. "Enzo disobeyed his orders?"

"Yes. He absolutely did. Kayden was concerned about him when he went missing, and he told me the details."

"It wasn't a hunt Kayden sent him on?"

"No. It absolutely was not."

She inhales and lets it out. "Adriel won't move away, because he needs to be close to all of this. And I won't move away, because I need to be close to him."

"What about moving out of the castle, where you aren't reminded of all of this so readily?"

"That's like giving Adriel a license to hunt."

"It's only a matter of time until he does that anyway. Let him be who he is, and give yourself permission to find out who you are, too. And just know this before you say no. Kayden sets ethical boundaries for his Hunters. He expects safety over money. He protects his people at all costs, and would die for any of them. He set up a massive trust fund for you to honor your father. How many people would do that?"

"You really believe in him."

"I believe in him completely. Passionately. And I won't lose him due to your risking his life and safety, like you did last night."

"And your life," she says. "Last night you said—"

"That you endangered all of our lives," I quickly insert, wishing I hadn't spouted off last night. "And you did."

"I'm sorry," she says. "I truly am, and I don't know how to fix this."

"We'll talk to Kayden—but I want you to think about what you really want to do, first. And talk to Adriel. *Really* talk to him."

She nods. "I will. Thank you, Ella. I'm glad you're here."

"Me, too."

A buzzing sound goes off and my eyes go wide. "Please tell me that's not a breach alarm."

"It's not. It's the buzzer to the front door for the store, and our pizza, I'm sure. Adriel ordered for himself as well, so I'm sure he'll grab the delivery, but knowing him, I'd better go get ours before he eats it, too." She stands but never makes it any farther before we hear, "The food has arrived."

Surprised to hear Marabella's voice, I shut my journal and twist around to find her entering the living area with several pizza boxes in her hands. "Had I made this, it would have been better," she declares. "However," she adds, setting the boxes down in front of me, then straightening, her hands settling on her robust hips, "I do know the owner of this restaurant and he's almost as good in the kitchen as I am."

"We're settling for his," I say. "When can I try yours?"

"You could have tried it today, but no one asked me," she scolds. "I'll make one for you and Kayden tomorrow."

And while her words are as warm and playful as ever, her energy is as uncharacteristically dark as her black dress, and, concerned that the death of Enzo has rattled her, with no one to offer comfort, I ask, "Will you join us? Aside from loving your company, I could use some help learning Italian." I glance between her and Giada. "Can you ladies help?"

"Of course we can," Marabella replies, crossing her arms in front of her and studying me. "You really do need to learn Italian to live here."

"I really do," I agree. "I hate it when people are talking around me and I have no idea what's being said. Why did you both learn English?"

"I learned when I started working here in the castle," Marabella replies. "And Giada was brought up bilingual by her father. She even went to one of the American colleges nearby."

"I'm a good teacher, too," Giada interjects. "In fact, I've been thinking about looking into a teaching job."

I flash back to my friend Sara's apartment, both of us sitting on her floor, with papers on her coffee table. *"It's going to be a long night of grading these papers for class tomorrow," Sara says. "How about we order pizza?"*

The memory is gone as fast as it begins, and I find myself frowning at the idea of me being a teacher. That doesn't feel right, though I am certain my mother was a dance instructor, maybe music, too, and I'm very maternal with Giada. But grading papers doesn't feel like music or dance.

"I'll get us all drinks," Giada says, snapping me back to the present. "We have Coke Zero and water."

"Water, please," I say, writing the word *teacher* in my journal.

"With or without gas?" she asks.

I frown. "Gas? Why would I want gas? What does that mean?"

"Bubbles," Giada says, her eyes lighting.

"Ohhhhh," I say, laughing. "You mean sparkling water. For Americans, *gas* means you ate something that doesn't agree with you. I guess I've just had my first language lesson. No bubbles for me."

"Gas for me," Marabella declares, and we all start giggling.

Then Giada joins Marabella, saying something to her in Italian before hugging her.

Marabella's eyes meet mine and we share a look of hope. Giada isn't completely lost, and it is then that even without my memories full recovered, a sense of family and belonging comes over me, which I'm certain I haven't felt in a very long time. Giada releases Marabella and walks toward the kitchen.

Marabella seems to decide to stay for lunch, claiming the chair next to me and softly murmuring, "You're good for her, Ella. For all of us."

"The feeling is mutual," I assure her.

"You're good for Kayden."

If only I knew that without any question, I think, fighting the urge to grab my journal and start reading through the notes I can't explain to her or Giada.

"Knives, forks, napkins, and drinks for three," Giada announces, returning and sitting down next to me before handing me a small box. "Four cheese. I hope that works. It seemed the most American."

"Any cheese is wonderful," I say, eagerly opening the box to find a delicious-looking concoction. Then I look at Marabella. "They didn't cut my pizza."

"We Italians don't pick up our pizza." She holds up a fork and knife and then hands them to me. "Our way is this way."

"You're making me work for my meal," I say, accepting the utensils. "I can live with that," and boy, do I. In one bite I'm moaning with the delicious, rich taste of the white sauce under the cheese, and as silly as it might be, I wish that I were experiencing this with Kayden for the first time. But I'm not and I'm eating it now, and eating it all, with a bonus of Marabella and Giada giving me a language lesson. And before long, the food is gone, and with Marabella and Giada's prodding, I'm repeating English words and their Italian equivalents, writing them down in the back of my journal, and I've lost track of time.

We're just talking about coffee when the buzzer at the door goes off again, and Marabella glances at her watch. "I bet that's your clothes for tonight," she says, having obviously spoken to Kayden. She heads toward the door.

"What's tonight?" Giada asks.

"Some political function Kayden and I are attending," I say, standing, my body stiff from sitting so long. "I'd better go help Marabella."

"I'll clean up our mess," Giada says, while I head toward the front of the store.

Rounding the corner, I come face-to-face with Adriel as he enters the living area. "It's football time, and since it's still my store, and my TV, I'm taking over this room."

"Never let it be said that I stood between a man and his football," I proclaim, "but your sister might be another story."

He grumbles something Italian that tells me I've hit a sore spot, and I laugh, stepping around him with a fond memory of my father and his pals sitting around the TV, yelling at football, carrying me to the front of the store. I find Marabella setting a collection of bags next to another collection of bags.

"What the heck is all of this?" I ask, noting several garment bags on top of the counter, as well. "Please tell me this isn't all for me? It's one party. I need one dress."

Marabella holds up her hands. “I didn’t do it. It was Kayden.” She offers me a black shopping bag with silk handles. “This came by way of a special, separate delivery, which seems to justify special attention.”

“You don’t know what it is?” I ask, accepting the bag, tons of black and white tissue paper sticking out from the top.

“No idea at all,” she confirms. “But there’s a card poking out of the top.”

Locating it, I remove it from the paper, and silently read the handwritten words *Open this package alone* printed on the front of it. As silly as it might be, what affects me is not the idea of a private gift, it’s the fact that it’s Kayden’s script on the note.

“Something good?” Marabella asks.

“I don’t know yet,” I say, stuffing the envelope back inside the bag. “I need to open it once I’m upstairs.”

Her eyes light. “Something good for sure. I’m sure you’re eager to get to your tower and explore all your new things. I think if we both load up we can get it all in one trip. Once you go through it all, you can let me know if you need anything else.”

“Hair color,” I say. “I have roots.”

She gives me a keen eye. “Oh yes. I see that now. What color is it naturally?”

“I have no idea,” I reply, Giada’s communication with Gallo dictating my noncommittal answer. “But the roots don’t lie. They need to be covered.”

“I’ll get you some once we get you upstairs,” she promises, draping one of the garment bags over her arm.

“Thank you, Marabella,” I say, reaching for some of the

bags, when I suddenly remember my journal on the coffee table in the other room, and drop the bags, my panic instant. "I need to grab something from the living room." As I hurry away I hear her call out, "I'll head on to the tower."

I cut left and quickly pass under the archway to the living area. A soccer game, Italian "football," is playing on the TV. I round the couch to find Adriel occupying my prior position, my gaze going to the coffee table where my journal should rest but does not, setting my heart thundering in my chest.

"Do you want to watch the games with us?" Giada asks from behind the kitchen island.

"I need to unwind for tonight and figure out what I'm wearing," I reply, still focused on Adriel, who arches a brow my direction.

"Something I can do for you?"

"Did you see the journal I left on the table?"

Irritation flints over his expression. "Unless it has to do with football right now, I not only have zero idea what you are talking about, I don't care."

"Oh, good grief, Adriel," Giada says, moving toward us. "You men and your football. You get so rude. It has to be here." She glances at her brother. "Get up."

He gives her a heavy-lidded stare, and she squats by the couch, looking around his feet, then stands and grimaces. "I don't see it, but it has to be here. I'll keep looking for it."

I want to ask Adriel to stand, but he's leaned forward, watching the game. "Thanks," I say, motioning toward the door. "Marabella is waiting to help me carry my delivery items upstairs." I turn and hurry away, running through the things I have inside that might be bad if they were discovered by any of the Hunters, who know I managed to get on Niccolo's radar in that alleyway, but not why.

I've just arrived at the front of the store to feel guilty at the discovery that Marabella managed to carry all of the packages, when I hear Adriel say, "Ella."

I turn to find him close, too close, towering over me, my journal in his hand. "Don't leave things like this lying around," he says, offering it to me.

"Thank you," I say, accepting it, only to find myself fixed in his hard, deep green stare, a lock of his curly black hair teasing his forehead.

"Let Enzo be a lesson," he stuns me by saying. "Mistakes have consequences." He turns and walks away, exiting the store into the main castle, as if he can no longer stomach the game that he saw as pleasure minutes before. And for the second time in twenty-four hours, I'm not sure if he's warned me or threatened me. Kayden isn't my enemy, nor am I his, but Adriel . . . I just don't know.

I wait a good two minutes before I exit the store, hitting the button to shut the door with my elbow, and my gaze travels down the hallway to the room where Enzo died. For several seconds, I relive the moment when Nathan declared Enzo gone. And yet, we've eaten pizza, told jokes, and I'm about to try on fancy dresses. Like he never existed. Like he didn't just die. My chest tightens and I think of Kayden, wondering how many times thoughts of Enzo have gutted him today. Suddenly, I really need to talk to him, and not giving myself time to change my mind, I unzip my purse and grab my phone, quickly punching in his number.

"Ella," he answers in only one ring, the deep textured tone

of his voice doing funny things to my stomach. "Is everything okay?"

"Yes. This isn't an emergency. Does that mean this is a bad time?"

"The only time it's a bad time is if I tell you not to call unless it's an emergency."

"I thought we both needed to know that it's not a crisis every time I call. And I thought you needed to know that I *will* call."

"Indeed," he says softly. "I did."

"But I know you're busy with whatever you're doing, and honestly, I just wanted to hear your voice."

"I'm taking that advice you gave me last night in the shower about closure."

My eyes go wide. "About . . ." I catch myself before I say "Enzo," not sure if the phones could be tapped. "You are?"

"Yes. I am, and at the moment I'm waiting on a few details to come together."

"I'm glad you're doing this. It's the right thing."

"But not the easy thing—and I wouldn't have done it if not for you." His voice is gravelly, exhausted almost. "Maybe you'll make me a better person."

I read that as the self-blame it is. "This wasn't your fault. You know that, right?"

"Responsibility and blame," he says. "The two walk the same fine line as love and hate."

He means us. I know he does. "I could come with you. Maybe I could help."

"Not this time. There's too much I don't want you near." He hesitates. "I know I'm protective."

I laugh. "Just a little."

"And bossy—"

"Ridiculously bossy."

"I just don't want this world to destroy you or us. It's going to take me time to ease up. Actually, I'm not sure I will."

"You will," I promise, "simply because I'm going to get better at taming the beast you are."

"The beast? Is that what I am now?"

"Yes," I say, "but at least you're a sexy beast."

He laughs, a deep rumble of masculine perfection that is good in so many ways. "Ah, Ella," he says. "We have a lot to talk about."

Matteo's voice rumbles in the background, and Kayden replies in Italian, followed by Carlo. "I have to go," he tells me. "I'll be there in time for the party." He murmurs something to me in Italian, following it with, "And then, we'll work on that understanding we talked about."

He ends the call, and I hear his promise in my mind: *I demand everything and more.*

nine

I find Marabella in our closet, and not surprisingly she's organizing my new wardrobe items. "Dresses and coats are here," she says, waving at a row of bagged garments. "Shoes are below and still in their boxes, in case you want to return anything." She shoves her hands into the pockets of her baggy black skirt. "Kayden wouldn't bother, but I will. The money should be spent on things you want to keep and wear."

I straddle the center bench and stare at the clothes hanging up and in boxes on the floor. "Good grief, the man goes so overboard."

"Well, he has the money," she says, sitting next to me, angled to face me, "and he clearly wants to make you happy and spoil you. He hasn't had anyone to do that with in a very long time."

"Since Elizabeth," I say, and I am reminded of Kayden's reference to some things as being better not remembered, and I know he does not mean her but rather the moments and years of pain that followed.

"Yes," she says sadly. "She lived here for three months before her death."

I give a grim nod. "I knew that."

"Oh good," she says approvingly. "He's talking to you. He needs to talk, and he hasn't for a very long time."

"He changed after Elizabeth and Kevin died?"

"Oh yes," she says. "He clammed up and seemed colder about life and his duty. But there is a shift in him since your arrival. He laughs and smiles with you. He kisses you, and some of those dark spots in his eyes fade."

"He makes the dark spots fade for me, too."

She tilts her head to study me. "You're different from Elizabeth. She was . . . gentler."

When I stiffen, she smiles. "That's not an insult. Gentleness is easily destroyed by this world, and I'm not talking about her murder. Kayden knew that, so he sheltered her—but he's sure not sheltering you."

"I'm not sure if that's by choice or circumstance," I say, thinking of the way he tried to protect me from the necklace revelation. "I think he'd prefer to keep me in the dark."

"Of course he would. Then he'd never have to know if you'd reject him."

"And ironically, I'm worried about my unknown past doing the same."

"Ah, the world of young lovers. Just remember that nothing easy is worth having."

"He said something very similar," I say.

"Because I've told him that his entire life. I taught that boy manners, and right from wrong. I never had kids. Just him." She grimaces. "Well, Giada in some ways, too, but I fear this relationship with Gallo is the breaking point. She can't stay at the castle. It's too dangerous."

"Please tell me you don't think there's a real relationship between them, that it's just an infatuation?"

"I'm afraid I do," she says. "At least as of Thursday, when I ran into him at the market, not long before Enzo died. Running into him in the middle of the day seemed odd enough, but Giada went off on her own not long after. I finished up at the butcher's, and was headed to the checkout when I found them huddled together." She purses her lips. "His hand was on her waist."

"That's not good."

"No. It's not, and I didn't let them know I saw it. I felt it was best I tell Kayden. He'll get to the bottom of it. I'm hoping he was just attempting to seduce her, and that we've shut him down now before he succeeds. You really influence her."

"I'm trying," I say. "I'm not sure it's helping, but I'm certain Matteo will tap both Gallo and Giada's phone and computer records, and we'll know for sure."

Her lips curve slightly. "I am pleased that you know the ins and outs of Kayden's world." She doesn't give me time to ask exactly what she means, already moving on and standing up. "I'll go get your hair color."

"I appreciate that," I say, following her out of the closet.

She runs her fingers over the edge of the giant white sunken tub, then turns to look at me. "This is unacceptable. You two need to decide what days I can come in and clean and cook. I know you want privacy, but this place is getting dusty, and you both need good food."

I smile. "I understand. It is unacceptable. How about Monday, Wednesday, and Friday mornings?"

"Plan on me being here all day this Monday. And be at the table for breakfast at nine."

"Yes, ma'am."

She motions to the closet. "Go try on clothes, and call me if you don't find a perfect dress."

"I don't know what that means for this event. Any idea as to what I should expect?"

"Arrogance, money, and power."

"Kayden," I joke.

"He has humility. Most of them do not. So expect these dresses to be outrageously expensive, since tonight there will be plenty of judgment of your worth." She starts for the door and pauses to look at me. "He never told Elizabeth the secrets of The Underground. He loved her but he shielded her, though ultimately he knew one day she'd see everything. And because that day never came, he never knew if she really loved *all* of him." She leaves without another word.

I stare after her, thinking of my encounter with Kayden earlier today, and one thing replays in my head. He has been alone in his guilt for a very long time, but then, wasn't he always alone, if he never allowed anyone to see every shade of right and wrong that he might be? *You have no idea how dark I can be*. It is then that I think, *I have a dark side, too*. That's why Kayden and I connect. We are alike in ways neither of us know. Surprised by these unexpected ideas, I suck in a breath and wait for my mind to show me some horrible atrocity—perhaps the very one I've been hiding from. But nothing comes to me.

What does come to me is Marabella's story about Giada and Gallo, and the journal I stupidly left lying around. I suddenly want to know how damning anything inside might be if it was shown to Gallo.

Exhaling, I hurry into the closet and sit down on the bench, pulling my purse over my head to remove the journal, and I open it down the center. The first page I turn to is a list of bullet points: *Tied to a bed. Cold. Scared.* I flash back once more to that night, and I can feel that man, whoever he is, naked against me as he declares, *"There is always a price for power, but losing you will not be mine. I protect what is mine." He leans into me, his cheek pressed to mine, his lips at my ear to add, "And you are mine."*

Swallowing hard, I read the next note. *As long as he is alive, that man will never let me go.* I slam the journal shut, deciding anything Giada read inside will cause me, and Kayden, problems. I set it next to me and remove Charlie from my purse, letting the cold steel comfort me. "He *will* let me go," I say vehemently, before I set the gun on top of the journal. "He will."

Welcoming an escape from the past, I pick up the black bag Kayden told me to open alone and pull out all of the black tissue. Inside is a rectangular red velvet box. My heart starts to pound with welcome excitement, and I pop open the lid, and suck in air. Inside is a gorgeous bracelet with a silver and black hawk in the center that looks incredibly like the tattoo on Kayden's wrist; the spread wings are etched with diamonds, while four thin delicate black strands on each side make up the band. This is not something he randomly picked out. I shut the lid, setting the box next to Charlie, and pull the card from the bag.

Wearing this means that you are mine to protect, and anyone who harms you will pay a price. Wear this tonight and choose to protect yourself. Wear it again, and choose me—but only when you understand what that means. Right now, you do not.

—Kayden

I stare down at the phrase, *You are mine to protect.* And despite the many ways every specific word Kayden chose changes the context and the promise of everything I've asked for and demanded, it's so eerily similar to those in my flashback that a chill runs down my spine.

By six o'clock, I've narrowed my dress choices to two, picked out my lingerie for the night, danced awhile, and Marabella has taught me a "party" list of Italian words while cleaning up the mess Kayden and I made in the living room the prior night. It's time to color my hair, and out of the three choices provided, I choose to be adventurous with a deep, chocolate brown instead of medium brown. If I can't be red, I want to find a shade I can love.

By seven o'clock, not only is my hair sleekly flat-ironed, it's a shiny, gorgeous brown that I think might just fit that "love" bill. Since Kayden has yet to arrive and I'm nervous, I decide to go ahead and get dressed. I start by putting on a long black Valentino dress, but the sparkle in the gown doesn't quite feel right and I change into a sleeveless, knee-length, velvet Gucci gown. Once I've zipped myself into the snug silhouette, I decide the exposed horizontal seams and yoke lace neckline, which matches the lace of the hemline, delivers a look that is elegantly sexy and understated, and I love it. The outfit is completed with Gucci heels and a small evening bag, both also lace-trimmed. Regrettably, the bag isn't large enough to allow Charlie to join the party, but Kayden will be with me, and I have no doubt he'll be well armed.

Next, I need to put on the bracelet, but I really want to wait for Kayden and tell him what it means to me. I set its box on the bathroom sink next to my purse, hands on my hips. Okay, then, I'm done until Kayden arrives. I walk to the bedroom and it's ten minutes until eight. Obviously, we're going to be late to the party, or just not go. My cell phone rings from inside my new purse on the bathroom counter, and I answer quickly.

"Hello."

"Are you ready?"

I glance at the velvet box. "About three minutes from done."

"I'm waiting in the center foyer."

"Oh . . . okay. I'll be right down." I end the call. Why didn't he dress here with me? He'd literally have to have showered and dressed elsewhere. I'm confused and I feel upset, and I tell myself I'm overreacting. He had important business today. Where he got dressed shouldn't matter, and I stare at the velvet box. Inhaling, I open it, staring down at the striking diamond-studded hawk in the center. So much for the romantic, dramatic proclamation I'd wanted to make when I put it on.

I reach for the bracelet and put it on, and it fits perfectly, as does the band, the hawk so like the one Kayden has etched into his wrist. He fits me perfectly, and in my heart and soul, I know that no past life will change that. I reach down and trace one of the diamond-studded wings, and this is truly the most unique, stunning piece of jewelry I've ever seen. The butterfly was gorgeous, but this is . . . Wait. My brows knot together. *The most unique, stunning piece of jewelry I've ever seen.* I smile with the realization that I *know* this to be a fact, when up to this point, most things have been uncertain. There was no "the best I ever had" or "the favorite thing I've ever done or seen" before this moment. My mind is shifting, opening up. I feel it, and suddenly my mood is lighter, and I am optimistic.

Eager to share this news with Kayden, I pick up my purse and walk into the closet, retrieving the Gucci dress coat I've chosen for the night before hurrying from the bedroom and down the hallway. At the bottom of the stairs, though, I am suddenly nervous about him not dressing here, wondering if I've read him wrong about where we stand. This idea has me pausing before opening the door separating me from the central foyer, where I know Kayden is waiting. Lifting my arm, I stare at the hawk on my wrist. I read it as a sign of a growing bond, but maybe it's really only about protection. I'll know when I see him, I decide. But I still find myself shifting my coat to cover it before pressing the button to lift the door.

I step to the center of the archway, waiting for the door to lift and reveal the main castle foyer. Seconds tick by, feeling slow when they are fast, and within a few breaths the barrier is gone, and Kayden is standing directly in front of me, a perfectly fitted tuxedo hugging every tall, broad, perfect inch of him. He owns it just as well as he owns denim and leather, like he owns everything around him. Like he does me—and that is trust. A deep, complete trust that my past says I should have for no one, yet I have it for him.

I want to tell him this, but all that comes out is, "Hi."

Those pale, pale blue eyes of his answer with a fast, intimate sweep up and down my body, before he snags my hips and pulls me to him.

"Hi," he replies, aligning our lower bodies and removing more than the space between us. I know now that we are not separate, but together. "You," he declares, his voice low and silky, "are breathtaking in every way."

"And you," I say, flattening my hand on his chest, feeling his heart thundering the way mine is, "really *are* beautiful, Kayden Wilkens." I search his face, finding starkness in his eyes that I want to erase but know I cannot. "How bad was it with Enzo's mother?"

"Bad enough that if you and I could be fucking it out of my head right now . . ."

"And yet you dressed somewhere else."

"I wasn't in a good place, and tonight, before this party we need to attend, was not the time for you to see that part of me."

"Is there ever going to be a time you show that part of yourself to me?"

"Yes. Or you wouldn't be going to this party with me."

"Promise me, Kayden."

"I promise you, Ella. Just not yet."

"I'd reject that answer, but I know we have a party to go to, so I guess we're just going to have to stick to the plan."

"And that would be what?"

"There's going to be some fighting before we get to the fucking."

He wraps me in his arms and presses his cheek to mine. "And what if I don't want to fuck you? What if I want to make love to you, Ella?"

I lean back to look at him, and in his eyes, the starkness of moments before is now tenderness and passion. There is an open door I needed so damn bad tonight. "Can we do both?"

"We *will* do both." He brushes his lips over mine, a whisper of a touch I feel everywhere, and I wish he were touching me now, not later. "Many times," he adds, seeming to reluctantly release me, before inching up his sleeve to check the time. But this time, instead of seeing the watch, it's the Hawk beneath it that has my attention, reminding me of the bracelet yet to be revealed.

"We need to get moving," he says, draping his arm around my shoulders and heading toward the main foyer. "Chief Donati will be there tonight and I don't want us to miss him."

"Please tell me Gallo won't be there, too," I say as we cross the foyer.

"He won't," he says, opening the door leading to the garage and allowing me to enter the stairwell and start down the narrow path.

"This event is by VIP invitation only," he adds following me down, "and mostly high-ranking politicians, elected officials, and all their cronies."

"Does that make us their cronies?" I ask over my shoulder.

"That makes us their biggest wish they'll never get." He catches up with me and opens the garage door for me. "And that's power, sweetheart. You'll see that at the party."

On that note, I enter the surprisingly warm, well-lit garage and see the ridiculously expensive shiny blue Pagani Zonda that ironically, considering the statement he just made, was given to him as payment for a job. "Why is the police chief's presence tonight so important?" I ask when he steps to my side. "Is it about the favor you owe him?"

"It's about the favor he won't get if he doesn't keep Gallo away from you. Which car, sweetheart?" he asks, indicating the four F-TYPE Jags lined up on the opposite side of the garage.

"I love the ice blue," I say, "but black feels very James Bond, like you in that tuxedo."

He laughs and walks to the rack of keys on the wall. "Just call me 007, sweetheart. And since we're talking cars, we need to get you one of your choosing soon."

"No, thank you," I say as we walk toward the black Jag. "I don't want to drive on roads the size of sidewalks, in a car worth more than some people make in a year."

"If you scrape it up, we'll fix it," he says, dismissing my concern.

"Jags are not meant to be scraped up and fixed. And I know these cars are your pride and joy."

He opens the passenger door for me. "I couldn't give a flying fuck about these cars. They're metal. They're replaceable. And they are not you. I'll put a driver on call for you until you change your mind." He opens the passenger door for me. "Then you can come and go as you please without the confines of what's walkable. Let me put your coat in the trunk." He takes it from me, already clicking the key chain and moving away.

But I'm not thinking about the coat. I'm not thinking about cars. My mind flickers with a memory, and I flatten my hand on the roof of the car. I know why I'd been tied to that bed for two hours, why I'd been punished, and it shakes me to the core. I'd gone shopping without permission. Who was I then? Why would I allow anyone to treat me like that?

"What are my boundaries?" I call out to Kayden, not even sure where the word *boundaries* comes from.

He returns and steps in front of me. "In bed or out, sweetheart?"

"Kayden. I'm serious."

"As am I. In bed, you always have the ultimate power, no matter how much I seem to claim for myself. Out of bed, safety dictates everything."

"Can I really come and go as I please? Because it didn't seem like it today."

"Today was complicated, and in hindsight, I handled it like shit and I'm sorry."

The apology, spoken by a man I do not think apologizes to anyone, surprises me in all of the right ways.

"In explanation, not defense," he continues, "Gallo talking trash about me to you fucked with my head. And I don't let much fuck with my head. You are not a prisoner, nor have you ever been. You are not my captive, nor do I want you to be. But protecting you isn't just a desire. If you're to be here with me, it's a need. I need you safe." He closes the small space between us and lifts my hand from on top of the car, revealing the bracelet, but he doesn't look at it. He looks at me, holding my stare, and letting me see the truth in his words. "This sends a powerful message to anyone who is, or who would be, my enemy. It says if they so much as look at you wrong, I will kill them. It says that you are mine, and even Niccolo will think twice before he touches The Hawk's woman."

"Your woman," I repeat, heat radiating up my arm from where he holds me. "Is that what I am?"

"Not until you say you are. Not until you wear the bracelet by choice, not public need. I want nothing you don't give me freely, Ella."

"The bracelet tells the world that you own me," I repeat, a tight knot of emotion in my chest. "Does it tell them that I own you?"

He pulls me to him and cups my head. "You do own me, Ella. The good, the bad, and the very damn ugly. And my worst fear is that you can't handle that. That's why I didn't come to you tonight. But I need you to handle it. Do you understand? I *need you* to be able to handle it." He kisses me, hard and fast, but it is passionate and deep, a short taste of torment and ecstasy, before he tears his mouth from mine.

He turns me to face the open passenger seat, his hands bracketing my waist, his mouth at my ear as he says, "Get in the car, before I pull your dress up and fuck you right here in the garage, which would be far more appealing than this party, which we can't miss."

I inhale on what has become his confession, and that is the trust that has me climbing into the car, breathing a little easier. And once I'm there, I look to my right, where he still stands, staring down at me, his gaze half veiled. His attention is like a warm blanket on a cold night. Heavy and addictive. He shuts the door and walks around the car, climbing inside with me, and I have this sense of us being together more than ever before. As if choices have been made, choices that will all end with us, here, tonight.

ten

Kayden cranks the engine and turns on the heat. "I have a gift for you," he announces, unbuttoning his jacket to reach inside, and produces a small leather pouch the size of a makeup bag.

My eyes light as he hands it to me, the steely weight familiar in my hands. "I know what this is, and it's perfect."

"You do, huh? What is it?"

I unsnap the pouch and remove the small handgun, fitting it in my small palm. "A Ruger LCP. Small enough for a bra strap and a garter. I freaking love it. Charlie just got retired."

"Who the hell is Charlie?"

I face him. "I remembered my father's name today. He was Charlie, and I named my Glock after the man who taught me to shoot." I hold up the Ruger, and right then my memory produces an image of my mother. "This is Annie," I say. "My mother, whose name I remembered just this second." I settle the Ruger on top of my lap. "Kayden, I'm starting to remember and it's really exciting and scary. Just random things—like I could say, this is my favorite gun or food or movie, and know it's right. I didn't think like that before today."

"Why exactly is that scary?"

"Because," I say, my tone turning somber, "I, too, need you to be able to handle the good, the bad, and the very damn ugly if there is some. And I'm pretty sure there will be."

"Nothing is going to change how I feel about you," he says, taking my hand and kissing my knuckles. "Nothing, Ella."

"Yet when I say that to you, you don't believe me."

He studies me for several moments. "I guess we both need to have a little faith in who we are together."

"It's hard, isn't it?"

"Nothing worth having—"

"Comes easily."

Approval lights his eyes. "Exactly."

"Marabella told me she used to say that to you."

"Marabella has said a lot of wise things to me over the years," he says, releasing my hand to pull his sleeve back again.

This time when I see his watch, I flash back to the memory I had in the shower. A man's wrist. That watch just below a starched white shirt and jacket sleeve. His hand on my bare arm.

"Donati should be arriving right about the same time as us," Kayden says, shifting back into his seat.

I blink back into the moment. "You know when the police chief is going to arrive?"

"Friends in high and convenient places," he says, hitting the remote above his visor to lower the wall behind us.

I turn to watch it slide away, in awe of this modern feature in the historical architecture. "I still can't get over how cool that is."

"Remind me to show you how to get to the visitors' garage." He backs up and turns the car toward the exit ramp, then faces the car forward as the wall slides back into place.

"There's a second garage?"

"That's right," he says. "Visitors, like Carlo yesterday, have a separate parking area and entry point."

"Some would say you're paranoid."

"Not paranoid enough," he says, driving us into a cloudless, dark night. "Otherwise Enzo would be alive right now. *Raul* is lucky he's not dead right now, but he will pay for what he did."

"Good," I hiss, remembering the moment Nathan set those paddles down and declared Enzo dead. "What are you going to do?"

"He's a fucking drug dealer," he says, driving toward the gate that's now sliding open. "Once I'm done with him, I'm going to get him the hell out of my territories and make him wish he never came."

"Are you doing a hunt for him?" I ask as he pulls onto the road and shuts the gate behind us.

"He thinks I am." He glances over at me. "And you know what for."

"The necklace," I say, my throat tightening. "Did he know about me?"

"No, and as of now, he has no information to aid our search for the necklace, either. He just wants to get to it before Niccolo does."

"Everyone wants what I held in my hands," I say, checking the safety on my new gun. "Thank you again for this little piece of cold comfort." I bypass the pouch and zip it inside my purse. "And the purse and clothes."

"Don't thank me," he says, turning onto a narrow road lined with cars. "Every one of those things was for me."

My lips curve. "The purse was for you?"

"It's where you just put Annie, right?"

"Gucci does hold her quite nicely," I say, stroking the lacy front. "I love this purse almost as much as I do her."

"And you learned to shoot Annie from your father?"

"No," I say, my brow dipping at the certain answer that isn't supported by memory. "I think . . . it feels like a Ruger was the personal weapon I carried. I'm actually surprised I wasn't carrying it the night you found me."

"You wouldn't have legally been able to carry, as an American."

"No. I suppose not. Still, I think I had a gun." I shake off the thought and change the topic. "Before we get to the party, Marabella told you about Gallo and Giada, I heard."

"Yes." He shifts gears and turns down yet another narrow road, where pedestrians force him to slow to a crawl. "And Matteo's initial search shows no call records, but he's digging deeper."

"That makes no sense, Kayden. Marabella said he was holding Giada's waist."

"It could be that he was trying to seduce her," he says, moving past the pedestrians and cutting me a quick look. "But I tend to agree. I have men following both of them."

"I talked to her today."

"Adriel told me, and it was quite the conversation, I hear."

I cringe. "I was hard on her, and I spoke for him. I didn't mean for him to hear it."

"You said what I hadn't, out of respect for Adriel."

"And I guess I didn't exactly respect that boundary."

"I'm fucking happy as shit about it, too. It needed to be said. And Adriel is relieved."

"Well, that's interesting to know," I say. "He's hard to read and like I said, he hasn't been overly receptive to my presence."

"You can thank Giada for that," he says. "She's been nothing but a pain in the ass that distracts him, so he doesn't, or he didn't, see how you could be anything but a distraction to me."

"Didn't?"

"He thought you'd go 'Giada' on me today due to Enzo's death last night, but instead you fought for me and him." We turn onto a double-laned street lined by sidewalks, and he adds, "But you should have told me he was giving you trouble."

"I won't win anyone's respect by your demanding it. I have to earn it myself." My eyes light on a massive white building with a red carpet in front and cars everywhere. "Is that where we're going?"

"That's the party," Kayden confirms, then cuts down a small street and parks by the curb.

"What are we doing?" I ask, the dim streetlight illuminating his stark expression.

"Every reason I've given you for bringing you to this party was true."

"But?"

"The group sponsoring this party is a powerful consortium that's behind much of the fractured state of the Italian government. They want the power themselves, and are controlled by—"

"Niccolo," I supply. "What is going on? Why are *we* here?" A bad feeling consumes me and I try to withdraw, but he catches my arm.

"Hear me out, Ella. There is nothing happening here that you don't decide to make happen. My stopping here, now, is about giving you the power to decide if we go to the party. This is your choice. You *always* have a choice."

"If that were true, you'd have explained this so-called choice before we were sitting in a car right by the party."

"That's not true. I did it this way because decisions that come with fear are easier made when you're one step from the fire. You are the kind of person who will stand by the flames and be empowered, instead of cowering."

"Is Niccolo the fire, Kayden, or are you?"

"I am the man who wants to keep you alive and by my side. If that makes me the fire, then yes, I am the fire."

"Is Niccolo here?"

"Niccolo does not attend political events, nor is he on the guest list tonight—or we would not be. He controls the puppets inside, and many of his loyal followers will be present. And if you really know Niccolo—"

"I know him. Someone close to him will be here. They will see me and us. This isn't hiding in plain sight. This is inviting Niccolo to find me."

"Yes, they will. And that's the point."

eleven

My fingers curl into my palms. "I don't even know how to process what you just said to me. No part of my mind can find a path to why you would want Niccolo to find me. Because 'hide in plain sight' seems to have become 'knock on Niccolo's door.' "

"Hiding in plain sight worked when I thought you were a random person who'd stumbled into Niccolo's line of fire. In that scenario, the interest in you would have faded. But now we know you're more than that."

"We've known that for a while, with my flashbacks."

"And I've had this on my mind for a while," he concurs. "When Gallo dragged you into the limelight today, it drove home what I knew needed to be addressed. Waiting for a hatchet to fall doesn't work in our favor."

"And that hatchet is Niccolo."

"We don't know who might think you have the necklace and be looking for you. We have to establish that you don't have it. We have to take control—not allow it to be taken from us by Niccolo, or anyone else."

"How do we establish that I don't have the necklace, when I have amnesia?"

"We go public, starting with tonight. Let Niccolo find us—and when he does, he'll call me."

"And he'll demand you hand me over to him, and probably try to beat the location out of me. And then he'll be dead because I'll kill him, and maybe life will be good."

He cups my face. "Easy, sweetheart. Niccolo will never touch you. I won't let that happen. I know you know that."

"*I* won't let that happen."

He takes my hand. "*We* won't let it happen. And Niccolo's a businessman. He wants the power that necklace represents, but so do a long list of others, and he doesn't want them to get it over himself. He'll negotiate in order to be the insider when your memory returns—and the bottom line here is that he'll tell us who you are. So we wipe out the unknowns and do just what I said: claim control."

A million questions come to my mind, but I settle on the one that makes all of the others unnecessary. "If you really think this is the right move, then why not just go to Niccolo directly?"

"For the same reason that I need real proof that he killed Elizabeth and Kevin, before I kill him. Long before my time, The Underground was at war with the Italian and French mobs. The end result was an uneasy truce where all of us mutually respect each other's business. If he thinks that I knew you were in that alleyway waiting for him, and I hid you, it could mean war. So we have to rely on the truth. I found you. I thought you were in the crossfire, and you have amnesia."

"But won't he be pissed that you were there for the necklace?"

"I'm a Hunter, and respecting that is respecting my business. I might not be willing to work for him, but he'll easily believe that I'm chasing that necklace, and not for a client. I'll eventually negotiate to find it for him, which, considering The Underground doesn't work for him, will feel like a big win to him."

"You say he'll negotiate to be inside when I get my memory back, but I thought you didn't want him to have the necklace?"

"We aren't giving him the necklace. He'll tell us who you are, and Nathan believes that will trigger your memories. We'll locate the necklace, return it to the British government, and this will be over."

"You make it sound so easy."

"Being in control is always easier than sitting and waiting. But this is your decision, Ella. I'm not forcing you, nor will I ever force you, to do anything. So: do we play it safe and go back to the castle? Or do we make a public statement starting with this party?"

"There is no choice here," I say.

"There is always a choice."

"No. There isn't. I can't hide in a castle tower like Rapunzel and expect this to go away. And even if I could, anyone close to me could get hurt if I try and fail. I have to do this. I need to make me the target, not someone else."

"We're not on the same page here, Ella, if you think I'm trying to make you a target. You already are one. We're going to get the bull's-eye *off* of you."

"I want the bull's-eye off everyone else. I can't live with putting anyone else in danger. But you should have talked to me about this the minute you considered taking me to the party!"

"I didn't want Niccolo to have time to get inside your head and control you before we could even get here."

"So you did, instead?"

"I knew you'd get to a *yes* eventually, so why give you more hours to worry, when all you do right now is worry?" He doesn't wait for a reply. "Do you trust me?"

"I did."

"*Do* you trust me?"

"Maybe I shouldn't."

"Ella—"

I sigh. "Yes. Beyond obvious reason right now, I do, and you clearly believe this is the right decision."

"I do. I absolutely believe this is a path to the freedom and the answers we both crave."

"And if Niccolo's people try to grab me?"

"Once we make a public showing, with you wearing that bracelet, there are politics in play. You don't touch The Hawk's woman. If he does every division of The Underground, every hacker, every ex-mercenary, everyone who is anyone, will be his enemies, and believe me, Ella, no one, especially Niccolo, wants that. This makes you safer than you've ever been. The only reason I haven't done it before is that it means you aren't just with me. You're with The Underground."

"You *are* The Underground," I say, thinking of what Marabella had revealed about Elizabeth today. "And why would you even want me by your side if I couldn't accept that and all that comes with it?"

His eyes glint. "I wouldn't," he says firmly. "And if I hadn't made that decision before now, I wouldn't have given you that bracelet to wear. But even more, I wouldn't have asked you to keep it and put it on again by choice, not necessity."

No part of me questions that I belong with him, and my father's advice about actions meaning more than words has never rung more true. I reach down and unhook the bracelet, catching it in my hand. "Now I'll put it back on, by choice," I say, my hand trembling with the swell of emotions I feel for this man, the clasp refusing the connection.

Kayden's hand closes over the bracelet and my wrist. "Until you know everything—"

"My father said to look in a man's eyes, and watch his actions, and you will know the true person. I have looked. I have watched. I know you. I know I want to stay with you."

"You don't know the things I've done. You can't know my actions or my reactions."

"I know all I need to know. Please, help me put it back on."

He stares at me, those pale blue eyes glinting a deeper blue, the air between us thickening before he leans in and cups my head for a deep, passionate kiss that's over too soon. When it is, he stares at me another few beats, searching my face for something I hope he finds. "I'm not going anywhere," I whisper.

"You're right. You're not." He reaches down and fastens the bracelet, and then does the most remarkable thing. He connects our palms, flattening The Hawk on his wrist against the one on mine, and in that moment there is understanding between us; there is commitment. There is a certainty that no matter what the future holds, no matter what the past reveals, we have decided we're in it together.

"There are many reasons I want this night to be over, starting with all the things I want to say and do to you," he says.

"There are many things I want to say and do to you, too."

His lips curve. "Well, then why the hell are we sitting here?" He kisses my hand. "Let's go get this over with." He releases me, shifts into gear, and pulls a fast, tight U-turn toward the party. "Any last-minute doubts?" he asks.

"No," I say. "I might not know all of my past, but I'm not Rapunzel in the tower. I want answers and freedom."

"Just remember that maybe nothing will come from tonight," he warns. "It could be another event or ten, for all we know."

"Considering neither of us is good at waiting for things to happen, I really hope tonight is it."

"If I could force it I would, but letting Niccolo come to us is the ticket to the outcome that we want—not what he wants." He turns into the half-moon driveway, and I lean forward to look at the incredible stone building hugged by six round pillars that seem to go on for miles and miles, the roof steepled and framed by two lion sculptures.

"It's almost castle-like," I say, noting the railings and overlooks wrapping the top of the structure.

"Try one of the oldest privately held palaces in Italy," he says, stopping behind the line of cars waiting to reach the doorman. "It's preserved in as much of the elaborate glory the royals that once occupied it chose to bestow on it."

"I've never been in a palace. But then, I'd never been in a castle before yours, either." And the very fact that I know those words are true has me facing him. "See what I mean about my memory? When did I ever say things like that before today?"

"You definitely haven't."

"I feel really hopeful. If I can recover my memory before Niccolo figures out who I am, that could give us an extra advantage to negotiate with him. I mean, how will we even know if what he tells us is true?"

"I'd like you to remember on your own," he says, pulling up a few feet and idling again, "and I'm happy you're feeling encouraged. But don't bury yourself in pressure, sweetheart. We have resources to confirm whatever Niccolo might claim, and we'll take everything with ten grains of salt."

"I want the control to be ours, not his."

Several valets in uniforms with yellow and green tassels dangling from the sleeves open the doors of the black sedan in front of us, and Kayden pulls us next in line for the door.

"Sometimes other people's control is the façade that gives you the power," Kayden explains. "And that's the kind of magic you use on a man like Niccolo."

I open my mouth when a woman exits the vehicle in front of us, her stunning full-length gown sparkling with white diamonds. "I feel underdressed, Kayden."

"Overdone is not the kind of attention we want," he comments, while another woman steps out of the same car, and to my relief she is dressed in a short, elegantly simple cream dress.

"Less is more," Kayden reminds me, pulling us to the front door. "Remember that tonight."

As one of the valets steps to my door Kayden holds up his hand, stopping the man to speak to me. "I'll get your coat before you get out. It's a long, cold red-carpet walk up stairs that rival the Spanish Steps." He exits the Jag to walk to the back of the vehicle.

I wait for him, and I am not nervous, but rather eager to embrace this night. Action is what we both need and want. Hiding, always feeling afraid of what's around the corner waiting to destroy me or those around me, wasn't going to work for either of us much longer.

Yet when my door opens, a rush of nerves overwhelms me, my mind flashing with an image of me on my knees, and that man, Niccolo or whoever he is, holding my hair. *Pulling* my hair.

"Ella."

Kayden's voice is silk on my nerves, where that memory had been sandpaper and razor blades. I look right and realize that he's kneeling beside me, his hand holding mine. "Flashback?"

"Yes. It was sudden and short but intense."

"We don't have to do this."

"Yes, we do," I say, irritated at having allowed an asshole from my past to control me in the present.

"We don't," he insists.

"Don't doubt me," I say fiercely, facing him, my skirt riding high. Cold air zips along my bare skin, but I am not cold. Not when Kayden and I are suddenly staring at each other and his hand is on my leg, fingers resting on the lace of my thigh-high, a hot touch I welcome and crave. Because it's him. Because he is right in every way that other man is wrong.

"I don't doubt you," he promises softly, the air charged between us. "I have never doubted you."

He isn't talking about this moment, any more than I was. Some part of me still fears the past and what it will do to us.

"I'm afraid of losing me and us. And I hate that fear, but you matter to me—more than I think you understand. I just want you to know that."

His eyes glint hard. "I keep telling you: I'm not letting you go, and he's damn sure not taking you from me." He stands, taking me with him, his big body shielding mine while he slides my dress down my legs.

"Thank you," I murmur as my coat and the scent of him, spicy and rousingly male, wrap around me at the same time, and I slip my arms inside the wool.

"Thank me," he says, his voice low, almost rough, his fingers branding my hips, "by ending the question of what you're wearing under this dress besides thigh-highs."

"Maybe I'm not wearing anything at all," I tease, sounding breathless, because somehow, some way, in the middle of my blackouts and fears I am oh so very breathless.

One of the valets says something to him in Italian, but before he responds to him, he leans in, his breath a warm fan on my skin as he murmurs, "Careful now, sweetheart. You tempt the beast and I'll take you to a corner of the party and find out myself."

Heat zips through me, darn near turning to fire as he walks

me to the curb with a quick, smoldering look before turning to the valet, and I'm left with the distinct impression he might just make good on that warning. I watch him talk to the other man, power and confidence wafting off of him, and I'm amazed by how this man makes me feel consumed. And I welcome it, when escape was all I craved with the man in my flashbacks.

Kayden laughs, a deep, sexy rumble from his broad chest, and the way my nipples instantly tighten proves how powerful a drug he is to me. I watch as he palms the man a ridiculously large bill before turning back to me, and I swear, the way he looks at me is like no one else exists. Like I am his moon, sun, and star, and I really do not believe anyone has ever made me feel that special.

"Was that a hundred euros you gave him?" I ask as he drapes his arm over my shoulder and pulls me into the shelter of his body.

"It pays to make friends with the staff." As we head toward the mile-high red-carpeted steps, two men with cameras start taking photos of us.

"And there's the press," I murmur. "Maybe we should stop and pose. That should make tonight the night."

"That would be a little too obvious," he says. "Though I have no doubt that Niccolo hacks the press photos for these events. Just not as effectively as I do. Directly or indirectly, I make damn sure The Underground owns every important event in this city, even when I'm not in attendance."

"Like you own the neighborhood."

"The neighborhood is like a family, and The Underground has been head of the family for a good fifty years."

"You mean The Hawk has been the head of the family for all of those years."

"Yes," he agrees. "Which means everything The Hawk does is watched, analyzed, and dissected. And as my woman, you inherit that attention. Be prepared to be badgered with probing questions from people with bad English."

It hits me then how much trust he's putting in me—and it strikes me how profoundly important it is that he has sometimes trusted me more than I have myself. "I can handle it," I promise.

He wraps his arm around my neck and leans down to kiss me. "I know, Eleana."

I grimace as he loosens his hold on my neck, wondering how he'll explain my new identity to Niccolo, but it's too late to ask. We reach the final step, and what amounts to a giant stone porch, where two guards stand at attention on either side of a roped-off continuation of the red carpet. One of the men greets us in Italian, then checks our names off a clipboard after asking for identification. Once he's satisfied with our identities, Kayden and I walk the remainder of the red carpet, where two additional guards monitor the tall double doors, opening them at our approach.

"Is my gun in my purse a problem?" I whisper, suddenly concerned.

"Not for us," he says, and I don't ask for details. This is Kayden. This is the power of The Underground.

Moments later we cross the threshold of the magnificent palace, green-and-beige-streaked marble beneath our feet, the room seeming to stretch onward for miles. "It's breathtaking," I say as we move to yet another check-in point, my gaze lifting to the curved ceiling adorned with green-and-beige-toned paintings of Roman armored soldiers on horses, while intricate trim work divides it from the beige walls.

"From the fourteen hundreds," he says, guiding me toward a pedestal where yet another man in a uniform holds a clipboard. "Obviously restored."

He tells me a bit about the royal family while we are once again checked off a clipboard, and a young woman in a long black dress takes my coat in exchange for a ticket.

"And now the games begin," Kayden says, linking my arm with his again and setting us in motion deeper into the palace.

"Is that what this is? A game?"

"These parties are always games about positioning. Someone wants something. Someone needs something. Expect them to hint at those things to you, and just soak it all in. Often what doesn't seem important now becomes so later."

"Well, I won't be a big help there since I don't speak Italian."

"The brilliance of their choppy English and your lack of Italian is that you'll speak Italian soon—while the people you meet tonight will assume you don't."

"And say things they don't think I'll understand near me," I supply. "That's devious."

"This crowd is devious," he says. "We have to keep up or get stabbed or shot in the back. We won't, but I'm sure a few people will try to come at me tonight through you."

"Gallo's given me plenty of practice dodging those kinds of bullets."

His cell phone buzzes and he reaches into his pocket to

glance at the screen, replacing it in his pocket as he says, "Matteo has a visual on the ballroom."

The unexpected announcement puts me on edge all over again and I don't know why. I want Niccolo to find me. And I must stiffen or react because Kayden wraps his arm around my waist and pulls me closer. "What just happened?" he asks.

"If you suspect bad things might happen tonight," I say, "just tell me."

"Bad things can always happen, and I won't pretend otherwise. What are you specifically concerned about?"

"You have Matteo doing live monitoring of the party."

He stops walking, facing me, his hands on my shoulders. "I always have a tech guy tap the security feed for these events. The playback makes for interesting viewing, which you'll see when we watch it tomorrow. I asked for Matteo specifically because you're here for the first time by my side, and I will always want the best for you."

We. It's a good word but it, and everything he just said, reminds me of just how protective he is. "Don't shelter me," I warn. "Don't put me in a situation without arming me with the facts, no matter how good, bad, or very damn dirty."

"I have every intention of letting you get very damn dirty with me, sweetheart. In all places, things, and situations. Okay?"

I study him, searching his face, and I don't believe for a minute that he's going to stand by those words if he thinks he can protect me from something. But I do believe that he *thinks* he will, and for now, that's enough. "Yes."

He wraps my arm around his. "We'll watch the videos together in the morning," he says, turning us toward the music, and under a giant archway that leads us to another stairway. "It'll help you get to know all the players."

"I'd like that." As we grow nearer to the sound of heavy chatter, and even louder music, a thought hits me. "I can't believe I didn't ask this. What if I see someone I know?"

He smiles. "Amnesia is like pleading the Fifth Amendment. You don't know who they are, or what they're talking about. And I'll be with you. We'll wing it together."

"Wing it," I repeat in disbelief, but as we reach the top of the stairs, and more cameras begin flashing again, it's clear that's the best plan I have right now. "I think I need a drink."

"Don't drink and drive," he replies, moving us past several reporters to enter a ballroom speckled with glitzy gowns and tuxedos, a dance floor in the center, and at least five hundred candles dangling from long ropes above.

We stop just beyond the crowd, which I guess to be in the hundreds, and we both scan the room, my gaze going toward the two giant ice sculptures framing the musicians to our right. "Butterflies," I say of their design. "That can't be a coincidence, can it?"

"Nothing with these people is a coincidence," he confirms. "It's a message to someone, and we need to find out who before we leave here tonight."

A waiter stops beside us and offers us champagne, which we both wave off. "What happened to needing a drink?" Kayden asks.

"It's better if I'm sober when I pretend to forget people I

just remembered, and ask subtle questions about things I'm pretty sure I shouldn't know about. And that statement was just so ridiculous that it sounds like I am drunk."

Kayden's eyes light with amusement and mischief, his fingers lacing with mine. "I'm hungry. I need either a private place to have you for a snack, or the only good thing about these events—the food."

"Where is the food? Because I'm starving."

He bends our elbows and places our connected hands together, my bracelet on full display, and then indicates the far corner. "The goal line is directly in front of us and to the right. That is where we find pasta and chocolate, and mock the crowd with full stomachs. Between us and it, though, are people who want to keep us from that reward."

I laugh. "So what's the plan?"

He gives me a serious, focused look. "An all-out American football attack. Straight up the middle. Got it?"

"Got it," I say, playing along, the nerves I didn't realize had attacked settling down to a tolerable level.

We start walking, and before we've gone three feet, we're tackled from the left. Then the right. Before I know what has hit me, I'm being introduced to people, struggling to understand questions and remember accented names.

Except one.

Suddenly, Kayden and I are standing in front of the politician in the photo Gallo showed me this morning.

"Eleana," Kayden says, his hand settling at my lower back. "This is Lino Conti. One of the only honest men in Parliament, which unfortunately earns him more enemies than friends."

On that unexpected tidbit of information, Lino, who happens to be a bit of a silver fox, offers me his hand, which I accept. "Nice to meet you, Eleana," he says, but rather than letting go of me, he and Kayden lean over me, sharing a quiet, brief exchange before Lino releases me and they separate.

"You have a good man here," Lino says, offering nothing more before he disappears into the crowd.

I give Kayden a questioning look that he answers by pressing his cheek to mine and whispering, "There are two sides to every story."

He leads me toward the food tables, which are finally in view, but his statement has me searching every passing face, looking for answers. My worst fear and hope is that one of them knows the other side of *my* story. Just the idea has me holding on to Kayden's hand a little tighter.

twelve

Finally, Kayden and I clear the crowd, the table of food standing in an alcove under a giant white stone stairway, filled with all kinds of goodies. I go for the spill-proof options of bread and cheese. Kayden fills his plate with a variety of items he then tries to feed me. "Try this," he says, picking up a ravioli.

I let him feed me the bite, and the creamy, cheesy center has me moaning in delight.

"That's not the way to keep my mind on business," Kayden warns, his lips curving.

"And pasta and cheese is not the way to keep me from outgrowing the clothes you bought me," I counter, dabbing my mouth with a napkin.

"I promise to help you work it off," he says, offering me another bite.

"No," I say firmly. "No more." A waiter passes and I hand him Kayden's plate.

Kayden arches a brow. "You know I wasn't done, right?

I laugh. "Oops. I'll get you another."

He shackles my waist, holding me in front of him, his

mood suddenly darker. "Why haven't you asked me about Lino?"

"Because just like I think we both needed to know I could call you just to call today, I think you need to know that I trust you enough not to need details."

"Niccolo had his wife killed, and made it look like Lino did it."

My eyes go wide. "Why? Or does he even have a reason?"

"Payback for him refusing a political favor."

I start putting the pieces together. "Lino tried to hire you to fix this for him."

"More like to exact revenge. He wants to destroy Niccolo."

"Did you tell him to join the club?"

"I told him, when his trigger finger cools off, to call me."

"And has it?" I ask.

"He says it has."

"But you're not sure," I conclude.

"I'm not, no, but we have a mutual enemy. Where that leads us, I have yet to decide."

"Gallo's placed you together. That means Niccolo can, too."

"I knew Gallo was snooping around, which forced me to call Niccolo after that meeting."

"What impact did that have?"

"Aside from amusing Niccolo, not much. But then, I didn't tell him everything, either."

"But you told me."

"Yes. I told you."

"Thank you," I say, a moment before a male voice says, "Kayden," from behind me.

I turn to discover a fifty-something-year-old man several inches shorter and stockier than Kayden, his gray hair a shade lighter than his eyes, which fall on me as he says, "And you must be Eleana."

"Meet Chief Donati," Kayden says, reaching for my hand and kissing it, the act exposing the bracelet. "He also happens to be Detective Gallo's boss." He eyes the chief. "Who threatened and manipulated Eleana today in an effort to turn her against me."

Donati eyes my bracelet and then me, surmising. "Obviously he failed."

"Miserably," I say. "But he did teach me that a bar means coffee in the morning, not wine."

"Wine is acceptable at all times in Italy," Donati corrects, his English heavily accented but nearly perfect. "However, coffee is a good remedy or preparation for the evening's wine, depending on how you choose to look at it."

Kayden's phone buzzes and he removes it from his pocket, inspecting the screen before announcing, "I need to make a call." He leans in to kiss me, lingering long enough to whisper, "Give him hell," before he straightens again. He then eyes Donati, gives a laugh, and says, "Good luck," before he leaves.

Donati arches a brow at me. "What does 'good luck' mean?"

"He thinks I'm a handful for everyone but him," I say.

"And why is that?"

"Apparently Italian men find self-proclaimed feminists intimidating."

He studies me for several heavy beats, stunning me as he asks, "Do you know what that bracelet means?"

"Do you?" I challenge.

"That you're his woman."

"Yes," I say. "I am very much his woman."

"And you know who, and what he, is?"

"I do know who and what he is. Do you know who, and what, Gallo is?"

"A man who doesn't like to color outside the lines, even when it might be to our benefit."

"And yet he threatens me, and seduces the young woman who lives with us. That's outright scribbling in all the corners."

"Are you telling me that Gallo is involved with Adriel's sister?"

"That's exactly what I'm telling you. She isn't part of any of this, and I respectfully request that you keep him away from her."

He studies me for several moments. "You are bold for a woman so newly inserted into Kayden's life." The word *inserted* hits a very bad spot in me, but I have no time to explore his meaning. "What do you think Kayden would do for me, should I grant your request?"

"I wonder what he will do should you *not* grant it."

A man in uniform steps to his side, whispering something to the chief. A moment later the newcomer leaves, and while the chief's expression remains unchanged, I don't miss the subtle tightening around his mouth. "I'm afraid I have a situation to attend to. I'll handle Gallo and we'll talk again."

He turns and leaves, and I have a bad feeling that "we'll talk again" translates to him calling on me for a favor. I scan for Kayden and start walking through the random clusters of sparkling dresses and tuxedos with no success. I finally spy him standing in profile, with a beautiful brunette woman, at the exact moment that she grabs his arm and leans her body into him. I suck in a breath and exhale as he immediately extracts himself. The woman looks at me and says something to Kayden, and I have déjà vu, remembering a similar incident in the bar with the bartender.

Sure enough, he responds as he had then, turning to seek me out. Rather than leaving, as I tried to do then, I hold my ground and he motions me forward. Not certain I really want to meet Little Miss Grabby Hands, who doesn't seem to be going anywhere, I force myself to sidestep several guests and make my way to his side. The instant I'm within his reach, Kayden shackles my waist and says in my ear, "You know—"

"Yes," I say firmly. "I do."

"Good," he says, approval lighting his eyes before he turns to face the other woman. "Eleana, this is Sasha. She's one of ours."

"You're so beautiful," Sasha gushes, reaching out and stroking my arm, her accent not quite like everyone else's. "I love your green eyes," she continues. "They're the color of grass on a perfect summer's day."

I'm not sure what to make of her, and Kayden laughs. "As you can see, Sasha is a toucher and a talker, with a big personality, which ensures that she's well known at these events."

Sasha points at her deep cleavage, and shakes her breasts. "These are why I'm well known." She waves down her body. "And all of these goodies, too. Do you like?"

The woman has me blushing. "You're fabulous. And I wish I had your confidence. Is your accent Italian?"

"I am the best French import Italy has ever seen." She adds, "*Je séduis les gens pour leurs secrets.*"

I blanch and repeat her words. "'I seduce people for their secrets.'"

Kayden turns to face me. "You understand French?"

"Yes. Or I think I do. Do you?"

"Fluently," he confirms. "*Comment a été votre rencontre avec Donati?*"

I repeat his question. "'How was your meeting with Donati?' Kayden, I know French! How? Maybe I took it in school, but that doesn't feel right."

"I have a thought on that," he says, "but we'll talk about it later. How *did* it go with Donati?"

"I asked him to keep Gallo away from Giada, and he was trying to manipulate me into promising him a favor when a man in uniform came up to him, whispered something, and Donati left."

Another interruption occurs as two men join us and start a conversation with Kayden that I of course can't understand.

Sasha listens a moment and rolls her eyes, stepping closer to me. "They want him to sit on some ridiculous board, which he'll never agree to join. I need to go to the toilet. You want to join me?"

"Yes," I say, glad for a few minutes away from the crowd.

She nods and then interrupts the conversation, announcing our departure. Kayden leans down and whispers, "I'll get us out of here soon," before Sasha links her arm with mine and leads me past the piano and violin, and then down a hallway that is blessedly free of other guests.

"Thank God," she says, releasing me, her silliness evaporating along with her heavy accent. "These events are exhausting. Everyone wants something, including us." She gives me a sideways look. "Be careful with Donati. Aside from his preference for quid pro quo, something about that man bothers me, and don't ask what, because I don't know. But I've been doing this long enough to trust my instincts."

"How long have you worked for Kayden?"

"Since he took over France a few years back, but my family is made up of generations of Hunters and Hawks, most of them now dead."

"So you transferred from France?" I ask, wondering if she's related to the prior Hawk in that region.

"A year ago, after I stupidly tried to seduce Niccolo's stepbrother." She snorts. "That went badly."

"Who is his stepbrother?" I ask, hoping a name might trigger a memory.

"He runs the French mob."

"Wait. So the French and Italian mobs are one?"

"Oh no," she says. "That was the idea when the two families married, but it didn't take long for the parents to end up dead, while their sons claimed control of their own regions."

I gape. "You're saying they killed their parents?"

"Without a blink of regret," she says.

"And who is the head of the French mob?"

She holds up a hand. "I'm sorry. I can't even speak that man's name. He's a monster."

He obviously hurt her and I hate to push, but . . . "Who—"

She shakes her head at the entry to the bathroom. "Not a topic for a public place."

Frustrated, I nod and we enter a huge bathroom with green marble floors and at least a dozen stalls. Sasha's phone rings and she digs it from the silver evening purse hanging from her shoulder. As she sits down on a leather couch, I keep walking toward the row of stalls.

Stepbrothers. Mafia. Murdering your own parents. It's all insanity, and I'm suddenly transported back to the kitchen of my family home, with my father lying in his own blood. I see the blood. I see the gun. I feel the trigger against my finger when I kill his attacker. Shaking myself, I blink, and I'm standing at a bathroom stall and don't remember how I got here. The same way I blacked out right after Enzo's death.

Concerned that Nathan shouldn't have dismissed that incident as trauma, I enter the stall, then lean my head against the locked door. I know that my flashbacks are always trying to tell me something. My father was murdered, ripped from my life, while these mobsters, these *monsters*, chose to murder their parents for personal gain. But what does that mean to me? Is this about the men who killed my father? Or . . . maybe this isn't about my father at all, but some lesson he gave me. I blink, and I'm transported back to the kitchen again, hiding in the pantry with my mother.

There are crashing sounds and muffled gunfire, like a silencer is being used, and my mother and I both jump. And then there is silence. Oh God, the silence is deafening, and I wait for my father to come to us, but he does not. I can't take it anymore. I jerk away from my mother, every instinct telling me my father needs help.

I open the door and gasp at the sight of him lying in a puddle of blood. I dash forward and fall to my knees.

"Dad. Dad."

My mother drops down beside me, bursting into tears as she starts begging him to stay alive. "Gun," my father murmurs. "Ella . . . take . . . gun."

I look down to find it at his fingers and I take it. "I have it."

"Two . . . men."

The kitchen door bursts open, a man in a mask and all black appearing, and my father hisses, "Shoot," and instinct takes over. I raise the gun and fire at the man in black, and he tumbles forward.

My eyes pop open. *Two men.* That's what comes to me. *Two men.* Is it the *stepbrothers*?

A knock sounds on the door and I jolt. "Open up," Sasha says urgently and I immediately comply. She shoves her way into the stall and shuts the door behind her. "We have a problem," she says very softly.

Alarm bells go off. Is she the problem? "What are you talking about?" I whisper back.

"Niccolo is here."

thirteen

Sasha might as well have punched me in the chest. "Niccolo can't be here."

"And yet he is," she whispers. "And don't say his name."

"You just did."

"*I* didn't have a choice; I needed you to know who exactly I was talking about."

"Right," I say, laughing without humor. "He who shall not be named. I thought that was his brother."

"They're named Bastard and Bitch," she says, "and this isn't Harry Potter. There is no magic wand to make the one that is here disappear."

"And just so I don't get confused. Is he the Bastard or the Bitch?"

"The Bastard."

"Are we just going to hide in the stall while the Bastard is in the building?"

"We're waiting for Kayden to call," she says, and as if on cue, my phone rings.

I reach for my purse and my shaky fingers fumble on the zipper. "Stupid adrenaline," I murmur, while Sasha reaches down and opens it, handing me my phone. "Thank you." I slide my finger across the screen to answer, and will myself to be my father's daughter and get a grip. "I just heard," I say. "What's the plan?"

"Are you okay?" Kayden asks.

"Peachy," I say, repeating a word I somehow know was my mother's.

Admiration fills Sasha's eyes with my flippant remark, but Kayden isn't as won over by my bravado. "Ella, sweetheart—"

"I'm fine. I promise. What happens now? Do I march out there and let him see me?"

"That is the last thing you will do," he says, his voice a hard command.

"It gets it over with."

"It puts you within his reach, before I can ensure that you won't be in the future. Sasha is going to take you out a side door, where Adriel is waiting with a car."

"Why not you?"

"If Niccolo sees me, and hears my woman is present, he'll want to meet you. I need to stay out of sight."

"Won't it be weird that I just disappear, and you leave alone?"

"We're going to make Niccolo think you're leaving with me."

"How is that possible?"

"Ella, I know you want to feel some sort of control right now, but I need you to find that in me. I had a plan for every possible problem that could be thrown our way when we came here tonight, including Niccolo." He softens his voice. "I've got you, and this. I promise. *Trust me.*"

"I do. Completely."

"Good. Then let's go home and get naked."

"Yes, please. How do we make that happen?"

"Sasha knows what to do. Follow her lead. She won't fail you."

"Got it." I look at Sasha. "I'll follow Sasha, and Annie and I will see you soon."

"Nothing is going to happen to you," he says, ending the call. "I'm ready," I tell Sasha.

"I need to know who Annie is," she says.

I reach in my purse and remove my gun. "My best friend."

"Good friends, good times. But right now I think you should zip it into your purse, out of temptation's reach."

She's right. I might shoot Niccolo, and while that would be enjoyable, it would probably mean I'd end up dead, too. And I don't plan to go down with him. I zip Annie inside. "Now what?"

"We go." Female voices sound outside the door and she grimaces, whispering, "Go along with my craziness. It's actually kind of fun." She releases me, and I nod.

She smiles, and then motions to let me know that we're a go. A moment later she opens the door and exits into the outer room. "Thank you, Eleana," she sobs. "Please don't tell him I got this upset. It makes me look bad."

I join her outside the stall to find her actually crying, while two thirty-something women stand a few feet away, gaping at her, and now us. "You don't look bad," I tell Sasha. "But you need to tell him what you told me." I glance at our audience. "And let's not do this now."

"Sorry." She swipes at her eyes, wiping tears that I'm actually not sure really exist. She's just so darn good at screwing up her face that I thought she was really crying. "I did say I'd stop this."

"We'd better go find Kayden," I say. "He'll be missing me."

"Of course," she says, and we head for the door, exiting into the blessedly empty hallway. "Nosy wenches," she murmurs as we start walking. "I should sleep with their husbands."

I gape. "Sasha. Please say you—"

"I'm kidding. Sort of." Her cell phone buzzes in her hand and she looks down at the screen, and the slight furrow to her brow has me asking, "What is it?"

"Hold on," she says, punching in a reply to the message, and then linking her arm with mine. "Niccolo is standing near the stairs we need to take."

"Can't we go another way?"

"Not if we're going to make them think I'm you, when I leave through the front with Kayden."

"We can't just walk right by him."

"Kayden's going to create a distraction right when we get into Niccolo's line of sight. So here's the plan." She locks our arms. "I'm going to hang on to you, and we're going to keep our heads low, like two new girlfriends chatting it up about pasta and coffee, and we'll zip right past him." We near the end of the hallway and she stops. "If you suddenly have a flashback that causes an urge to stop, shout, or shoot, just hold on to me and let me get you through it."

Stunned that Kayden would tell her anything at all, I look over at her. "What do you know about me and Niccolo?"

"That you have amnesia, and think that he did something

horrible to you or someone you love. And I get it. He did something horrible to someone I love." Emotions knife through her eyes, and she cuts her gaze away. "Don't ask for details." She squeezes my arm. "Let's get this over with."

I nod, and as we reenter the party, I decide that death really is too good for Niccolo. Destruction. Disgrace. Jail. Those things sound good. "Head down," Sasha warns as we pass the piano, then laughs as if I've said something funny. I laugh, too, and, needing a place to put my nerves, I say, "Pasta, pasta, coffee."

She snickers and says, "Coffee, coffee, and pasta. We're going up the center stairs and he's to the left by the food displays."

"Got it. How is he even here when he's a criminal, and Donati is here?"

"We're with politicians," she says. "They're all criminals."

"Right," I say, and we both fake laugh as some man stops in front of us, gazing down at her cleavage while she waves him off, and drags me around him. "Bastard," she mutters. "Here we go. Niccolo on our left. Coffee. Coffee. Coffee. Assholes everywhere. Coffee. Your turn."

"Pasta. Pasta. Pasta. Assholes everywhere and I swear my skin is tingling like he's looking."

"We're gorgeous. Of course he's looking. And one of us is Kayden's woman. Someone will have told him, but there's about to be a planned distraction. Don't react." We reach the steps and start our climb, and the sound of glasses crashing to the ground fills the air.

"That was a tray of champagne being dropped right next to Niccolo," she tells me. "Kayden promised the waiter extra if Niccolo got wet." The sound of an angry, familiar male voice rips through the air.

"And I'm betting the waiter is getting that tip," Sasha quips.

Niccolo's voice lifts in the air again, and his voice, his anger, is familiar, but not quite right for some reason. A niggling memory begins to come back to me. Images flicker and then take control. *I am in "his" bedroom, and I'm holding the gun, pacing, certain of what I have to do. Decision made, I walk to the bathroom and grab my purse, then open a drawer and grab the cosmetic bag where I've stashed the cash I've been collecting for weeks. I head for the door and open it, exiting to the hallway, when I hear two male voices raised in anger, his and another coming from the office down the hall. The office door opens and I hurry back into the bedroom, peering through a crack as they approach and then stop on the stairs in front of me.*

"Ella," Sasha says, jolting me back to the present. "Are you okay?"

"Yes. Sorry. I'm fine." I realize that I blacked out again, and we're now at the top of the steps.

"This way," she says, dragging me to the right, behind a wall, but I can still hear Niccolo's voice, and I know—I just know—that if I see him, I'll remember everything I have lost and need to find.

I jerk free of Sasha's hold, turning back toward the party and stepping just to the edge of the wall, my gut clenching as I find Niccolo in profile. "Ella," Sasha hisses, closing her hand down on my arm again.

"One minute," I whisper, planting my feet and holding on to her. "Just one minute. I have to see his face."

And in that moment, as if he senses my presence, he turns and looks toward us. Sasha and I both jolt backward and start moving down the hallway, but I saw his face. "You're a crazy person," Sasha chides. "Crazy, insane, and did I say crazy?"

"Amnesia sucks," I say. "I had to try and jolt my memory."

"Did it work?"

"No. It didn't work."

"Some things are easier forgotten anyway," she declares, echoing Kayden's sentiments and turning us around a corner into a narrow hallway. "Here," she says, opening a door, and we step inside a dark room that I think is a library.

"What are we doing?" I ask as she locks us inside.

"Undress," she orders, reaching for her zipper. "We're switching clothes so the staff thinks you're leaving with Kayden."

I don't argue, wasting no time complying, and in about sixty seconds, I'm stepping into her silver gown while she does the same with mine. "Gorgeous," she says, running her hands over the velvet. "I might forget to return this." She eyes my feet. "What size?"

"Seven."

"Perfect," she approves, and we quickly make the exchange, trading purses as we head to the door, where she pauses and grabs my arms. "Ella. I hate this, but I have to have that bracelet. People have noticed, and they'll know it's not you—"

"Right," I say, feeling sick to the stomach. "Of course." But I can't seem to make myself reach for it, and I'm not sure why.

Understanding fills her face, and she takes my arm and

turns my wrist over, unlatching it. "I promise you," she says, as it slides off my arm, "I'll get it right back to you, by way of your man." She closes her hand around it. "The stairs are directly in front of this door. Go down them and exit the palace. Adriel will be waiting at the curb."

"How are you going to get down the stairs without Niccolo seeing you?"

"Kayden has a plan, but timing is everything, which means I need to move, and move now." She opens the door and we exit to the hallway, where she shocks me by giving me a quick hug. "We'll make him pay," she vows, releasing me. "Go now."

I grab the doorknob and open the door, entering the stairwell, and by the time the door has closed, I've lifted the silver satin skirt of Sasha's dress and started down the steps. Niccolo's face, his voice, try to claim my thoughts, but I shove them aside. Right now, I want to be out of this palace, and to know that Kayden and Sasha are as well. Three flights of stairs, and a blister on my right toe later, I exit the palace and step onto a sidewalk, and into the chilly night without a coat, the cold quickening my already fast steps. But there is no Adriel. I'm about to call Kayden when a black Rolls-Royce pulls to the curb, but I don't breathe easier until a man in all black steps out.

"Adriel," I whisper, hurrying forward as he rounds the hood of the car and meets me at the passenger side.

"You okay?" he asks, opening the door.

"Great. Peachy." I start to get in, but he grabs me.

"Sorry," he says, "but Sasha and I are fuck buddies. We need to make this look good." He molds me to him, pressing his forehead to mine, while I fight shock and the urge to shove him away. He notices, warning me, "Don't react. And please keep all weapons away from Kayden when he sees this film."

"Don't even think about kissing me," I warn, "or I *will* bite you."

He laughs and lets go of me, turning me toward the car. I step toward its sanctuary, but he grabs me, holding a hand on my belly, his mouth by my ear. "Count to five and it's over."

"Four, five," I say. "Enough."

He releases me and I disappear inside the car, thankful when he shuts the door. Mechanically, I pull on a seat belt and sink into the seat, while Adriel joins me and puts us in drive. "I'm sorry, Ella. I had to do that."

"It's fine," I say. "I just need to think." I shut my eyes, and I'm back in my memory of minutes ago. *I peek through the door and the two men*, him *and the other, stop on the stairs, and they are speaking in Italian, fighting. Niccolo's voice echoes through the room, angry.*

My eyes pop open and I know then that "him" is not Niccolo.

fourteen

I've barely come to the conclusion that *he* is not Niccolo when Adriel's cell phone rings, and he surprises me by speaking in English to his caller, "Yes. I have her here. She's safe." He listens a moment. "She wants you to call us once you're out of the palace." He listens again and then ends the call.

I turn to face him. "Thank you, Adriel. I know you could have spoken in Italian, but you knew."

"That you need some kind of control," he supplies. "Yes. From one control freak to another, I get it."

He glances at me and then back at the road. "I watched you on film tonight. You handled yourself well in there. I was wrong about you. Kayden chose well."

"How can you know if you're right or wrong, when none of us know my past?"

"I thought you were starting to recover some of your memories."

"Randomly, and too few and far between for any of you to know who you're dealing with."

He glances at me briefly once again. "Where is this coming from?"

"I don't know how to answer that—because I don't know what you know, or what Kayden wants you to know."

"Caution, like you just showed, is exactly what would be expected of the woman Kayden would give that bracelet to," he says, while I grab my wrist, which feels more naked by the moment. "I was with Kayden when we found you," he continues. "I know there are no fingerprints on file for you, despite the fact that you would have been fingerprinted for your passport. I know that Matteo created a new identity for you. I know Niccolo is looking for you, and I know why we were in that alleyway. That leaves open a lot of possibilities that I'm smart enough to figure out."

"You know almost as much as I do, which is kind of scary since this is my life."

"Did something happen with Niccolo at the party that I missed on the film?"

"No. Yes. I don't know. I saw him, and instead of confirming he was this other person I though he was, I now know he's not. I know he's looking for me, but it's not because he's the person I thought he was. It's because he either thinks I know something I shouldn't, or I have something he wants."

"Do you?"

"I have no clue."

"And who did you think he was?"

"A very powerful, brutal man in my past who won't let me just walk away. I was sure it was him, so now I have no idea of who's coming for me—and he might hurt anyone I allow into my life."

"We are powerful, and Kayden is a force to be reckoned with."

"But he *is* human, and I can't be the reason something happens to him."

"There are many people who watch over Kayden, Ella. And the people who watch over you are all his people. The Underground is family, and you are now one of us. Your problem is our problem."

"I'm not worried about me. I'm worried about everyone else. Kevin was a Hawk, and he's gone."

"Kayden learned from Kevin's mistakes. He brought together and united Hawks around the world, and created a new, well-known, highly feared program called Evil Eye."

"What is Evil Eye?"

"The wrath unleashed from around the world on anyone who hurts a Hawk, or their family and extended family. Your wearing that bracelet tonight told the world that you are in that protected circle now. Even Niccolo fears Evil Eye."

"And Kayden developed the program?"

"He developed it and heads it."

"He didn't tell me this. Why are you?"

"Because I've seen how stubborn you are. If you think the answer to protecting him is leaving, you will go at your own risk. And that answer is not the correct one. Kayden is well insulated, virtually without weakness."

"Except you just told me that I am the one unknown he's allowed into his world, and yours. I'm a weakness."

"Holy fuck, that is *not* what I just said."

"It's a fact."

"It is not a fact, Ella." His phone starts to ring. "We're not done with this conversation." He answers his call and has an exchange in Italian, and by the time it's over we're at the castle gate, watching it open. “That was Kayden,” he says. “He and Sasha are out of the palace and headed here now.” Lights flicker behind us, and I twist around to spy not one but two motorcycles. “Matteo and Carlo,” Adriel supplies before I can ask.

I face forward as Adriel pulls inside the castle gates, plotting my escape from the cavalry. While appreciated, they will ask questions that I don’t want to answer right now. My hand goes to the door handle beside me, and once the Rolls-Royce halts in front of the porch, I pull it, exiting to the driveway. By the time the two motorcycles park behind us, I’m already up the stairs with my key in my hand. I pause at the security panel, punch in a code, and unlock the door, entering the foyer.

There I shut the door, lifting the skirt of Sasha’s dress to run to the security panel for our tower. Once I’ve keyed in the code I wait for the door to lift and scoot under it the instant I can fit. I immediately punch the button to seal myself inside, lifting the skirt of my gown again to walk to the stairs.

“Ella.”

At the sound of Adriel’s voice, I whirl around to find he has snuck under the door. “What are you doing, Adriel?”

He walks toward me, stopping toe-to-toe. “It’s ‘come to Jesus’ time, Ella. He claimed you tonight, which, considering he’s been alone with his demons a very long time, got a lot of attention. And if his woman can’t trust him to protect her, why will anyone else trust him to protect them?”

“I do trust him. I just don’t trust me. I don’t know me.”

“Fear is a demon, and you no longer have the luxury of it winning. You’re strong enough not to let it. Is it better if you get your memory back? Hell yes. But if you don't, we'll deal with it. Because that's what we do, and because that's what he does. Deal with it.

"Now. I'm leaving before he gets here. Don't make me have to come kick your ass." He turns and walks to the door and punches the button, leaving me momentarily shell-shocked.

"You're an asshole," I say, emotions balling in my chest and belly.

He faces me. "And your point is?"

"Thank you."

His lips curve and he gives me a quick nod before ducking under the door. I punch the button to seal it behind him, and, lifting my dress, I hurry up the stairs, his words heavy on my mind.

He's right. Fear can't be the winner here, and it is, or I wouldn't still be suppressing things. I have to own my past; it can't own me. If I don't fear it, I can remember it. If I don't hide from the pain I have to relive, I can remember it. I'm going to go to our room, grab my journal, my ballet slippers, and whatever else feels right, and instead of hoping I remember, I *will.*

But when I hit the top step, the dimly lit tower stops me in my tracks, an icy sensation overcoming me. Like I'm being watched. Like I'm not alone. And while I know it's the spooky way this hallway always affects me, without a conscious decision to do so, my purse, or rather Sasha's purse I've claimed as mine, is unzipped, my hand covering Annie. I scan all visible areas. The hall at my right toward the spare bedroom. The also dimly lit living area directly across from me, and finally toward our room. Everything appears fine.

Of course it's fine. We have security, and damn it, I'm jumpy again because of Niccolo. I just lectured myself about fear, and he's still on my mind. And that man. *He* is at the root of this.

No, I amend. *I* am the problem because I'm letting him win again. Every day I let him stay nameless, he wins. I look down at Annie and have the gut-wrenching memory of my mother in her hospital bed. Oh the irony of me insisting that everything is better remembered, when I want to keep remembering her smile, but not her death.

I stick Annie back in the purse and head toward the bedroom, where apparently I left in such a hurry that the door is cracked open, the heat from the fireplace spreading into the hallway. Entering the room, I have an urge to look down the hall I just traveled, and refuse to give in. Then I change my mind. Isn't a refusal to look behind me my problem? I face the hallway, stare down the emptiness, and sigh in relief. I faced one fear, and I will face them all.

Shutting the bedroom door, I seal in the warmth and kick off Sasha's painful high heels. I lean against the door, leaving the lights off, the glow of the fireplace illuminating the room. Unbidden, a tingle of unease slides through me. Did I turn the lights out when I left? No. I don't think so. I didn't. My brow furrows. But maybe they weren't on in the first place? Or Marabella was up here? Or . . . am I having blackouts I don't even remember? It's a scary thought, and it's simply unacceptable if I am. I have to remember everything. Now. It's time, but the silence in my head and the room are damning.

Shoving off of the door, I walk to the foot of the bed, setting my purse on it. Glancing down at my deep cleavage, I unzip the dress, rejecting it as nothing I would ever choose, and step out of it. The lacy black bra, panties, and thigh-highs I chose for Kayden can stay. Facing the bed, I press my hands against the mattress, letting my head fall forward, my now-darker brown hair shielding my face. I've accepted it as part of me, but I reject the weak person in my flashbacks. She *isn't* me. There is something I'm missing. My gaze catches on my naked wrist. The Hawk's bracelet belongs on the arm of someone strong and brave, and hiding from my past is neither of those things.

Straightening, I turn and step to the center of the thick pile rug in front of the fireplace. Shutting my eyes, I will that part of me that has started to remember things to blossom and become a full exploration of my past. And so I wait. And wait. And stand there doing more waiting. Frustrated, I shove my fingers through my hair. I need a trigger. An idea hits me, and I walk to the bed and grab my phone from my purse, searching for a music app. Finally, I download "Take Me to Church," a song that reminds me of *him*, and not in a good way, and set it to replay over and over. Leaving my phone on the bed, I return to the center of the carpet again, and close my eyes, praying that the lyrics speak to me.

Take me to church. I'll worship like a dog at the shrine of your lies.

And they do. They knife through me in a jumbled explosion of images and emotions, attacking me, but none that solidify to one thing or one feeling. But my knees tremble as if in warning, and I suddenly wish that I had wine. Lots of wine, and until this moment I didn't remember that I like wine. Why am I thinking of it now?

"Take me to church," I whisper. "Come on. Take me to church."

Suddenly, I'm back in his home, in his room and my room? No. That place, with that man, was never home. I never had a room, and I hate his room. But I have to go there to get back to here. I know that. The word *wine* comes back into my head, and I realize it wasn't a random thought. I had wine the night I seem to want to visit. Expensive wine with an expensive dinner. I drank to forget, yet I want to remember now. I drank to get through what I knew would come later, after we left the restaurant. I drank because I wanted to leave him, but it wasn't time yet. I was working on how and when. I know why. Or I did then, but I don't know now. Nothing comes to me and I let the song permeate my thoughts again.

"Take me to church," I whisper as it plays. "I'll worship like a dog at the shrine of your lies."

His bedroom comes into view. I can't see it yet, but I am there. It is chilly. He always likes it chilly, but then, I'm usually naked and he is not. There is the woodsy scent that clings to his skin and hair. I hate woodsy so fucking much. And then I see the life-sized statue in the corner of a tiger, which is so a part of him. It's about power, control, and a willingness to do anything to defeat his enemies. Like I have to be willing to do anything to defeat him.

I open my eyes and stare into the fire without really seeing it, two thoughts in my mind. I was planning to stand against him long before the night I'd pulled that gun. And someone must know that statue. Encouraged, I shut my eyes again.

The taste of sweet rosé wine lingers on my tongue, melding with the bitterness of being naked while he is dressed in one of his favorite gray suits. It's expensive, like everything he likes, including the dress I'm no longer wearing that he bought me. I hate his suit and I hate that dress, but even more, I hate the way my nipples tighten when he stares at them, like he does now. He thinks he arouses me. Sometimes he does, and that makes me confused, after what he has done to me. Maybe . . . it's just survival.

I inhale and open my eyes, my knees trembling harder now. I hate this. I hate *him*, but I need to know why he was my survival. I force myself to shut my eyes again and go back to that moment.

And the fact that I do, that I can, is both comforting and uncomfortable. I am on my knees now, my hands on the carpet in front of me. He's above me, and I can feel him staring down at me. I'm aware of not wanting to do this, of pretending to be submissive, but I can't understand why. I hate this. Why am I allowing it? He squats beside me and his hand flattens on my back between my shoulder blades. My skin crawls, and every part of me wants to get up, to knock him away. But there's a reason I don't, and it's not fear, though I know he would hurt me. I know he has hurt others.

"Ella."

I blink and Kayden is squatting in front of me, and I'm somehow on my knees, his hands under my hair, warm on the skin of my neck. His jacket is gone, his tie loose, his hair is a sexy rumpled mess, and he is beautiful. He is right in ways that other man is wrong, and a calmness fills me that wasn't there moments before. I reach up and grab his wrists. "I'm glad you're here, and I'm glad I'm here. Even if it meant I had to go through *him* to get to you."

"Niccolo?"

"No, it's not him. I heard the man's voice in a flashback where he met with Niccolo, but *he* is not Niccolo. But this song makes me remember him, and I'm facing it and him. I'm going to—"

He tilts my face to his. "Are you telling me you're in your underwear, trying to relive what he did to you?"

"I have to."

"No, you don't. I told you. Some things are meant to be forgotten." He scans the room and his gaze lands on the bed. He starts to get up, and I grab him.

"What are you doing?"

"Turning this fucking song off."

"No! It was working. I need to do this. For us. For you. For me."

"I don't care if you ever fucking remember him."

"I *have* to remember him. The time bomb that is my mind will haunt us both, and I don't want that."

"It's only a time bomb because you say it is."

"In my gut, I am certain that we need to know who that man is—and tonight is all about taking control. You said that yourself. *We're* taking control, and we're doing it together. So take it with me now. Help me go to those bad places and face them. Re-create what this song is to me."

He stares down at me, the seconds ticking by like hours, his expression unreadable, until I can't take it anymore. "Kayden—"

"Why are you on your knees?" he demands.

"I was acting out the flashback."

"Tell me about that memory," he orders softly.

"Do you really want to hear this?"

"Yes," he insists. "I absolutely do, but only if you want to tell me."

"I don't even want this part of me to exist—but if I don't tell you, I can't ask you to help me face it." I inhale and let it out. "He made me undress while he did not. That's how he operated. He wanted me to be exposed and vulnerable. Once I was naked, he ordered me to my knees and stood above me, watching me."

"What did you feel?"

"At that point, I knew he was dangerous. I played submissive to survive, while I was plotting an escape. I think . . . I did escape."

"What did you feel, Ella?"

"Dread."

His hands come down on my shoulders and he stands, taking me with him. "Whoever he is doesn't matter. I know Adriel told you about Evil Eye. I know you doubted me—"

"No. No, that's not it. I was worried about you. I wanted—I want—to protect you."

"There are many things I want from you, Ella, but protection's not one of them." He cups my face. "He doesn't own you. He doesn't own your past. He damn sure doesn't own me. And he doesn't even get to own this song." He turns me, placing my back to his chest, his lips near my ear. "You said I could have everything. Now I'm going to take it."

fifteen

"Everything, Ella," Kayden repeats, his fingers splaying wider on my belly, while his other hand moves to my bra, unhooking the front clasp and then flattening between my breasts. "And *everything* includes your fear, Ella. And the shame I know he made you feel. I'm going to take those from you tonight. I'm going to hold them so you don't have to. And I'm going to give you permission not to remember, since you won't."

Shame. That word radiates through me with cutting accuracy, and I know then that I've not even touched where that comes from, or what that man did to me. I squeeze my eyes shut, and for a moment, I'm back in *his* bedroom, holding that gun, wanting to kill him, and battling a war inside me of right and wrong, and a desire to punish *him* for punishing me. Emotions well inside me, so many emotions I cannot contain or name, and the stupid music I wish I'd never turned on lifts in the air. *Take me to church. I'll worship like a dog at the shrine of your lies.*

"Whatever this song means to you," Kayden declares, his cheek pressing to mine, "it won't be the same the next time you hear it." He cups my breasts, his lips dragging down my cheek, to my ear. "And that means I'm going to take you places you don't know you want to go."

"Yes," I say, not because I refuse to remember, but because I hate what it makes me feel. "Take me there."

He nips my shoulder, a sharp erotic bite that he follows with the pinch of my nipples. "What are you thinking of?" he demands.

"That I want more."

He runs his tongue over the wounded skin. "And now?"

"That I want your tongue other places."

He drags my bra off of my shoulders and turns me to face him, reaching down to grip my panties and yank them off, one hand cupping my backside while his fingers slide into my sex. "Now what are you thinking?"

Sensations rip through me and my hand flattens on the hard wall of his chest, my head tilting forward. "I *can't* think."

His thumb twirls against my clit, while the fingers of his other hand tangle into my hair, giving it an erotic tug that lifts my gaze to his. "That's the idea," he says. "Don't think unless it's about me or us. Just fuck. And fuck some more." His mouth closes down on mine, his tongue licking against mine, stroking it, taking me deeper into the haze of lust and desire.

I lose time, blocking out the song and clinging to him, filling my senses with the taste of him, the masculine scent of him. Then we are on our knees, and he has pressed my hands behind me and onto the carpet in that way he likes to anchor me and take my control. He leans over me, the delicious heavy weight of him pressed to me. He lingers there, the promise of things unsaid and undone between us, and the chorus of the song lifts in the air again.

"Time to go to church, sweetheart," Kayden declares, his voice gravelly, affected, his hands on my body now, caressing up and down my sides, over my breasts.

With a moan I arch into his touch, panting as he leans down and licks and sucks my nipples, teasing, driving me crazy before he sits up, his hands bracketing my hips, his smoldering stare raking over my body. "Any man who had you naked and kept his clothes on is a fool—and I'm no fool, sweetheart. Don't move. Wait for me."

He releases me, leaving me naked, aroused, and willingly exposed with my breasts thrust in the air. And what I feel in this moment, in every moment with this man, is so many things beyond the word *love* that I don't even try to understand right now. But some part of me worries that by taking the escape he offers me, I am hiding, and I don't want to hide. He stops at the bed, his back to me, and in the next moment, his shirt is off, that ring of skull tattoos on his back reminding me of all he has lost before me. We could lose each other so easily, and I'm not denying myself every moment I can have with him.

He faces me again, and my phone is in his hand, and suddenly the song is playing louder, blasting through the air, and I am reminded that this isn't an escape. This is him planning to mute the pieces of the past that incited me to dread. When he steps away the music is in my mind, stirring dark emotions, and I shiver, sitting up straight and hugging myself against the ice sliding down my spine. Suddenly I'm on my knees in another place and time, again. *He* is standing over me. *He* is planning what he will do to me next. He grabs my hair. He drops his pants. He makes me—

"Ella."

Kayden's voice once again brings me back to the present, and he's squatting in front of me again, beautifully naked, his cock thick at my hip, his hands on my shoulders. And damn it, I've missed him undressing, because the past has controlled the present again.

"Please turn off the song," I say, grabbing his wrists. "I need to cope with the past, but the night we went public should not be about that part of my life, no matter what pushed us to do it."

"We are not turning it off," he says firmly, his hand closing around mine. "We're turning *him* off. Understand?"

"Clearly it's not that easy."

"I never said it was easy." His arm wraps my waist, his palm on my lower back. "I haven't even begun to show you how to make sex that dirty, dark escape I promised once before. But now is when you learn how to create a rush of adrenaline that wipes out everything, yet somehow forces you to deal with it at the same time." He cups my backside. "I'm going to spank you, Ella."

"What?" I gasp, and my hand flattens on his chest, panic rising inside me. "Kayden, I—"

"This isn't the first time I've brought this up."

"I know, but—"

"I would never do anything to lose you or hurt you, Ella." He cups my face. "Trust me, and then let's tear down every wall we can between us, and put one up in front of him."

My fingers curl on his chest, and I wait for rejection of his idea to come to me—but it doesn't. "I'm scared," I admit freely, and I know it means something that I can voice this to him, and know that he will listen.

"Because it's new, and because of what he did to you. But I am not him, and we are not controlled by him."

He's right. "What if I don't like it?"

"Then we won't do it again." He lowers us to the carpeted floor, facing each other on our sides, his thick erection pressed in the V of my body, his leg tangling with mine. His hand possessively splays on my backside. "*You* are what I want and need. Pleasing you. Experience what we are together, Ella—and that's better than apart."

It is then that I step outside the circle of my demons and into his, realizing that this isn't just about me. It's about him. About those dark and dirty parts of him. "This means you have to have faith in me, when you're the one coming unglued. I hate that you dressed somewhere else tonight."

"I'll face my demons with you, like you are with me now, and we'll figure out what that means then."

Considering the torment I'd seen in him earlier tonight, I know what this promise means. My fingers curl on his jaw, my decision made. It being my choice, rather than something forced on me, changes everything. It's sexy and intimate and still scary as hell. "What happens next?"

"We let it happen," he says, his mouth closing over mine, and in the depths of that kiss is trust, and I don't need my memory to know that it is something I have never felt, any more than I've felt the kind of bond I have with this man. And this isn't about the spanking. It's not here, between us, but so much more is. He takes his time getting us there, touching me, letting me touch him, and I can feel his need growing, expanding, and with it, my own. We become feverish, our touches, our kisses, and he turns me, placing my back to his front. Adrenaline spikes through me with the certainty that he will roll me to my hands and knees, but he keeps touching me, stroking my breasts, between my legs, and my backside. And then he curls my legs in front of me, keeping me on my side, stroking my bottom, back and forth, up and down, until I'm going crazy, wanting his hand between my legs. Wanting *him* between my legs. "Kayden," I plead.

He stills his hand, flattening on my cheeks. "I'm going to spank right here, just above your sex, so that you feel it everywhere. Five times, Ella. I'll do more another time, but for now, just five times. And then I'm going to fuck you hard and fast and ride that adrenaline with you. Are you ready?"

"Oh God. Now?"

"Now." He starts caressing my backside again, back and forth. "Are you ready?"

"Kayden—"

"Ella, say it. Are you—"

"Yes," I pant out. "I'm ready."

And then he does it.

One. Oh God. It stings, and sends spikes of pleasure through my sex and up my spine.

Two. Blood rushes in my ears.

Three. Four. Five.

It's done and he presses inside me, his thick cock stretching me, entering me. His hand flattens on my belly, and he thrusts hard, burying himself in the deepest part of me, an explosion of sensations erupting in my body, consuming me. *He* is consuming me. I arch into him and his fingers slide to my clit, his cock pumping and pumping, and every nerve ending in my body is on fire. And the world fades, leaving only him inside me, his cock stroking me, his hand stroking me, the sensations . . . so many sensations, that sweet spot building and building until it's *just* there. I stiffen and suck in air, my sex clenching around Kayden, spasms erupting so fiercely that they make my body quake.

One of Kayden's hands closes around my breast while the other anchors my hip. He pulls me into a deep, pulsing thrust, the wet, warm heat of his release filling me in so many ways. Seconds tick by or minutes, I do not know, and slowly we both sink into the rug and each other. Kayden envelops me with his body, his cheek finding mine. "How are you?" he asks.

"I'm good."

"You're sure?"

"Yes. Positive."

"I'm going to get you a towel."

"Thank you."

He kisses my temple, the way he did at the party. Tender. Loving. Then he pulls out of me and stands. I breathe in on the tight ball forming in my chest. The song is still playing, but I don't think of the other man when I hear it. I think of Kayden holding me, spanking me, fucking me, and I know the gift he has given me is freedom. I will never hear this song again and think of anything else.

Kayden returns, sliding a towel between my legs, and then something cold rests on my hip. I look down and find my bracelet lying against my naked skin. My hand closes around it, and I face Kayden, finding him in sweatpants and holding a black silk robe.

"I hated taking this off." Tears prickle my eyes and I turn away. "I'm going to cry, and I don't know why. But it's not about what we did, or you."

He moves in front of me, wrapping my robe around me. "It's the adrenaline from the spanking. You're trembling. Put your arms in." I do as he says, and he reaches down and ties it for me before repeating what he said earlier. "Adrenaline seems to wipe out everything, yet it somehow forces you to deal with it at the same time."

"How is crying 'dealing with it'?" I swipe at a tear that escapes. "I still don't know who he is."

"This wasn't about you remembering him. It was about not giving him the control." His lips curve. "And giving me an excuse to spank you when I want to."

"That's not going to happen." I laugh.

"Never?" he asks, turning somber. "Did you not like it?"

"It was . . . I . . ." Blood rushes to my cheeks.

"You can say anything to me, Ella."

"That's the point. I believe I can, and it seems I can *do* anything with you, and it's good. And it was kind of sexy."

"Trust is what's sexy." He takes the bracelet from me and wraps it around my wrist. "I want that in every way for us." He closes his hand around the bracelet. "This was my mother's."

I look up at him. I'm stunned and honored.

"I didn't give it to Elizabeth, Ella. Kevin left it in my inheritance with a note. But he didn't give it to me, even when he knew I was going to marry her."

"He was The Hawk. You weren't."

"But I was the successor and she was supposed to be my wife."

"What are you saying?"

"He called her a delicate flower and said delicate flowers don't survive. She didn't survive."

"That wasn't your fault."

"You didn't cry from the adrenaline rush," he says, giving me whiplash with the apparent change of topic. "Most people would have, especially with the baggage you're carrying."

"Most people didn't have a father who made a habit of screaming in their faces to shoot straighter, run harder, and suck it up."

"I don't want you to have to shoot straighter, run harder, or suck it up—but the truth is, I need you to do those things."

"I *am* those things. Kayden."

"I know you are." He holds out his right arm, displaying the tattoo of a box with the king's chess piece inside, reading the script tracking a line up his powerful forearm. "'Once the game is over,'" he says, "'the king and the pawn go back in the same box.'"

"In life and death we are equal," I say, and realize I said once before.

He catches my arm at the elbow, resting my bare skin on top of the saying on his arm. "How did you know that?"

"My father," I say, once again knowing something for no definable reason.

"How?"

"I don't know." My brows furrow. "Wait. Do you think he had a connection to The Underground?"

"It's a long shot, and I don't have enough to go on. Just the year that he died, and that he had a wife, and a daughter he left behind, with red hair."

"Would that make me a Hunter?" My eyes go wide, and I dismiss the fleeting memories of being a teacher that just didn't feel right. "Could David and I have been on a hunt for another division of The Underground, and I was never really engaged to him?"

"I've made absolutely certain that you, or any incarnation of you, have no connection to The Underground prior to meeting me. Could you have been working for someone else? I've considered it, but turned up nothing."

He stands and takes me with him. "I need to throw on some clothes and be ready to debrief with Matteo before we go to bed. I'll have him cautiously do some digging around about your father. But grab some slippers. There's something I want to show you."

sixteen

"What is it?" I ask, concerned that the bombshell of Niccolo showing up tonight isn't the one I face.

"Relax," he says, brushing my hair behind my ear. "It's just something special to me."

"Now I'm really curious," I say, letting him lead me to the closet. "Where is it? What is it?"

"I left it in my jacket in the other room," he says, grabbing a long-sleeved gray T-shirt from a hanger and pulling it over his head. "And you have to wait to see."

Eager to find out what his version of "special" is, I ditch my robe for black leggings and a black sweater, while he pulls on sweats, and it's not long before we're stepping into the chilly, creepy hallway.

"I swear I hate this hallway," I murmur, snuggling close to his side, his arm wrapping my shoulders. "It always gives me a haunted feeling."

"Ghost and goblins are part of the charm of the place," he teases. "As is a great kitchen stocked with food, where we are headed. I haven't had anything I'd call a meal since lunch." He glances at his watch. "And it's midnight. No wonder."

"My stomach is actually growling," I reluctantly admit, letting him turn me toward our kitchen, but hating that our "special" something is delayed by food. We make it all of two steps through when it hits that I would have noticed the kitchen light being on as it is now, earlier. "Wait," I say, stopping us, and turning to face him. "You said the kitchen light was on when you got here?"

"Yes. It was."

"It wasn't on when I got here," I say. My brow furrows. "And our bedroom door was open and the light was off when I got here, too, and that didn't feel right."

"It had to be Marabella."

"She doesn't leave things out of order. And why would she enter after I did and not check on me?"

"I'm sure she was afraid you'd be asleep. As for why she might leave things out of order, Giada and Gallo have her pretty rattled. But we can use the iPad in the kitchen to check the security footage, after you feed me."

I laugh. "If you think I'm cooking, we had better call Marabella, because if I know how to cook, it's traumatic and I've blocked it out."

He laughs. "Traumatic. Yes, well. For a feminist, I can imagine it would be."

"Don't even go there," I say as we enter the kitchen and he leads me around the island. "Because the whole point of being a feminist is that I can choose to cook or not cook."

"You sure know a lot about this stuff," he says, stopping us in front of the fridge and opening the door.

He's right. I do, and I have no idea why. But before I can really analyze why, he's already offering our dinner choices.

"We have a new batch of spaghetti," he says, glancing from the fridge to me. "I'm guessing that's why Marabella came in earlier."

"Which reminds me. She wants to set up days to cook and clean for us."

"You two work it out," he says. "And how do you feel about skipping the spaghetti and eating Kellogg's Coco Pops?"

"Coco Pops? Are they like American Cocoa Puffs?"

"Basically the same thing, different name. And much to Marabella's distress, I love the damn things, which means I have to sneak them in when she's not watching."

"Coco Pops it is, then," I say, laughing, and together we gather bowls, the cereal, and a jug of milk before settling at the table.

"So when did this Coco Pops obsession start?" I ask, filling my bowl with cereal and eager for a further glimpse into the man behind The Hawk.

"College," he says. "The whole 'get drunk and eat an entire box of cereal' routine."

"Drunks are not in control," I say. "You are, therefore I can't imagine you drunk."

"Neither could Kevin, which is why that phase lasted about three months."

"So you went to college here?"

"Right here in this neighborhood," he says, pouring milk into my bowl and then his. My gaze catches on the watch, and just that easily, I'm in the past. There's another hand. Another watch. *He* touches my arm. *He* says my name, *Ella*, and I hear his voice, *really hear his voice*, for the first time since my amnesia. It's deep, accented. Dominant.

"Ella?"

At the sound of Kayden's voice, I blink and shake myself, only to realize that I'm holding his arm, right above the watch. "Please tell me I didn't black out."

"I think you did," he says. "Is this happening a lot?"

"A few times since Enzo got shot. Nathan says it's trauma, but I want to talk to him again." I release his arm, and he catches my hand.

"What does the watch mean to you?"

"*Him*," I say without hesitation. "And I just heard his voice for the first time ever in my mind. He's not American. His English is good, but he has an accent."

"What else?"

"Nothing else—other than you just happen to wear the same watch."

He stares at me a moment and then faces forward, seconds ticking by before he stands. I twist around to follow his progress as he makes his way to the island, and then, oddly, presses his palms on the counter, seeming to contemplate the wall before him.

"Kayden? What are you doing?"

He seems to shake himself back to the moment. "Just thinking," he says, removing his watch and sticking it in a drawer. He then returns to sit with me, an iPad in his hand, scooting his chair closer to me. "Let's look at the security footage."

"Why did you take the watch off?"

"Because we're done with that man tonight."

"What happened to facing things?"

"It's a watch," he says. "I can replace it."

"But—"

He leans down and kisses me, his lips lingering over mine. "One step at a time, sweetheart. The song tonight. The watch another. Okay?"

There is something stark in him, something suddenly shut off, like I've somehow put a wall between us he doesn't like. Or maybe that he has. "What just happened?"

"Nothing happened."

"It did, and I don't like it." I curl my fingers on his jaw. "I need you to know." Nerves flutter in my belly with the confession I'm about to dare, but think he might need to hear. "Kayden, I want to say that—"

His cell phone rings before I can say *I love you*, and my lashes lower in frustration. Kayden kisses me, and murmurs, "Me, too, sweetheart. Me, too." And then he is standing, digging his phone from his pocket, and leaving me wondering if we . . . Did we . . . just say we love each other?

He sits back down, talking in fast, irritated Italian, and I use my nervous energy to stuff my face with Coco Pops. Kayden powers up the iPad while he talks, and finally ends the call. "That was Donati," he says, officially leaving love confessions behind.

"What did he want?"

"To negotiate Gallo's extended vacation. I told him to go fuck himself after hearing his terms."

"That's not good, is it? Did I do something wrong?"

"You killed it tonight, sweetheart. This is how Donati operates. We're a good three more phone calls away from him being reasonable."

"Sasha says she doesn't like him."

"Sasha doesn't like men who won't sleep with her."

"She likes you."

"If that's your way of asking if I've slept with her—"

"You haven't," I say. "I know. She all but told me that, and if I wanted to know, I'd ask anyway."

"Of course you would," he says, approval in his eyes. "She likes me because I saved her from Niccolo's stepbrother."

"She implied that as well," I say.

"That woman can imply a lot in little time. However, she's good at choosing her words cautiously. She wants you to call her tomorrow. She seems to consider you her new friend."

"Is that okay?" I ask. "Can I be friends with one of the Hunters?"

"As long as you keep in mind that less is more regarding what you and I share, there's no reason you can't." He sets the iPad in front of us. "And there's every reason to want them to like and respect you." He brings up the security feed. "Let me show you how to find the real-time views and past footage. I'll load it onto your phone in the next few days." He tabs through screens. "Just remember that no one else can see this, or even knows it exists, including Marabella." He freezes on an image of her in the kitchen, talking on her cell phone. "Time stamps three hours ago," he says. "So we have confirmation that she brought the food in then." He glances at me. "She's your light switch bandit."

"I guess so," I say, "but it seems so unlike her to forget anything. I mean, I don't know her all that well, but even I know that she's anal."

He hits the "play" button and we watch her pace as she talks on the phone, her words too muffled to make out even if

I could understand them. "She seems very upset," I observe. "I don't want to be nosy, but is everything okay?"

"I can't make out what she's saying, but I'd bet that she's talking to Giada. She's a topic I don't have the energy to deal with tonight, but it's time she moves out."

"I echo that sentiment," I say, brow furrowing. "I just realized that you said I did well at the party, but you never mentioned how things went for you. I assume you got out without incident?"

"Everything was smooth." He smirks. "Niccolo was so pissed about the champagne that got dumped on him, he was distracted during our departure."

"Why was he even there?" I ask, taking another bite of my cereal.

"That's a good question I'm working on answering," he says.

"Can I help you work on it?" I ask. "I'd really like to get more involved, Kayden. I can't hang out in the castle every day."

"According to Adriel, you don't intend to."

"He told you I want the store."

"Of course he told me," he confirms dryly. "He wants to go back to hunting, and he's all but packed Giada's bags."

"I have some ideas on how to make that happen. But, most important, are you going to let Adriel hunt again?"

"Once we decide how to deal with Giada, yes. I am. He's ready."

"What does that mean? He's ready?"

"Adriel was a renegade, trying to end up like Enzo for the six months after his father died. He fucked everything that moved and took every job he knew might get him killed. Giada going off the deep end gave me an excuse to ground his ass, so she's pissed me off, but she saved Adriel. For that, I've been patient, but I'm out of space to give her." He holds up a hand. "But I really fucking do not want to talk about that woman tonight."

"Can we go back to the store, then? Is it mine? I'm learning Italian, and I can use the store to get to know the neighborhood crowd. And I could hunt for things for the store, and who knows how I might be able to help you in the process."

"You aren't hunting."

"But—"

"No."

"Kayden—"

He turns our chairs to face each other, his hands settling on my legs, surprising me when he doesn't repeat the word *no* but says, "Give me time."

I am instantly softened, reminded that he has stepped into my circle of demons tonight, but his still exists. They're still breathing fire on him and me. "Yes," I say. "The store only, right now."

My understanding is rewarded with the warmth that fills his expression. "I brought you in here to show you something, remember?"

"I thought that was just your way of trying to find out if I would cook for you," I tease, while I'm really started to wonder if he's changed his mind about showing me at all.

"Since you opted for cereal, I'm assuming that's never going to happen."

"Marabella would be offended."

"We can't have that," he jokes, lifting his jacket from the next chair and removing a white, rather worn, envelope from the pocket. The moment his hands touch it, I swear his energy shifts and darkens.

"What is it?" I ask, suddenly nervous.

He offers it to me, and I take it. "That's the letter Kevin left in the lockbox with the bracelet. I think it pretty much sums up why I chose to give it to you."

Stunned, I ask, "You want me to read it?"

"Yes."

Not sure what to expect, I open it and he says, "Out loud."

I nod and start reading.

Kayden:

This is for your queen, should you find her. I never told you that I found mine. Olivia was strong and brave, and my biggest fear was her death. So I did something she could never forgive, and she left. A year later she was killed in a car accident and died thinking I was a bastard, when in truth, I was just a fool and a coward. You, like your father, are not those things. Maybe I could have saved Olivia, or maybe I just could have loved her until she was gone. Whatever the case, guilt gutted me every second of the rest of my life. Once the game is over, the king and the pawn really do go back in the same box. In death they are indeed equal. But in life, we are not. In life we are a product of more than our decisions. We are the consequence of how we cope with those decisions, and too often that is fear and guilt. Don't let it be fear and guilt.

I lower the letter, my chest tight, my eyes burning. "Even as a child hiding in a closet," Kayden says, coming down on one knee in front of me, "I knew the moment my mother died. My father let out a roar that was from his soul. I'm struggling with all the feelings I know Kevin had, and the pain my father lived in that moment of loss, which was the same emotion. They both felt they failed the woman they loved. I love you, Ella, so I can't let you go."

"I love you, too," I say. "I love you. And if you tried to let me go, I wouldn't let you."

"Says the woman who hasn't experienced just how protective I can be yet."

"I think I have."

"You haven't, but I have a feeling I haven't experienced the full wrath of your anger yet, either." He wraps his arms around me. "I have a feeling we're going to do a lot of that fighting and fucking, and then making love. But I'm in if you are."

"I am. Completely in, Kayden."

His phone rings and he grimaces. "Obviously, I could have timed this better," he says, pulling me to my feet. "That's going to be Matteo telling me he's here with video from the party. Do you want to watch it with us?"

"Yes," I say, pleased that he's included me. "Thank you."

He cups my face and stares down at me. "I'm not losing you, Ella. No matter what that means." He kisses me, a deep, passionate kiss that is over too quickly. He answers his call, and I put the food away, but as we head down the stairs to the central tower to meet Matteo, his statement comes back to me: *I'm not going to lose you, Ella. No matter what that means.* And suddenly those words feel foreboding—as if I come with a price he has to pay.

seventeen

I wake the next morning to find Kayden gone, and shocked to discover it's nearly ten o'clock. Kayden has likely long been awake, so I hurry to the bathroom to brush my teeth and hair, and throw on my leggings and sweater from last night. I won't be surprised if I find Kayden at the kitchen table, drinking coffee and watching the tapes Matteo left us last night. Kayden's downright obsessed with knowing every detail that happened to every single person at the event, down to the coat-check girl and the waiters. He leaves nothing to chance, looking for any detail that might be useful now or later, and I wonder if he learned that from Kevin or, as with the creation of Evil Eye, it's a manifestation of his need for control.

Opening the door to the hallway, I am greeted by a loud banging sound that seems to be coming from upstairs. Frowning, I head up the narrow steps, the noise leading me to the gym and my new dance studio. Once I've nearly reached the gym, the sound of American country music, specifically Jason Aldean, one of Kayden's favorites, touches my ears. Smiling at the certainty that he's working out, I hurry through the remaining steps to the training area and equipment. The radio is playing from inside my dance studio.

"Holy fuck, Kayden," I hear Adriel grumble. "Can we listen to something other than country music?"

"You're American. You should appreciate this."

"I'm not fucking American."

"You just tried to get transferred there," Kayden says dryly.

"Because you wouldn't let me hunt."

"Because you were being a dumb-ass."

"Yeah, well, I'm over that now," Adriel states, not even bothering to deny Kayden's claim.

"Because I'm letting you hunt again," Kayden counters.

"You're letting me hunt again because I'm over it."

A Blake Shelton song starts to play and I hear Matteo say, "I have one word for you. Headphones."

"I have three words," Carlo interjects. "Shut the fuck up."

"That's four," Matteo says, laughing. "Good thing you aren't in charge."

I grin and at this point I'm dying to know what they're doing in there, especially since Kayden never lets anyone into this tower. Stepping to the doorway of the would-be studio, I'm shocked to find the men installing a new floor. Kayden is kneeling by the far wall, nailing a rail down the center. My heart squeezes with the knowledge that he is behind this, but that they are all willingly helping.

"Hi," I say, and everyone's attention jerks up to me, putting me in the center of a circle of fierce male speculation, and random greetings.

Kayden stands and walks over to me, leaning down to kiss me. "Morning, sweetheart."

"I can't believe you're doing this." I glance around. "All of you. Thank you so much."

Kayden urges me out into the gym area and pulls me to him. "How are you?"

I wrap my arms around him, tilting my chin up. The pale blue T-shirt he's wearing is a perfect match for his eyes. "How can I not be good right now? Thank you."

He brushes the hair from my eyes. "Anything to make this home for you, Ella."

My heart squeezes all over again, both from his meaning and the idea that somewhere, someplace, I do have another place that was a home I don't remember. "You are my home, Kayden," I say, flattening my hand on his chest. "You know that, right?"

"Kayden," Carlo calls out, and Kayden gives me a weary but amused look, motioning back to the dance room.

"What is it?" Kayden asks, joining the other men and returning to his work location, while I linger in the doorway.

Carlo stands and stretches, chains hanging from the pockets of his black jeans. "A man's wife hid his million-dollar car to pay him back for fucking around on her. Want me to find it?"

"Who's the man?" Adriel asks.

"Aldo Tucia," he says, and Kayden whistles. "Sweet. Get the man's car back."

"Who is Aldo Tucia?" I ask.

"One of the Italian soccer greats," Kayden explains. "Which means our price is top of the scale."

"I'll add ten percent for speedy service," Carlo tells Matteo. "That's your cut for finding me a place to start this chase."

Matteo cuts Kayden a questioning look. "Do it," Kayden answers. "Go make the money."

Matteo stands and walks toward me, a dark, wayward curl dropping to his brow, pausing when he reaches my side. "Even Sasha liked you last night," he declares, heading out of the room and leaving me with a frown at the odd comment.

"Sasha's a bitch," Adriel supplies, clearly noting the exchange. "But when she likes you, you've earned it."

"And she likes you," I point out.

"Bella," he says dryly. "I earned it. Why do you think she and I weren't around to watch the video?"

I laugh, my cheeks flushing with his obvious meaning. "That was very bad," I reprimand, and when he chuckles good-naturedly I decide that scar down his cheek and his big, burly body have become a little less intimidating. "I did wonder where you two were."

Carlo steps between me and Adriel. "I hear you can dance and shoot, and if I piss you off, you'll shoot me."

I hold up my finger and pretend to shoot. "Because I'm a bitch, too."

He stares down at me, seconds ticking by, all Italian-stallion intensity before he bursts into laughter, winking at me as he exits. Kayden's eyes meet mine, and the approval in his expression tells me that I'm being tested by his men, and so far, I'm passing.

"I want to help," I say, but before I can join him and Adriel, a buzzer goes off.

"What's that?"

"Matteo installed security panels in several parts of the tower for you this morning." Kayden motions for me to join him by the door, where a new mini TV has been mounted. He hits a button and shows me the tower door, where Marabella is now entering. "She has a passcode, but if there's someone else you want to let in, just punch the button on the top right."

"But you don't like people in the tower."

"You should be able to choose when you want visitors."

I glance up at him, knowing this is another effort to make me feel at home, and I push to my toes and kiss him. "Thank you."

He grabs me and kisses me hard. "Thank me when we're alone."

"Alone is good," Adriel says, reminding us he's here.

Kayden and I laugh, then I eye the panel again. "I think I should go check on Marabella. But since you're both here . . . Am I pushing Giada to move out, or what?"

Adriel stands, hands settling on his hips. "Yes, but I want her in the neighborhood, where we can watch over her. Can you teach her to shoot?"

"Ella already suggested that," Kayden says. "But are you sure you want your sister with a gun?"

I say, "Yes, you do. Because if she feels in control, maybe she'll stop acting out of control." The two men exchange a long look and then nod at the same time. "Okay, then," I say. "I'll call her and see if she can do lunch tomorrow. We'll talk and then go to the range."

"I'll go with you," Kayden says. "I have a few words I want to have with her."

It's an encounter I've encouraged, and I tell myself his agreement is not about Niccolo and our public outing but

Giada, though it's hard to completely follow that train of thought. Whatever the case, it's a good thing. "I don't have my phone, so I'll call her when I get downstairs."

Adriel offers me his. "Have at it. The sooner we get her in line, the better, considering Gallo's pursuit. The less she knows, the less she can tell."

I accept the phone with Giada's auto-dial already pulled up. "I've seen enough of Gallo to know that he's going to pursue her harder, when she's easier to access."

"And the more we try to keep them apart," Kayden says, "the more Gallo will want to keep her close."

"I see," I say. "So remove the forbidden and it's no longer interesting to Giada."

"And no longer useful to Gallo," Kayden says. "Which is why I'm going to give Giada my Gallo blessing at lunch tomorrow."

Now his attendance at lunch makes sense, and I press the key to dial her number. "I'm headed to the store now," Giada answers, after two rings.

"It's me, Giada."

"Ella?" she says. "Why are you on Adriel's phone?"

"He and Kayden are installing a floor for my new dance studio, and I borrowed his phone."

"Dance studio? What dance studio?"

"It's for my private use here."

"I didn't know you danced."

"I'll tell you all about it," I offer. "How about lunch tomorrow? I want to go to the shooting range, and I thought you might want to learn to handle a gun."

"You know how to shoot?" she asks incredulously.

"Very well, and carrying a gun is empowering."

"You carry? Can you even legally do that? Never mind. You're Kayden's woman; you can do what you want. But hell yes, I want to learn to shoot."

"Great. How about noon tomorrow? We can meet in the store?"

I chitchat with her for a minute and then end the call. "All set." I hand Adriel's phone back to him, finding his expression grim. "What's wrong?" I ask.

"You're a better sister to her than I am a brother."

"Blood trumps all," I say, hating the heartache beneath those words. "I'm just a cool friend who's new, and therefore exciting. I'm going to check on Marabella." And for reasons I can't explain, I suddenly need to touch Kayden. I reach out and drag my hand down his arm. "I'll be in the kitchen."

He catches my hand and kisses it. "Thanks, sweetheart."

My heart does a little flip-flop at the tenderness in his eyes and voice, and I head for the door. "Yes," Adriel calls after me. "Thank you. Sweetheart."

I call over my shoulder, "Thank me by being nice to me."

"I'm always nice."

We all laugh, but as I hit the stairs, the words "blood trumps all" hit me hard and I stop dead in my tracks, catching the wall with my hand. What if Kayden and I have a blood feud? What if my family hurt his family, or his hurt mine? What if my dad was a Hunter? What if—

No. No. No. Don't go there. Don't do this. I glance down the hallway toward Kayden's office, where the photo of the necklace rests in his drawer, a sure trigger to some kind of memory. Needing answers, any answers, I head in that direction and don't stop until I'm sitting behind the heavy wooden desk, that folder open in front of me again.

I stare down at the necklace, the butterfly with diamonds set in its wings, and words start to come to me. Wishing I had my journal, I grab a pen, and I'm suddenly back in the past. I am back in that hotel room, moments after David left. It's the moment after he left me alone and I ripped the butterfly from my neck in anger.

Appalled at what I have done, I stare at the necklace on the floor, falling to my knees. I pick up the butterfly, and frown as I find a piece of paper sticking out of the back. I tug on it and stare at the handwritten words. What the heck is this? Pierre Remy—Marc—0000. That's very odd. This has to be some sort of serial number and the manufacturer. Right now, I just need to figure out how to get the chain fixed. I need to find a jewelry store before David gets back.

I open my eyes and write down *Pierre Remy—Marc—0000.* Then I underline it. This is important. The air shifts and I glance up to find Kayden entering the room. "Kayden," I say, and one look at his intense, hard expression has me popping to my feet to meet him as he rounds the desk. "I just wanted to look at the photo. I didn't mean to invade your private space."

"My space is your space, Ella," he says, his hands coming down on my shoulders, and he pulls me to him. "Ella—"

"I remembered what the piece of paper from the necklace said."

He blanches. "What? When?"

I grab the folder and show him the note. "Pierre Remy—Marc—0000." I glance at him. "Does that mean anything to you?"

"A place. A person. A code of some sort. We'll figure it out later."

"But it's important—I know it is."

"Niccolo called."

My heart falls to my feet. "Oh God. Already? What happened?"

"Just what I said would happen. He wants to meet."

"You're nervous. You're worried. You're things I never see in you."

"*You're* nervous. *You're* worried. *I'm* calm. I have this under control. I promise." Adriel appears in the doorway. "Adriel is staying here with you and locking down the castle," Kayden says. "He knows how to get you out of here if he should have to."

I don't let myself think about what might make that necessary. "Who's going with you?"

"Nathan. He's done work for Niccolo and Niccolo trusts him. Matteo and Carlo will have our backs."

And there it is. Proof of what I suspected. My doctor is so much more than just a doctor. "What do you think is going to happen?"

"As I told you, we'll negotiate. We'll come to terms, and he's going to tell us who you really are." He eyes Adriel, who disappears, and the instant he is gone, Kayden snags my hips and drags me to him. "This is good, Ella. This is answers and freedom. You know this."

"I do," I say, sounding strong when I have to fight back the urge to tell him how scared I am. He has to focus right now, and he needs me to be strong, not a weak distraction. I grab his shirt, balling it in my fingers and ordering, "Damn it, you will make this go the way you said it would. You will be safe and come back alive. *You will.*"

"I will," he promises, cupping the back of my head and kissing me, a deep, drugging, too-short kiss that ends with him releasing me. Before I recover, he's disappeared out the door. No goodbye, no *don't worry*, but then, I'm not sure those things make me standing here, rather than chasing after him, any easier. And it's not easy at all. I fight the urge to go after him, to scream for him to come back, when I know he can't and won't. I know my pleas won't help things or stop what has to be done. But this isn't me supporting him in a hunt or his duty as Hawk. This isn't even about him getting the necklace and returning it to the British government. This is about him trying to protect me, and that's a bitter pill to swallow. If anything happens to him, I have only myself to blame.

I'm still staring at the doorway, willing Kayden to reappear, when Adriel steps inside. "Come with me," he orders.

"Where?"

He grimaces. "Just come with me."

I grab the folder and place it in the desk. Adriel steps back into the hallway and allows me to pass. "We're going back to the gym," he instructs.

That seems like an odd location to huddle down and wait this out, but it is one of the higher locations in the castle. Maybe that translates to safer. I cut left and take the steps, and once I'm in the gym I turn. "Now what?" I ask, as he joins me.

"Now we finish your floor," he replies, walking into my dance studio and disappearing.

Frowning, I stare after him for a moment, then follow him. He's already on the floor, fitting a piece of wood into place. "Is it safer up here, or something? I mean, shouldn't we be doing something to support Kayden?"

"We are," he says. "It's called staying safe and not bugging him. And keeping you busy means you won't climb the walls and drive us both bat-shit crazy."

"That's your plan? Keeping me from driving you crazy?"

"That about sums it up, so get your ass over here and help me."

Grimacing at his bossiness, I decide he's right. I settle onto the floor next to him but freeze as a low electronic hum fills the air and the room darkens. "What the heck was that?"

"Kayden just left the castle and locked it down."

"What does that mean?"

"The doors and windows are now securely shuttered. No one is getting in or out, unless we hit the emergency exit buttons."

"Which are where?"

"If I tell you, I'll have to kill you, and Kayden wouldn't like that."

"That's not funny, Adriel."

"Put the code nine-two-eight-seven in any of the panels by any of the doors. But no one except you, me, and Kayden knows that. We don't need Giada armed with that information."

"What about Marabella?"

"Not even Marabella."

"But they're on lockdown, too?"

"Yes, and this isn't their first rodeo, as you Americans say. They've done this several times."

My hands settle on my knees. "Does this mean we can expect an attack?"

"It means Kayden doesn't take chances with what's important to him, and neither do I, and that means you."

"In other words, we're safe while Kayden is on his way to meet with the head of the Italian mafia, who might kill him."

"Kayden thinks Niccolo killed Elizabeth and Kevin. If anyone is going to die today, it will be Niccolo."

If he means to comfort me by reminding me just how volatile the relationship between Niccolo and Kayden is, he fails.

eighteen

For the next hour Adriel and I work in silence but for the sound of country music and his occasional grumbles about country music, until he finally says, “That’s it,” and grabs the phone, turning off the music.

“My turn now,” he declares, using his phone to tune into a succession of songs from Imagine Dragons that remind me of something Kayden once told me. “I hear you forced Kayden into going to one of their concerts.”

He arches a brow. “Forced? Is that the story he told you?”

I laugh and fit a wooden piece into the floor. “Tell me your version.”

From that point on there’s conversation, laughter, and lots of scowling over Giada’s behavior by both of us, but I notice that his voice always softens a bit when he’s talking about her. His love for his sister is obvious and powerful, and with each story he shares about her, I grow even more committed to helping them find a middle ground I’m certain they once had.

Three hours later, the floor is done, and we stand up to inspect the finished product. “It’s perfection,” I say, but I can't revel in the gift of the room when Kayden's silence is deafening.

Adriel clearly notices. "How about we raid the kitchen and watch football?"

"He's been gone forever, Adriel," I say, ignoring his attempt to distract me. "Shouldn't we check on him?"

"He went to Niccolo's country estate, a good two-hour drive."

My eyes go wide. "What? That's got to mean secluded and dangerous."

"Evil Eye, Ella, remember? He's protected. He's fine. And Niccolo is known for long negotiations that include a meal or two. He draws things out to make people nervous, hoping they'll make mistakes. But most people are not Kayden."

"No," I agree, "Kayden is not most people." My eyes meet his. "And I do believe in him, if you're thinking I don't. But we're all human."

"Some of us less than most, and pretend that he's not."

"And get sideswiped when he's hurt?"

"Find a place to put it. You have to, or this won't work for either of you."

"You're right. I'm failing at that right now, but I'll find a way to handle it."

"I told you how." He indicates his T-shirt, which I now realize has an Italian logo on it. "Football. And food. Those two things are miracle drugs."

"Fine," I say. "Food and football, but it's Sunday. That also means American football. If I watch Italian football, we have to find some American football, too. And I need to get my phone in case Kayden calls me." My eyes widen. "What if he already called and I missed it? How did I not think about this?"

I start for the door and he grabs my arm. "He didn't call and he won't. So get your phone, but don't go working yourself up again staring at the screen." He releases me. "Calling isn't his way. He focuses on what he's doing, which is why he stays alive."

This time, he's managed to say something comforting. Kayden's focused. He's staying alive. As I head toward the stairs Adriel calls out, "I'll meet you in the kitchen." I waste no time heading down the steps and entering our bedroom, snatching my phone from the nightstand just as it rings. Hopeful that it's Kayden, I glance at the caller ID and frown at the unfamiliar number. Not sure what to expect, afraid it's Niccolo, or somehow related to Niccolo, I press the "answer" button and will myself to sound calm. "Hello?"

"Eleana, it's Chief Donati."

"Chief," I greet him cautiously, assuming Gallo gave him my number, and considering I'm now worried he's calling to tell me something is wrong with Kayden, I somehow manage a cool, "This is a surprise."

"Why don't you tell me why Kayden is at Niccolo's country estate?"

Alarm bells go off in my head, and I choose my words cautiously. "I'm watching football and stuffing my face, Chief Donati. I don't involve myself in Kayden's business."

"That bracelet you had on last night says differently."

"The bracelet is about commitment. That doesn't equal conversation to a man like Kayden."

"Don't fuck with me, Eleana," he shocks me by spouting. "Why is he there?"

"Everyone wants a favor from Kayden, so it's likely that," I say. "And you know as well as I do that Kayden listens to all requests but doesn't hand them out freely."

"No one turns down Niccolo."

"Then you don't know Kayden well."

"On the contrary, I know him better than you think. Perhaps better than you. Gallo was right. You're either blind, or a problem we have yet to understand."

The line goes dead and a chill runs down my spine, and I wonder at his statement: "No one turns down Niccolo." What did *he* give Niccolo? And why do I think he's afraid Kayden is about to find out?

By nine o'clock, football, Italian lessons, and food have all filled the hours, but news from Kayden has not. "I'm going to nap," Adriel says, lying down on the living room couch.

"Then I'm going to take a shower," I say, but his arm is already over his face, and he's tuned me out.

Retreating to the bedroom, I shower, dry my hair, and, still feeling that I need to be prepared for anything, I dress in pink sweatpants, a black T-shirt, and tennis shoes. The clock now reads nine thirty, and I'm going crazy. Surely Kayden will call on his way home? Or will he still be concerned about an ambush? Not sure what to do with myself, I grab my journal and phone from the nightstand and check my call log, but there is nothing. I sit down on the big brown chair between the security room and the bed, and set the journal down next to me. What's the point in tormenting myself to remember my past, if Niccolo is sharing that with Kayden? And oh God.

What if Kayden learned something about me that wasn't good, and that's why he hasn't returned? I lean forward and press my hands to my face. What if we are enemies? What if—

That same low electric hum that sealed the castle begins again, and I drop my hands. Sure enough, the lights flicker and brighten. We're out of lockdown, which means Kayden must be here! I rise and enter the security room, sitting at the built-in desk and keying the computer in the center to life. Tabbing through several screens, I all but shout for joy when I see Kayden entering the main castle foyer, with no one by his side. A good sign, at least for now, that trouble has passed.

"Yes, yes, yes!" I stand up and enter the bedroom, tossing my phone on the chair and rushing out of the room into the hallway just in time to find Adriel disappearing down the stairs. Fully intending to follow him, I move down the hallway, and as soon as I reach the top step, the sweet relief of hearing Kayden's voice lifts in the air, followed by Adriel's. Almost instantly, footsteps sound, traveling in my direction, and my gut knots in fear that somehow, some way, whatever he has learned about me has changed us. I've barely had the thought when Kayden appears, looking ruggedly sexy in his black-and-gray leather biker jacket, his hair a light brown rumpled mess, his expression weary.

I forget dread and worry, launching myself in his direction. The few steps between us feel like an eternity before I am finally in his arms, wrapped in the warm cocoon of his embrace, his powerful body absorbing mine. The hours of worry fade and I melt into the hard lines of him, sliding my hands beneath his jacket and inhaling the deliciously spicy scent that is so wonderfully Kayden.

My gaze goes to his, and I feel the punch of our connection. "I was so worried about you," I whisper.

His mouth closes over mine and I can taste his urgency, the fear that he's not dared speak to me, but which I recognize as my own. A fear that he'd go to this meeting and something would go horribly, terribly wrong, and we'd never be here, like this, again. I arch into him, drinking in his passion, instantly, willingly consumed by all that he is. I shove my hands under his shirt, absorbing the hot feel of taut skin over hard muscle, pressing closer to him. A rough sound of desire rumbles from Kayden's chest, and I gasp as he tears his mouth from mine, staring down at me, his hand cupping my face, his gaze meeting mine.

"We're fine," he says, speaking what our bodies have already tried to answer. "I told you. No one is going to take you from me, no matter what that means. And that hasn't changed. Everything went as planned."

"'No matter what that means'?" I repeat. "What does *that* mean? What did he tell you about me and us?"

"Nothing we can't deal with," he promises, lacing his fingers with mine and leading me down the hallway.

I let him, asking nothing else, dread becoming a living, breathing monster I cannot escape. I'm not going to like what he tells me.

We enter the bedroom and he shuts the door, releasing my hand. I walk to the chair by the bed and sit down. I can't explain why, but my heartbeat is now slow and steady. I am calm, icy even, like I've shut down my mind and emotions. No doubt it's an extension of my amnesia. Kayden shrugs out of his jacket and tosses it on the arm of the chair, settling on a knee in front of me, his hands resting on my legs.

"Easy, sweetheart," he says, catching my legs, which seem to be trembling. Okay, maybe I'm not so calm. "I told you everything is fine."

"What did he tell you about me?"

"He knew your name and how you connected with him, and not much more."

"My first and last names?"

"No. He just knows you as Ella."

"That's all? Just . . . Ella?"

"That's not all. You went to him for help."

"What does that mean?"

"You were trying to escape the other man. You met Niccolo and knew he was very powerful. You wanted escape and safe passage, but Niccolo does nothing without a price."

"He wanted the necklace and knew I had it."

"He didn't know you had it. You somehow figured out that he, like the man you were living with, wanted it."

"So this other man was using me for the necklace."

"Niccolo says he believes that was how it started, but that you became property."

A dark sensation claws at my chest. "Yes. I was his property, and he doesn't let his property be taken from him."

"Do you know who he is, Ella?"

I wet my dry lips. "No. I still don't."

"The head of the French mafia."

Ice fills my veins. "Sasha said the French mafia is run by Niccolo's stepbrother."

"That is correct."

"That's how I know French. I came here to escape Paris."

"That's correct, too, and where my mind went last night when you started speaking French."

"Sasha told me the two stepbrothers killed their parents."

"It's widely believed that they did, though they deny it. The murders divided the mafias again, and the reluctant brothers became enemies, each looking for a way to destroy the other. In the position you were in, you were smart enough to know that Niccolo was one of your only ways out."

"Going from one mobster to another was smart? That doesn't even compute."

"The good news is that he is motivated to deny his brother anything he wants, including you."

"And the necklace I still can't remember. You aren't saying his name. You can say his name. Please say it and make me remember it."

His lips thin, but he doesn't deny me my request. "Garner Neuville."

"Garner Neuville," I repeat, drawing a hard breath and then letting it out. "I know his name, but nothing else comes to me. I still can't remember. I need a picture." I grab my phone to Google him.

He takes my phone. "I have photos, but do you really want to see him right now? Are you ready to remember? Because I've worked things out with Niccolo. There is no imminent threat."

"Until Neuville shows up."

"Neuville will not step in Niccolo's territory. Niccolo is the stronger brother, which is why Neuville wants the money that necklace represents, and why Niccolo doesn't want him to have it."

"I'm done fearing unknown monsters that are about to jump out at me from around every corner, Kayden. I want my enemy to have a face and a name."

He hesitates and then reaches behind me, removing a folder from his jacket. "We're going to do this slowly."

"I don't want to go slowly," I object. "Just show me the asshole's photo."

He hands me a photo of an expensive-looking gray stone building. "What is this place?"

"His home," I bite out. "In Paris. There's a view of the Eiffel Tower outside his bedroom window."

He replaces that shot with one of a black Mercedes, and I say, "One of his cars. Kayden—"

"Who is this man?" he asks, handing me a photo of a dark-haired, athletic-looking man.

"I don't know him." I glance at Kayden. "Should I?"

"He's been showing a photo of a red-haired woman around Paris."

"He's looking for me."

"It would seem that way, which means he'll know who you are. I'm trying to find him."

"Ferguson," I whisper, the name coming to me from out of nowhere.

Kayden's brow furrows. "The man is Ferguson?"

"No. That's my last name. But there are tons of Fergusons, and my identity has been wiped out."

"We will find you with that last name. I promise you."

I give a choppy nod. "Let's go on."

He studies me a moment, seeming to weigh my state of mind based on "just bad" or "too bad," and "just bad" must win, because he slips another photo in front of me. I inhale with the image of a man's wrist and a watch that looks just like Kayden's. "Neuville's watch," I murmur.

"That I made the unfortunate decision to buy for myself, and will be donating mine to charity."

I set all of the photos aside. "Just show me his photo, Kayden. Stop softening the blow. It's going to suck, and that isn't going to change by leading up to it."

"I have more than his photo, Ella. Matteo hacked a few security cameras in areas he frequents."

My hand goes to my throat. "You have photos of me with him."

"I do, and I can show you one of just him, or I can show you all of them. Or we can just get naked, make love, and forget this until tomorrow."

I grab the folder from him and open it, sucking in air as I stare down at a man who is devastatingly handsome, with thick, slicked-back dark hair. "Neuville," I whisper, and my stupid hand starts to tremble. I grab it and will it to stop, forcing myself to look at the photo again. Images flit through my mind: Him kissing me. Him touching me. Him staring at me with brutally sexy eyes.

"Bastard," I hiss, flipping to the next photo, my spine stiffening at the sight of me sitting across from him at a table in a café. Laughing. God, I was laughing. "What a fool I was," I whisper.

Kayden's hands slide around my calves. "Ella."

I look up at him, into eyes that are a hundred times sexier

than Neuville's, but just as brutal. Kayden can kill. Kayden can be cold. But there's a kindness and fairness in him that made me fall in love with him. "Just so you know, I never loved him. I had this hero complex when he rescued me."

"How did he rescue you?"

"David disappeared, I think. I'm not sure yet. I know he's dead, but at the time, he'd just disappeared. All I know is that he was gone and I had no money or passport. Neuville rescued me. Only . . . I think I found out that he had arranged for me to end up with no money or passport. Yes. I don't know how I know this, but he arranged it all."

Eager for more to come to me, I refocus on the photos, flipping to yet another image, this one of me getting into the Mercedes, with Neuville's hand intimately placed at my back. I flip to the next and I'm trembling, inside and out. It's me and Neuville sitting at a table in a highly exclusive restaurant, with a woman standing at the table talking to us. And that woman is *the* woman. My trembling becomes shaking, and suddenly I'm back in time, reliving a memory, but with far more detail than before.

He is angry. He is always angry. He is also at my back, stalking me as we walk down a hallway in a club he says I'll soon enjoy as he does. There was a time when he would have said such a thing to me and I'd have believed him. That time has passed. The hallway ends and he punches a code into the door panel. An odd thing in a club, but of course he wouldn't frequent anyplace that isn't exclusive in every possible way. The door buzzes open and I enter what looks like a small, round coliseum, stepping past two huge pillars to find a naked woman with long, dark hair resting on her knees, her arms tied to some sort of posts. I gasp and turn to leave, but he steps in front of me. "Where do you think you're going?"

"I don't want to be here."

"You need to see what happens if you disobey me again."

"I already promised I'd listen from now on."

He caresses my cheek and I cringe. He notices and is not pleased, his fingers digging into my arm as he turns me to face forward. "You watch. You learn. If you move right now, you will become her." He shoves me to my knees, his legs at my spine, and my gaze meets the woman waiting for whatever punishment is soon to be hers. But she isn't afraid, as I am. She welcomes it. She wants it. A door opens to the left, and a beautiful blond woman in leather holding a whip enters the room.

"No!" I stand and face him. "No. No. No."

He grabs my hair and drags me toward the two women, glancing over my shoulder to say, "She goes first."

I inhale and try to pull myself out of the memory right here, where it normally stops, but I can't.

"Ella," I hear Kayden say, and on some level I am aware of being in his arms, but I still can't get back to him. I am back in the past.

Both of my arms are tied to the posts, stretched wide, and my back burns with the punishment it has taken. "Please stop." And it does stop. There is silence. So much silence, and then Neuville is in front of me, cupping my face, his thumb stroking over my lips. "You are so fucking perfect."

He kisses me and rage rises inside me, and every part of me that has faked it with him disappears. I bite his tongue, hard and fast, and he yelps, pulling back to glare at me. "You little bitch!" he says, fury filling his eyes before he slaps me. The pain radiates in my temples, and everything goes black.

The next thing I remember, I'm in a bed, lying on my stomach, and that woman is stroking my hair. I moan and she kneels on the edge of the bed beside me. "You cannot ever cross him again. He's going to come in here. He's going to want an apology. You must give it to him. Give it to him."

"Please help me."

"There's only one person who can help you, and I'm not sure that's help."

"Who? Who can . . . help?"

"Niccolo, but think long and hard before you ask for his help."

"I want help. When? How? I have something. . . . I have . . ."

The door opens and she leans to my ear. "Fuck him and fuck him good, honey. For your own safety."

She is gone then, and I hear her talking to him in French, something about me being beautiful, and him being lucky. And then Neuville's hand is on my head. "You should not have bitten me."

My skin crawls, but I see an image of my father yelling at me to run another lap. "Don't be weak! Push! Push! Push!"

"I got scared," I whisper. "I thought . . . you were someone else. I was disoriented and I didn't want a stranger to touch me."

And then he is pulling me into his arms, cradling me, and touching me.

I blink back to the present. "Ella. Sweetheart, you're scaring me. Nathan, she's trembling and I can't get her to wake up, just like in the dressing room that time."

"I'm okay," I say, pushing out of his arms, tears streaming down my cheeks. "But I'm sick. I'm going to throw up."

He scoops me up and carries me to the bathroom, setting me down on the thick rug in front of the toilet.

"Please go," I whisper, grabbing the seat, willing myself not to be sick until he does. "Please—" I heave. And I heave again and again. I lose time and place all over again, but when I come back to the present, Kayden is holding my hair, his arm around my waist.

"I told you . . . to go," I pant out, taking the towel he offers me and wiping my mouth.

"And I told you," he says, sitting against the door and cradling me in his lap, "I'm not ever letting you go."

"It's okay to let me go when I'm throwing up."

"No," he says, tightening his arms around me. "It's not ever okay to let you go."

I sink into him, suddenly okay with that. He strokes my hair and my back, and I shut my eyes. "He did horrible things to me, but I wasn't weak. I made my father proud. I did what I had to survive, but . . . it was horrible."

"I've never known anyone braver, Ella," he says, and in that moment I flash back to the kitchen the moment after I had shot the last of my father's two attackers. *I drop the gun and look down at my father, and he looks at me, blood running from his mouth. "My brave little girl," he whispers, before shutting his eyes and never opening them again.*

I sob, and Kayden does what he promised. He doesn't let go, and I finally fall asleep.

nineteen

I wake in bed, still dressed in my sweats, and Kayden is holding me. Memories flow back to me. Him carrying me to bed. Him holding me while I slept off the adrenaline and shock over remembering Neuville. Me waking up in the middle of the night to find Kayden wide-awake, watching over me. We talked for hours then, trying to make sense of the random memories coming at me, with no completion or logical order.

"You're awake," Kayden says, nuzzling my neck.

Smiling, something I'd not thought possible before our middle of the night talk, I face him. His jaw is shadowed, his light brown hair mussed up, and the pale blue T-shirt he still wears remains a striking match for his eyes. "You're even beautiful when you wake up," I say, sighing. "While I'm a puffy-eyed mess from all the tears."

He kisses my forehead. "You make puffy gorgeous, sweetheart."

I laugh. "You get an A for suaveness, because if you'd said I wasn't puffy, I'd never have believed a compliment from you again."

His cell phone vibrates on the nightstand and he rolls

over to grab it, settling on his back to eye his messages. "Nathan checking on you again," he says, keying in a reply.

"You freaked him out when you called him and told him I wouldn't wake up."

He sits up against the headboard. "Because *I* was freaked out. You scared the hell out of me, woman."

I sit up and pull my legs to my chest. "Well, considering all the things I remembered last night, I'm pretty incredulous that I still can't remember where the necklace is."

"You remembered what the note said from inside the necklace," he reminds me. "That's a start."

"Do you have any idea what Pierre Remy—Marc—0000 means?"

"Pierre Remy is a restaurant, but it has many locations in France. I assume Marc is a person, and 0000 some sort of code. We have to be cautious about asking too many questions, so we don't spook 'Marc' and send him and the necklace underground. I trust Sasha, and she's good at using games to get answers."

"But I thought she left France because of Neuville?"

"Against my orders, Sasha tried to seduce Neuville in order to retrieve something he took from someone. She's lucky she didn't end up like Enzo. But that was years ago, and she won't be there as Sasha, anyway."

My brow furrows. "You know, I initially didn't think I could read the note because it was in another language, but 'Pierre Remy—Marc—0000' is pretty easy to make out. So maybe there's more to the note."

"Or maybe you were just blocking it out," he suggests. "You obviously didn't want to remember Neuville."

A memory from the club tries to surface and I shove it aside. “But I said I couldn’t read the note because it was in another language. Since I speak French, wouldn’t I be able to read it?”

“Speaking a language and reading it are two different things.” He sits up and grabs a pad of paper and a pencil next to the bed, scribbling something down and handing it to me. “Let’s see if you read French.”

I study the sentence. “The sky is blue and the sun is yellow.” I hand him the paper back. “I can definitely read French. Something feels off about this restaurant theory. Could Pierre Remy be Italian? Does it translate to here?”

“It could be, but you were in France and the restaurant has no franchises here. And there’s every indication that Niccolo had no idea you were connected to the necklace, but that Neuville did and set the entire David situation up himself.”

“I don’t have clarity on that, but yes,” I say. “I believe I somehow found out that Neuville set up the David situation.”

“Pierre Remy therefore somehow connects dots between David and Neuville.”

“That makes sense, but I can’t help but feel like it’s something different altogether.”

His phone buzzes again and he reads the message and eyes me. “Marabella has hot croissants just out of the oven, and wants to know if we want some.”

“Are we even considering an answer other than yes?”

“Exactly my thoughts,” he says, typing a reply. “I’ll tell her to bring them up.”

“Wait, though. What time is it? We’re supposed to have lunch with Giada.”

He glances at the clock on his phone. "It's ten o'clock, but I cancelled with Giada and told her tentatively tomorrow. I didn't know how you'd feel today."

"Thank you. I'm eager to talk to her, but today is not the day. And is it even safe, anyway?"

He scoots closer and slides his arm under my knees. "Neuville won't come here. And now not only do you have me and Evil Eye protecting you, which Niccolo knows, by the way, but he himself has any number of reasons to do so, as well."

A knock sounds on the door, and we hear, "Brunch in bed! Are you decent?"

Kayden and I both smile, and he murmurs, "For once, we are. You up for this?"

"Are you kidding? Who wouldn't be?"

He kisses my nose and calls out, "Come in, Marabella," and that silly, tender action has me ridiculously giddy when he releases me and gets up to help her.

A few moments later the room is enveloped in the scent of hot bread and coffee, as well as Marabella's chattiness, and I have this surreal moment of family and belonging. My mind shifts to Sara, my friend in the States, and I know then that she's as alone as I am, but we've found a sisterhood in each other. A bit like what I hope I can give Giada. Thoughts like that remain on my mind after Marabella leaves and Kayden and I head to the bathroom to shower.

"How about we have a date day?" he suggests, tearing his shirt over his head, giving me a distracting view of his naked torso. "We'll go buy us both ridiculously expensive watches, explore the neighborhood, and then go to dinner." He steps to me and reaches for my shirt, pulling it over my head before sliding his arm up my back and molding me to him. "You need to know your neighborhood."

"Right. I want to, but I think . . . I'm just feeling gun-shy."

"That's why we need to do this. And know this, Ella. I hate Niccolo, but I will partner with him to destroy Neuville, if that's what it takes to give you peace."

"Niccolo killed Kevin and Elizabeth. You can't—"

"Patience is a virtue that keeps people alive and gets you what you want. Niccolo will get what he has coming to him, but right now, you are what matters. Neuville is in my sights, and he has no idea what is coming his way."

"What are you going to do?"

"The list is long. Think kid in a candy store of weapons, and I'm the kid." He lifts me and sets me on the sink, pulling my arm and the bracelet between us. "This is a showpiece you can wear anywhere and anytime, but today we'll also get you a Hawk tattoo to match mine. A message to anyone who dares touch you, that they will die." He tangles his fingers in my hair, dragging my gaze to his. "They will die painfully." Then he kisses me, and that promise of protection is on his lips, but there's more. Something darker. Something that makes me kiss him deeper and, once we're in the shower, fuck harder. Something that feels way too much like dread.

Kayden and I dress casually, both ending up in black jeans and T-shirts, with lace-up black boots. While I feel quite chic in my Chanel coat, he's ruggedly handsome in his black-and-gray biker jacket. We take a car service to the Spanish Steps and spend the afternoon shopping, walking around the high-end stores nearby, where he indeed buys a ridiculously expensive Rolex for himself and tries to buy one for me as well, but I refuse. I want my tattoo on one arm and my bracelet on the other, a choice that warms his eyes. We are growing closer, stronger. We laugh and talk easily, my memories of my mother and father blossoming, and I share them as they come to me.

At one point we sit at a tiny café, waiting for espressos. "I already have someone working on connecting you to your last name," he tells me.

"I know," I say. "That's why I didn't ask. I have that much confidence in you, Kayden. My mother had that kind of faith in my father."

Our espressos arrive in tiny cups, and on a shared smile we down them. I choke on how strong they are, and he laughs. "That's why I have a coffeepot at home." He looks at his new watch, which has a thick black band with a gold face and stirs absolutely no memories. "I want to show you around the neighborhood both before and after dark, so you can see how it changes."

We pull our coats on and start to get up, when I realize I've forgotten something important. "Wait," I say, grabbing his arm. "Where the hell is my head? I can't believe I forgot this. Donati called me yesterday while you were gone."

"How does Donati have your number?" he asks, settling back into his seat.

"It has to be Gallo—so he's not working to get Gallo off our backs at all."

"What did he want?"

"He demanded I tell him why you were with Niccolo."

"And you said?"

I relay the entire conversation. "But what was weird was the way he said that no one turns down Niccolo. It was almost offhanded, and I'm not sure he really meant to say it. I think he did something for Niccolo and was worried you were going to find out what."

He thrums his fingers on the table. "Donati is a good man. He means well, but he thinks he can play on a field he's not skilled enough to play on. So somehow he crossed Niccolo, and now he's indebted to him. He wants out. And as Kevin used to say, a caged man is a stupid man."

"He was worried about you being with Niccolo, Kayden. So that stupid you're talking about involves you."

He pulls his phone from his pocket. "Which means we attack directly."

"By doing what?"

"We go to Niccolo."

As we walk down a sidewalk, on our way to meet Niccolo, I ask, "Are you sure it's smart for me to meet this man? You met with him alone for a reason."

"We met leader to leader, and established that our boundaries had not been crossed, which ensured that you weren't caught in the crosshairs. Now, it's another day and time. As my woman," he says, "you look him in the eye, and you do not blink."

"What if he puts me on the spot about the necklace?" I ask as we enter the square with the Spanish Steps directly to our left.

"You'll handle it. If I didn't think you could, you wouldn't be my woman." He stops in front of double wooden doors, one open and revealing a long hallway. "Now we wait."

Several horse-drawn carriages sit about three feet away, while cabs line up to our left.

"Will he just walk up and greet us? I mean, how does the head of the Italian mafia have a casual meeting?" At that moment three black sedans pull up in front of the walkway, where I don't think other cars are allowed.

"I guess I just got my answer," I murmur, my heart racing.

"He'll be in the center car," Kayden tells me, "and the last to exit."

Sure enough, doors pop open from the sedans at the front and back, and several men in trench coats exit, eyeing the surroundings. "I think they've been watching too much TV," I murmur.

"TV is imitating them, sweetheart, not the other way around."

One of the men eyes Kayden and inclines his chin.

"Inside," Kayden instructs, and we step inside the hallway. Almost immediately two of the trench-coated men enter, one motioning someone, Niccolo I assume, forward.

Kayden's hand settles at my back and a tall, gaunt bald man I guess to be fifty enters the hallway, his pin-striped suit fitted and expensive. The other two men go back outside and shut the double wooden doors behind them.

"Niccolo," Kayden greets him, and I am shocked at the confirmation that this man is the mafia king who in photos appears younger and more attractive.

"Hello, Hawk," Niccolo replies, his lips twisting sardonically before his cold, dark stare lands on me, and he shocks me by taking my hand. "Ella. So good to see you, dear. Any woman who holds a gun to Garner Neuville's head in front of his staff and disgraces him is damn near blood to me."

I blanch, shocked. "I . . . did what?"

"Ah yes," he says, folding his arms in front of his chest, flicking his gaze between the two of us. "The amnesia. Such a shame to steal that pleasant memory from you. I was concerned you wouldn't make it out of his home, let alone his country, alive, but here you are. Without my necklace."

"I don't remember it."

"So I hear." His eyes harden, and he looks at Kayden. "I'd hoped you'd remedied that problem."

"If only I could command her to orgasm or to return from amnesia," Kayden replies dryly, "but I'm not guaranteed either." He changes the subject. "What do you have on Donati?"

Niccolo's lips quirk. "Good man. Morals. Conscience. All that good stuff that makes men do stupid things. I have ammunition on him and he knows it, but I do on most people. Why?"

"He seems rattled about you and me spending yesterday together."

Niccolo presses two fingers to his jaw. "Rattled, you say. Isn't that intriguing?" He eyes me and then Kayden. "Us together. You with her. Could be a deal with Neuville, which means we have a problem."

"You have a problem," Kayden says. "Because whatever

Donati is doing, it's in response to this leverage you have over him. And it's a situation we don't need while I'm locating the necklace."

"Hmm," he says. "Yes." He holds out his hands on either side. "Handle two assholes, or get the insanely expensive necklace delivered to me by The Hawk himself." He drops his hands. "I'll handle the assholes. Whatever the case, go back to your romantic frolicking and consider it handled. And somewhere in the middle of the kiss kiss, bang bang you two are enjoying, find me my damn necklace." He knocks on the door and it opens, but before he exits he gives Kayden a pointed stare. "It occurs to me that I am the reason your woman made it out of France alive, and now I have graciously forgiven her costly amnesia. That is two favors you owe me."

The comment sounds almost like a joke, but it isn't. He's deadly serious. As he turns away, Kayden snaps, "Mafia king," the way Niccolo had called him Hawk, and I now know that means business.

Niccolo freezes, but does not turn. "Yes, Hawk?"

"We both know you owe *me* times two," he says, and it's clear he means Elizabeth and Kevin.

He pauses. "He who laughs last is dead," he says, and then disappears.

Understanding comes over me in a quick jab. "He means he's dying."

"What are you talking about?" Kayden asks. "Is this something Neuville told you?"

"No. But it's in his eyes. They're my mother's eyes."

"And a dying man is worse than a caged man."

"What are you going to do?"

"Right now we need him and he needs us. But after that, I'll be making the long kiss good night I've planned for him a little shorter."

We take a car service back to our neighborhood, and begin to explore Trastevere on foot. Kayden seems determined to introduce me to the locals, all of whom know him well, and they look at him with respect that swells me with pride.

Come five o'clock we make our way to the tattoo parlor and I start to get nervous, asking Kayden a million questions about the pain before we arrive.

"This place is a hole-in-the-wall," he says, as we arrive at the location, "but Drago is the best in the business."

He holds the door for me, and we enter, greeted by dangling plastic jewels from the ceiling, seventies-style purple and orange splatters all over the walls, and loud Italian rock music. A woman who doesn't speak English takes our coats and leads us to a private room where Drago, a fifty-something man with a toothpick in his mouth and tattoos on pretty much every part of his body, greets us.

Thirty minutes later, I'm in a chair with him working on my wrist while Kayden holds my other hand, and we've decided my Hawk gets pink wings. A prospect I'd be excited about if not for the pain of Drago carving out my skin. I don't like that thought. "He's carving my skin," I tell Kayden. "Literally carving it."

"Let's talk about dinner."

"Carving my skin."

Kayden smiles and kisses me. "Pasta. Wine."

"Lots of wine." Pain sizzles down into my fingers and I grimace. "*Lots* and lots of wine."

He laughs and begins teaching me Italian curse words, and he and Drago commend my quick grasp of the language.

Finally, I'm done, and my wrist is bandaged. Kayden helps me to my feet and pulls his T-shirt off. "My turn." He straddles a chair that allows him to lean forward, his back exposed. "Two more, Drago."

I grab a chair and sit in front of him. "Two more skulls?"

"That's right. Annie and Charlie."

"My parents?"

"Yes. Your parents."

"You don't have to do this."

"I don't do anything because I have to."

I cup his face. "I love you so much." I kiss him and he cups my head, holding me to him for a long, drugging kiss that has Drago yelling at us.

I laugh as a sense of rightness comes over me. Everything I have ever been has been leading me here, to this man. And I would die for him, but I know him enough to know those aren't words he wants to hear from me.

Kayden closes his eyes as Drago goes to work, and unbidden, Neuville's voice is in my head. *I own you. You are mine. I will find you.* I don't even remember when he said those words, but I believe them.

He will find me. He will come for me. And I fear that he will come for Kayden. And I can't let that happen.

twenty

By the time we finish up at the tattoo parlor the bond between us seems to expand with every look, touch, and word, and I decide to simply enjoy this time with him, and bring up Neuville tomorrow. Arm in arm, we exit the shop into a chilly night, and the streets have transformed from the calm of earlier to walkways filled with tourists, street vendors, and a few performers.

More and more the neighborhood has become like hands to me, with side streets that are many fingers. We cut down one of them now, cafés and outdoor seating lining our path.

"I can't believe there are people eating outside in this weather," I say, eyeing the busy tables.

"You should see it during the warmer months," he says. "Italians like their outdoor dining, and for the most part that's because there's no air-conditioning." He pulls me a little closer. "How's your wrist feeling?"

"Just a dull throb," I say. "It turned out beautifully, so I'm excited about it. How's your back?"

"Nothing some wine won't cure." He stops us at the door to a place that looks rather busy. "This is one of the more modern restaurants in Trastevere. Very American in its size and atmosphere. Very Italian when it comes to the food."

We enter the main dining area with pale wood floors, and modern-looking steel-and-glass steps up the center, and a hostess seats us in a corner booth in the back. Fifteen minutes later we are drinking wine, eating bread, and, at my urging, Kayden has ordered his recommendations for us.

We laugh and talk, the way we have all day, in spite of Neuville, Niccolo, and even Donati. Once our plates are gone, Kayden laces his hand with mine, leaning in close and turning somber. "Do you know how few people could go from where you were on that bathroom floor last night to where you are right now? You are brave."

That memory of my father calling me brave comes back to me and guts me just a little. "Which means I'm scared, but I do it anyway. I *am* scared, Kayden. I didn't want to talk about this tonight, but Garner . . ." I cringe. "I just called him by his first name, as if I actually had a relationship with that man."

"You did, sweetheart, and he might be a dark spot on your life, but it's the way we deal with those dark spots that makes us who we are. And they made you special."

"I'm not special, but they brought me to you, and I'd live them again to be here now." I sit back and drink some wine. "I didn't want to bring this up tonight, but he's coming for me and the necklace—and that means you."

"He hasn't come for you because he doesn't know where you are."

"He'll find me."

"But we've found him first, Ella. That's what matters.

We've found him, and we will hurt him in ways he's never imagined."

"Translate that."

"Evil Eye will be evoked. You are mine and they are yours. The attacks will come hard, fast, and vicious. His people will doubt him. His world will crumble."

"When?"

"I have key members flying in for a meeting in a week for the vote."

"So it's not guaranteed that they'll take him down."

"The meeting is more about planning than approval. I lead Evil Eye—and if I can confirm that Niccolo is dying, that makes the dynamics of this interesting," he says. "A shift of power from both mafia leaders has to be handled with care, but if done right, it could weaken both organizations."

I study him closely. "Why haven't you sent them after Niccolo, Kayden?"

"I set this organization up based on order and honor. Not an easy thing to do, when not every Hawk is about honor. There are rules and a burden of proof. If I step around that, then everyone will expect to do the same, and that can lead to dangerous places."

"What proof do you have of what happened to me?"

"Niccolo is providing me proof."

"Which is what?"

"Do you really want to hear this?"

"Yes. It's my life. I don't want to be sheltered, and I'm not going to have a meltdown here."

"The woman at the club helped you reach out to Niccolo,

and she owes him a favor. She says she took a picture of you after the beating and I have to use it, Ella."

I have a fleeting memory of her stroking my hair the night I'd bitten that bastard's tongue. Anger overrides shame, and I drink the rest of my wine. "Have you seen the photo?"

"Not yet."

"Won't it make me look weak to The Underground?"

"You survived and escaped a mafia king. You do not look weak."

"I'm not weak," I repeat, maybe trying to convince myself, which really sucks. "I don't want to see the photo." I down his wine, too. "Do they have tequila? I have some noise in my head right now I'd like to mute, and since we can't have sex, it seems like a good option."

He lifts his hand and a waiter appears, and after a short conversation, Kayden stands up. "Come on."

"We're leaving?" I ask, letting him pull me to my feet.

"I want to show you a taste of Italian nightlife next door. They'll hold our coats here."

"Okay," I say, feeling slightly dizzy. "But I'd better skip that tequila. Apparently the wine did the job." He wraps my waist to steady me and leads me to the back of the restaurant and down a hallway. We reach a door he opens and suddenly there is loud Italian pop music, dim lights, and a narrow stairway.

Kayden puts me in front of him, his hands on my hips, and we walk up the stairs. I'm greeted at the top level by a blue-hued darkness and a dance floor filled with people. Scanning, I find an oval bar to the left, and some sort of sky bridge up above. Kayden steps to my side and drapes his arm around my shoulder, leading me to the bar, where he orders drinks.

"This doesn't seem like your kind of place," I say, leaning on the bar.

"Bars are gutters of information," he says, leaning on the bar next to me, his arm pressed to mine. "And as a bonus, there are drunk people divulging it left and right."

"Now it seems like your kind of place," I say, and not for the first time, I think of his skill as a chameleon.

Two shots appear in front of us and Kayden stuffs euros into the ticket tray before lifting both of the glasses and facing me. "Bottoms up, sweetheart," he says, offering me mine.

I accept it but don't drink. "I'm pretty tipsy."

His hand slides around my hip to my backside, easing me closer. "I'll protect you." But the way he says it is more like, *I'll give you ten orgasms.* Motivated, I down the drink, grimacing at the taste.

He laughs and downs his shot, then sets our glasses on the bar. "Come on," he says, leading me past the dance floor and through the crowd, our destination a set of stairs leading to the sky bridge. Again, he places me in front of him and holds on to my hips, and it's a good thing he does. The steps are narrow and I really, really feel a buzz now. Once we're at the bridge level, Kayden leads me down a hallway away from the bridge, and then to another set of stairs with a chain across them.

"Doesn't the chain mean this area is closed?" I ask.

"I know the owner." He lifts me over the chain, joins me, and we climb yet more stairs until we reach a closed area of the bar. "Our private party," he says, snagging my fingers and leading me to the railing that wraps around the center room below.

"This is the best place to be in a bar," Kayden says as we gaze down at the crowd. "Above the world."

I face him. "You can't get those drunken secrets up here."

"From up here, you target those who have them and are drunk enough to talk about them."

"You always have an angle," I say, and suddenly my head spins and I sway. Kayden catches my waist and walks me backward several feet until I'm leaning against a big beam, his powerful legs holding me steady.

Then an American song starts playing. *I can't feel my face when I'm with you. But I love it. But I love it.* I start laughing. "I really can't feel my face, Kayden. But I like it. If I didn't trust you, I couldn't let myself be like this right now."

"Because you know—"

"I know that you are all kinds of tattooed hotness, Kayden Wilkens. Hawk."

His lips curve. "Is that you talking or the wine?"

"It's called liquid courage."

"You're adorably drunk."

I stroke his cheek, which feels much better than mine. "But you're here, and you are The Hawk and I know I'm safe."

"You *are* safe with me, Ella."

"I am, but you're dangerous to everyone else."

His expression sobers. "Is that what you think of me?"

"Don't go getting serious on a drunk person. I didn't mean that negatively—you're everyone's protector." I grab his T-shirt. "I meant that the bad guys are in trouble when they piss you off. And I meant it like you're a badass, thus the 'you're sexy' comment. Wait. Did I say that or think that? I'm saying it now. You're sexy."

He flattens his hand at the small of my back. "Badass?"

"Badass."

"Do you know how badly I want to be inside you right now? Right here?" His hands go to my sides, traveling to my breasts, his thumbs stroking my nipples to hard peaks.

I grab his hands as my cheeks flush. "Too bad I wore jeans. You'll have to behave."

"Will I?" he asks, flicking my nipple.

I grab his wrists, firming my voice. "Stop, because yes, you do. I am not getting undressed in public."

He reaches down and fingers the easily undone laces that line the front of my jeans. "I'll settle for you having an orgasm until we get home."

I reach for his hand. "I can't have an orgasm in public, either," I say, but my body betrays me, my sex clenched and wet.

"That sounds like a challenge—and this is barely public." He pulls several of my laces loose. "I told Niccolo I couldn't command you to orgasm. I want to try."

"You can," I assure him. "You can pretty much just look at me and I'm wet."

"Are you telling me you're wet now?"

"Very—so take me home and do something about it."

His hand goes to my jaw and he drags my gaze to his.

"I never thought I'd use the word *home* again—let alone have a woman I want to use it with. I love you, Ella."

"I love you too—" He slips his fingers beneath the laces and suddenly they're intimately pressed to my sex. "That was unfair!"

"You're not wearing panties," he observes, slipping a finger inside me.

"Kayden—"

"And you are very, very wet." His head lowers, lips at my ear. "I would kill to feel you around me right now."

I pant, and my sex clenches around his fingers. "You're about to embarrass me."

"No one can see us."

"That's not what I mean. I mean—" He thumbs my clit and presses another finger inside me. "I'm going to come really fast." He kisses me, a deep slide of his tongue, and oh . . . oh . . . I stiffen and come. That fast, hard. My body shakes and quakes and I collapse against him, burying my face in his chest. "See? Embarrassing."

"Try sexy as hell, and I'm hard as fuck. Now I'm taking you home." He goes down on a knee in front of me and starts lacing up my jeans, and a shadow catches my eye on the other side of the room.

"Kayden," I say urgently. "I think someone is here."

He stands and turns to scan the room, wrapping his arm around my waist. "What did you see?"

"A shift in the shadows. I know I'm drunk, but someone was watching."

He unzips my purse and puts my hand on Annie. "Probably a kid, but stay here. I want to be sure."

I lean against the wall and watch as he walks the entire floor, and Garner's words play in my head again. *I will find you.* I shake off the memory and hug myself when Kayden returns with no evidence of our voyeur. "Nothing?"

"Nothing obvious," he says, "but if you say someone was there, I believe you."

"It felt—"

He cups my face. "I know what you're thinking, but it wasn't him. Garner Neuville is not here. But I am. Okay?"

"Yes. It's the rawness of my memories and the alcohol."

"Which is understandable." He takes my hand. "Let's get out of here."

We head for the stairs, and I have such a strong feeling of being watched again that the hair on the back of my neck stands up. Which makes no sense. Kayden just checked the room. I'm officially done with drinking.

Bundled up again, Kayden and I exit into the cold night. "This way," Kayden says, turning us left, his arm around my waist. "We have two left turns to reach the castle."

"I'm never going to figure out these small clusters of streets."

"Landmarks," he says. "Look for restaurants." He points to a green sign. "That's a pharmacy sign. They're always easy to find."

We turn left onto another busy street lined with restaurants, and my head spins a bit. "I'm still tipsy, so I'm not likely to remember it tonight." I sober a bit with memories of the bar. "I really thought I saw someone back there, Kayden."

"And I really do believe you."

"But I had this moment when I thought it was *him*. I hate that I'm letting him get to me." We turn left onto one of the streets that's more alleyway that road, with parked motorcycles in clusters along the walls and little alcoves here and there, and I'm immediately uncomfortable. "I know I'm drunk, but—"

"I feel it, too."

I reach under my coat and unzip my purse, just in time. Someone jumps out at me from an alcove, and instinct kicks in. I throw an elbow, whirl around, and shove my knee into my attacker's groin. He grunts and falls to his knees, and I point my gun at him.

"Kayden?" I call, glancing over my shoulder to see him slam a gun into the head of another man, who collapses next to yet another who's already on the ground.

The man in front of me groans and rolls to his back. Kayden is there instantly, shoving his foot into the man's chest. "Are you okay?"

"Yes," I say, while Carlo and two other men appear seemingly out of nowhere and point weapons at the fallen men.

"Bitch," the man on the ground growls at me.

"That bitch took you down while she's drunk," Kayden tells the man. "Who sent you?"

"Fuck you," the man grumbles.

"I'll be your bitch," Carlo offers, placing his foot on my attacker's hand and giving it a crunch, apparently pretty hard because the man makes a horrible sound.

"Who sent you?" Kayden demands of the man.

"I don't know," the man growls and when Carlo starts to apply pressure again, he says, "It was a cash pickup. I never saw the person."

"What were your instructions?" Kayden asks.

"We were supposed to scare the girl and make her feel like you can't protect her."

Carlo laughs. "And then *the girl* beat your ass." He glances at me. "Remind me not to piss you off."

Kayden tells him, "Tie them up and dump them on Gallo's doorstep." He turns to me, and it's only then that I realize I'm still pointing my gun. He takes it from me and sticks it back in my purse. "It's done." He links my arm around his, and sets us walking toward the castle, removing his phone to punch in a number.

"Detective Gallo," he says a moment later. "You have a special delivery coming your way. And thanks for making me look good. Your men were idiots, and Ella is more convinced than ever that I'm the greatest warrior on the planet." There is silence, then Kayden laughs. "I'm thinking you should arrest those guys and look like a hero. I'll come file a police report tomorrow if you like. And I'll even bring Ella." He ends the call and sticks his phone back in his jacket.

I cut him a curious look. "How do you know it was Gallo?"

"Because he's the only person I know of who has a motivation to scare you, and is stupid enough to hire the kind of idiots who thought this would go well." He scrubs his neck. "I'm going to have to do something with him."

"Like what?"

"Create a scandal that forces him to leave his job and the city."

"That's horrible."

"I'm just trying to shut him down before he ends up dead."

"That *does* seem like where this is headed. On another note, your men got to us fast. So maybe having Giada stay close is a good idea."

Kayden stops walking, his hands settling on my shoulders.

"Our date night started with a mafia king, and just ended with us being jumped—not to mention that I've just told you I'm going to pretty much ruin a good man."

"And I'm pretty sure the creep who jumped me watched me have an orgasm in the club."

"And all you have to say is that staying here is good for Giada?"

"What do you expect me to say?"

"Most women would be freaked out, Ella."

"I'm actually not at all. I had a great day with you. We just found out I know how to fight, which I think is a great asset. I got a very special tattoo, and so did you. I'm warm with booze and I had an orgasm with the promise of another. Plus we won whatever that was back there, so I'm not going to be crying anytime soon."

He stares at me for several beats, then kisses me. "You're the badass, and I find new reasons to fall in love with you every day." He wraps his arm around my shoulder and turns us forward. "Let's go home."

I smile at his words, feeling pretty untouchable. And considering where I was last night, that says a lot. It's like there is a storm raging around us, but together, Kayden and I have found our little sliver of peace.

twenty-one

I blink awake the next morning with a smile on my face and a memory of dancing with my mother. It's like a ball of light in my mind and heart, and it feels like I've faced my demons and now I can see everything else. Eager to share this with Kayden, I roll over and my hand hits a note.

> I worked out and showered, and you were still passed out. I'll either be in the kitchen or my office. And since we need to deal with Giada today, there will be more tequila.

Laughing, I head to the shower, then dress in light-colored jeans and a supersoft light blue sweater. Tending to my tattoo is another smile-worthy moment, and I'm eager for tomorrow, when I can remove the bandage. I walk into the bedroom and grab my phone and journal. Maybe reading my old notes will dislodge the remaining cobwebs in my head and finally reveal the location of the necklace.

Heading to the door, I open it and find Kayden standing

there, his big, muscular body filling the door frame, his hair a bit mussed. He's also wearing his black-and-gray biker jacket.

"You're leaving."

"Not by choice," he says, dragging me to him for a long, drugging kiss. "Definitely not by choice."

"I thought we were doing the Giada thing today?"

"I'm going to meet you two. I made reservations at a new firing range by the Spanish Steps. A car will meet you at three, and since it's later than planned, we'll have an early dinner afterward."

"That's fine with me, and I'm sure it will be with Giada, but is everything okay?"

"Niccolo called and told me the situation with Donati was 'contained,' whatever that means. And surprise, surprise, Donati called and wants to meet with me. This time, I agreed."

My brows dip. "That's weird."

"It's questionable timing, but I'm guessing he now wants help dealing with Niccolo."

"He seemed more concerned about you than about Niccolo when I talked to him."

"Niccolo has a way of shifting the dynamics in his direction."

"And he won't tell you what's up, I guess."

"Not a chance in hell. But on a positive note, Carlo got proof that Gallo hired the men who attacked us last night."

"Are you going to get him fired?"

"I'm going to give him thirty days to leave town first."

"That is more than most people would do."

"It's more than I would have done a month ago." He pulls me to him and kisses me. "Just remember. You've made me a better man." With that very odd statement, he releases me and starts walking. I follow his path. I decide we've come way too far for me to read into that, and rather than chasing it in circles, I'll just ask him about it later.

I head on to the kitchen, and find a pot of coffee already made. Filling a cup, I doctor it my way and sit at the table. After texting Giada and setting up our afternoon, I'm left with hours to read and write in my journal. I start flipping through it, reading my underlined notes and looking at one butterfly drawing after another, until I freeze. A page is torn, a portion of it missing.

I stand up. How could a page get torn? I flip several more pages and find another that's torn. I don't remember what was written there. Who the hell took those pages because I didn't black out and take them myself. No way. I did not. Someone took them. I sit down again and start making a list of all the people who might have been near my journal.

Adriel
Giada
Nathan?
Matteo?
Marabella, though she isn't really a consideration.
Who else?
Carlo?

Once again, I have too many question marks.

At two forty-five, I'm in the main foyer waiting for Giada when my cell phone finally rings. "Kayden! I've been dying to know what's going on!"

"A fucking gaggle. I moved the shooting range reservation to four o'clock, so take her shopping or whatever you want beforehand. You have your credit card I gave you, right?"

"Yes. What does 'a fucking gaggle' mean?"

"Gallo tried to play dirty. He told Donati I dumped the men and tried to use our phone records to prove it. Then I was forced to prove he hired them. He's now suspended and angry, and that makes him dangerous. I'm sending Sasha to lick his wounds."

"Sasha knows Gallo?"

"She's about to and I don't know why I didn't connect them before. If anyone can contain that man's anger, she can. But Donati is my main concern. He was acting nervous, and he doesn't do nervous. Niccolo contained him, but he's still afraid I'm going to find out what he did. And I am. So I'll meet you at four."

We end the call right as Giada appears, looking adorable in a long bright pink jacket and pink pants. "This is how you go to the firing range?" I ask, laughing.

She struts to the front door. "This is how I get the hot men at the firing range looking in my direction."

"Something tells me today is going to be interesting," I say, and we head outside to meet our driver.

"Is Kayden really meeting us?" Giada asks once we're on our way.

"He is, and I'm excited for you two to spend time together."

"I'm nervous. I haven't exactly been the best houseguest."

"You aren't a guest. The castle is your home."

She inhales and looks out of the window. The silence that follows tells me she's hurt, but I let it go.

After the ride ends, we stroll past the shops. "Any store you want to go to?"

She perks up and links her arm with mine. "There's this really affordable makeup store down the road I adore."

"Affordable? You do know you're a millionaire, right?"

"It's a trust fund, and I don't feel like I have money. But I am excited about having my own place."

"Well, that's new," I say as we cross the road and step onto the sidewalk, the crowd bustling around us.

"Yes, I—"

A man steps in front of me and grabs my arms when I have to stop suddenly. "Sorry about that," he says, his black shades hiding his face. "American without a clue here."

"It's fine," I say, stepping back from him, but he's still standing there.

"Hi," Giada says, smiling at the man, who has this tall, dark, and deadly thing going on in all black. The *deadly* is the part I don't like.

I grab her arm and step around the man, putting us in motion again. "Don't flirt with strangers."

"Then how do they become bedroom buddies?"

"I'm not going to try to answer that question."

"Because the answer is they can't," she argues. "And he was hot. Why do hot men never bump into *me*?"

"It seems Gallo does. I hear he was touching your ass at the grocery store."

She stops walking. "That's wrong. I stumbled and he caught me."

"By your ass?"

She grimaces. "He's kind of hot, but he's hateful toward Kayden, and I've been thinking a lot about that. If he hurts Kayden, he hurts my brother and you. Tell Kayden he doesn't have to meet us just to lecture me. One of the neighborhood guys has an apartment for rent. I took it today."

"You're kidding. Is it safe? Is it nice? Is it—"

"You will approve, and it's right around the corner from the castle." She looks skyward. "Finally I can walk to the fridge naked and no one but the hot guy I bring home will care." She motions behind her. "This is the store. Kiko. It's divine."

I sigh in relief. One problem seems to be on the mend, but as we enter the store, I can't help but scan for the man in black. There are a lot of unusual things going on today, Giada's transformation being one of them.

Come four o'clock, Kayden sends me a text message that he's on his way and I take Giada to the shooting range in the upper level of a cobblestone building. There, we ditch our coats and wait in the entryway for someone to help us.

"I can't believe I'm going to shoot a gun," Giada says. "Which is kind of crazy, considering who I live with. How did you learn?"

"My father taught me. And don't forget a gun can either be dangerous, or be a girl's best friend."

"Hopefully dangerous to anyone who tries to hurt you,"

she says. "I admit, living alone makes me nervous, which is why staying close to the castle is so appealing to me and Adriel. I told him today that I was moving."

"How did he react?"

"He gave me a deadpan look. That's what he does." She imitates said look, and we laugh.

Another few minutes pass and a man comes out to talk to us. He insists Giada needs to sit through a class, which is doubtless of Kayden's or Adriel's making.

"I'm going to shoot while you learn," I say, ignoring her grumbles and making my way to another room, and it's not long before I have goggles, hearing protection, ammo, and my own booth.

I unload a round, and the fact that my memories of my father teaching me to shoot feel more like everyday thoughts than flashbacks feels huge. I'm just reloading when I get a tingling sensation on my neck. Cutting a discreet sideways look, I catch the reflection of a man in one of the glass panels separating me from another booth, and he is familiar. He steps in my direction and I turn and aim my weapon at Mr. Tall, Dark, and Deadly himself.

"Wow, sweetheart," he says, holding up his hands. "If I was hitting on you, this would be a major turnoff."

"But you aren't hitting on me. We both know that."

"No," he agrees, removing his shades so I can see his eyes. "I prefer redheads, but don't tell my wife."

My blood runs cold. "Who *are* you?"

"Your friend Sara hired me to find you."

"Sara hired you?"

"Yes. And you weren't easy to find. We can call her."

"No. Sara can't be involved in this. She needs to stay away."

"I know. I told her husband—"

"She's not married."

"She is now, to a very powerful, famous man who spent boatloads of cash to find you. And for the record, it gutted her not to have you at her wedding."

"Damn it, Blake," a female voice says. "This is *not* a friendly approach."

"That would be my wife, Kara," Blake says. "You'd never know I'm the bossy one." He calls out, "I was friendly. She's trigger-happy."

"If she were trigger happy, you'd have a bullet in you already."

At the sound of Kayden's voice, Blake curses. "Holy fuck. This is not going as planned."

Kayden steps to my side. "Was the plan that I not be here?"

A pretty brunette steps to Blake's side. "Yes, it was. Because frankly, we wanted to know that she's safe."

"Can we put the gun down?" Blake asks.

"Put it down," Kayden tells me. "I have the entire staff here on payroll."

"Of course he does," Blake grumbles, eyeing me. "You're still holding the fucking gun, and you seem to follow orders about as well as my wife."

I keep the gun aimed at him. "How do I know Sara sent you?"

"Let's call her," he suggests again. "She won't know where you are. She just needs to hear your voice."

Kayden's hand comes down on my back. "Ella, sweetheart. If she did hire him, he can fill in the blanks you want filled in. And you can give Sara her peace of mind."

"You believe him?" I ask.

"I believe I do," he says, reaching out and taking my gun while telling Blake, "There's a room upstairs where we can talk."

"That works for me," Blake says. "Not my wife." He eyes Kara. "Wait outside and if I don't come out alive in an hour, I guess start the funeral arrangements." He grabs her and kisses her.

"Don't say things like that. They aren't funny."

"Yes, wife." He turns back to us. "I'm ready."

Kayden talks to the man at the door who's now watching us, then to Blake. "He'll take you there. I need to talk to Ella for a moment alone."

"Understood." He starts to walk away.

"Blake," Kayden says, halting him. "If you are who you say you are, you have my protection, and so does your wife. But if you're not—"

"Protection it is," he says, turning away.

Kayden turns me and removes the goggles I didn't even know I still had on. "You okay?"

"I have these weird, crazy emotions going on that I can't even lock down."

"That's understandable. I can talk to him alone."

"No. I want to do this."

"Well, then," he says, placing Annie in my purse and zipping it up, "let's go see what he can tell us."

Five minutes later, Kayden and I are sitting at a round table with Blake in a small room.

"First," Blake says, "who I am. My brothers and I run Walker Security. I'm former ATF, my older brother Royce is former FBI, and Luke is a former Navy SEAL. We not only have our own team, we also worked with a group of local investigators to get here today."

"How did you find her?" Kayden asks.

"I'm a damn good hacker. She was on the grid and she disappeared. When she disappeared, I knew we had trouble. When I couldn't find her despite my skill, I knew we had *big* trouble."

"So I ask again," Kayden says, "how did you find her?"

He keys his iPad to life and flips a photo around to show us. "That's Ella crossing the Italian border. That was our first big break. I then hired a group called The Jackals, who gave me a lead that brought me here."

"Fucking Jackals," Kayden bites out.

"You know them?" I ask, glancing up at him.

"We're Treasure Hunters," he says. "They're the pirates I fired." He eyes Blake. "They'll sell her out."

"They were paid well."

"Pirates never get paid well enough. What do you know about David?"

"A doctor with nothing remarkable in his background," Blake says. "Pretty average. He vanished with Ella, and I haven't gotten a ping on him at all."

"He's dead," I say. "Don't ask details; I can't remember how. I just remember that I ended up with no passport or money."

"I actually know that part of the story," Blake tells me. "And that you ended up with a man named Garner Neuville. He told our people that he spooked you and you ran. He's been looking for you."

"And he can't be allowed to find her," Kayden says. "But The Jackals will help him in two seconds flat. So you, Blake Walker, are just good enough to find her, and just bad enough to get her in trouble."

"I'm good enough to save her ass, just like you. The Jackals don't know I found her. I'll redirect them back to France."

"Do that," Kayden says. "Do it now."

"Consider it done." Blake flips to another screen on the iPad and hands it to me. "Sara's wedding."

Tears instantly form in my eyes at the sight of Sara in a gorgeous rose lace dress, next to a man in a tux. "She looks gorgeous and he's hot." I swipe at tears, and Kayden squeezes my leg. I hold his hand and ask Blake, "Who is the man? Is he a good man? Does he love her?"

"Chris Merit is his name, and he's a world-famous artist who's passionately in love with her."

"Artist." A memory comes back to me. "Did I . . . Was there a storage unit?"

"Yes," he says. "You bought it during summer break to make extra money, and it had artwork and several journals in it. Sara took it over when you eloped, and it led her to Chris."

"Summer break. You're saying I was a teacher?"

"Yes."

Memories ebb and flow. "I was teaching. . . . But that isn't me. Something doesn't add up." A thought hits me. "Do you have photos of my parents?"

"I do," he says, taking the iPad and showing me a shot of my mother.

I smile and show it to Kayden. "My mom."

"Swipe," Blake says. "The next one is your father."

The fifty-something, balding man in the photo is the one I remember being in my mother's hospital room, long after my father died. "That's my bastard, drunk, asshole stepfather. Not my father."

"Sorry about that," Blake says. "Swipe again."

I swipe and inhale at the sight of a red-haired man with strong features. "That's him." I show it to Kayden.

"Mr. Badass himself," Kayden says. "I wish I could have met him."

"Interesting that you call him a badass," Blake says. "He was CIA and at such a high level that I can't get to him—not by hacking, or with my contacts. And that's saying a lot."

My gaze jerks to his. "CIA? Not military?"

"No, not military."

"I'm not a schoolteacher," I say, certain of it.

"You were one." Blake reaches for his iPad. "I snagged your records before they were deleted."

"I know I was teaching when I left for Paris—but it's not who I really was." I consider that for a moment. "I think I was CIA. I took a time-out, or was suspended." I glance at Kayden, suddenly afraid of what that means for us. Then I turn back to Blake. "Can you find out?"

"There's no record of you being CIA," he says. "None. Nothing that indicated a hiccup in your record." He pulls a thumb drive from his pocket and slides it over to me. "That contains everything I have, but I'll dig further."

"Be careful," Kayden warns. "Garner Neuville is a problem that we can't have erupt."

"I'm always careful."

"The Jackals," Kayden replies. "That's all I'm going to say."

"I'm handling them." Blake sets a phone on the table. "This is a disposable phone that we can destroy after we use it. I'd like to call Sara and put her on with you."

I glance at Kayden. "Is it safe?"

"If we destroy the phone, yes."

"But I don't know if I can ever see her again. Neuville will never stop coming, and—"

Kayden cups my head and kisses me. "Neuville is going to expire. He's a temporary problem, and remember what we talked about. He doesn't get to own you or your friend." He glances at Blake. "Make the call. Ella, this is as much for you as for Sara."

My heart starts pounding as Blake dials the phone. Then I hear, "Chris, it's Blake. Listen. I need you to prepare Sara for good news. I have someone for her to talk to." A pause. "Yes. She's alive, but hiding. Right. Yes." He hands me the phone. "He's prepping her, so it will be a minute."

I reach for it with a trembling hand and put it to my ear, standing and walking to the corner, listening to the silence. Kayden steps behind me, his hand at my waist. "Blake and I are going to step into the hallway. Talk as long as you like, but—"

"Less is more."

He kisses my temple and walks away, the door closing behind them.

Another beat of silence follows, and then I hear Sara's excited voice. "Ella!"

I start grinning and crying. "Yes! Yes, it's me!"

"Oh my God. Oh my. God. Oh. My. God. Why can't I stop saying 'Oh my God'? Chris, it's really her! I can't believe it's you, Ella!"

"Well, I had amnesia, so I wasn't me for a while."

"You're in danger."

"Yes, but I met a man and he's amazing and—"

"Not David or Garner, right?"

"His name is Kayden. And I hear you have a sexy painter now. I saw his picture. He's hot."

"He's so hot," she says. "I'm so lucky. I wish you could have been at my wedding."

"One day I'll meet him, and you can meet Kayden. Tell me about him."

"There's so much I want to tell you about! About the storage unit, and Rebecca, the girl who owned it, and Chris—"

"I want to hear about Chris."

She starts talking, and I talk, and we talk forever. Finally, though, it's time to hang up. We say teary goodbyes, and I promise to call again. I break the phone open and pull out the chip inside, running it under water and then breaking it. And I know how to do that because I'm CIA. Or *something* that could mean I was after the necklace for my own reasons. And maybe I was investigating The Underground. Or Garner Neuville. Or both.

I walk to the door and open it, and the minute Kayden sees me he pulls me into his arms. "We are not enemies," he says.

"But the CIA—"

"I have allies in every agency." He cups my face. "And I've said it before and I will say it again. We choose if we are enemies." He kisses me, and in that kiss there is demand. So much demand. And his demand is that I refuse to be his enemy.

To be continued in *Surrender*. . . .